The Dancing Tortoise

Naaotua Swayne

authorHOUSE®

AuthorHouse™ UK Ltd.
500 Avebury Boulevard
Central Milton Keynes, MK9 2BE
www.authorhouse.co.uk
Phone: 08001974150

First published by AuthorHouse 7/31/2008

ISBN: 978-1-4343-9633-4 (sc)

Printed in the United States of America
Bloomington, Indiana

This book is printed on acid-free paper.

To my three children,
Ophelia, Kwaku, Zinobia

*C*hapter *O*ne

---

*E*SSENAM CAME RUNNING INTO HER MOTHER'S bedroom after her elder sister Emefa had put her to bed.

"Mum, mum! You have forgotten to tell me a story, "

"I am busy at the moment," Jiffa replied. I'II tell you a story tomorrow." She was tidying her wardrobe and feeling miserable after weeks of quarrelling with her husband.

"Yesterday you promised me a story today. Today you say tomorrow. Please tell me a story now!"

Jiffa stopped what she was doing and sat on her bed. She lifted six-year-old Essenam on to her lap and spoke to her quietly. "Go back to bed and I will come and tell you a story there."

"Mum, where is Daddy?" asked Essenam, as she was about to leave.

"He's not yet back from work" said Jiffa.

"Will he tell me a story, too?"

"I will tell you a story today, and daddy will tell you a story tomorrow"

"Alright, Mum, but please come soon".

On her way out, Essenam bumped into her elder sister Emefa.

"What are you doing here, Essenam? Didn't I tell you to stay in your bedroom? Said Emefa angrily.

"Mum promised to tell me a story, so I came to remind her," Essenam replied humbly.

"Go to bed, mum can not tell you a story today, she is busy."

Jiffa overheard them talking, but did not intervene. She went back to her wardrobe, humming a hymn.

1

"But, sister Emefa, mum just said she is coming to tell me a story," said Essenam sadly.

"Listen to me," said Emefa, wagging her finger. "Mum is busy. Go to bed. Even Kobla is fast asleep." Essenam went away quietly. She was upset, but knew she must not challenge her elders.

"I promised to tell her a story," said Jiffa when Emefa came in to help her. "Now you have upset her"

"I only told her to go to bed. Why should that upset her?"

"You were too harsh with her," said Jiffa.

"Well why didn't you say so?"

"I don't want to tick you off in front of your younger sister, because that would destroy her respect for you. But please treat her kindly."

"Mum, I love Essenam dearly," said Emefa quietly. "But if you give in to her too much she will become spoilt."

"But I don't."

"I'm sorry, but at times you do," Emefa replied.

"All Essenam has done this evening, is to ask me to tell her a story. I don't want to talk about it any more, I have enough problems already." Jiffa was almost in tears.

"Have I upset you,?" asked Emefa anxiously.

"Of course not."

"Then why are you crying?"

"I'm fine," said Jiffa, turning away, They finished tidying the wardrobe and sat down on the bed.

"You're not alright, Mum. Please tell me what is troubling you?"

"I don't think you are old enough, Emefa..."

"Yes I am."

"Alright, then. Your father and I haven't been getting on well recently. You remember he went to Italy last month?"

Emefa nodded.

"Since he came back he has changed." Jiffa continued. "I am tired of his behaviour and I cannot take any more."

"I have noticed you've been arguing, but I didn't know why. Mum, please don't say you're tired of him."

"What else can I say?"

"For our sake, don't give up. But you're right. Before Daddy travelled, life was fun - he used to play and chat with us. Now everything has changed."

Jiffa sighed, and was silent for a while. "Emefa, please ask Ajovi to come in," She wanted to be alone to think. After Emefa left, Jiffa lay back on her bed, sighing deeply. Why had Vincent changed? He had not spoken to her all the previous day, and when he left for work this morning he did not even say goodbye. They had had disagreements in the past, but he had never behaved like this. So why now? She decided to talk to him as soon as he got back.

Then Ajovi came in with Emefa , and Jiffa told her to lock up the house. When she left, Emefa sat down beside her mother.

"Mum, I'm so sorry you feel depressed. What can I do to help?

"You are only seventeen, my dear. You should not be burdened with such things."

But I want to know. I love you and dad very much."

Jiffa gave in. "Look, it's almost ten o'clock, and where is your father?" she said. "Usually he gets back from work by six, but these days I'm lucky if I see him before midnight. And when he comes, he doesn't eat his supper."

"Don't you ask him where he has been?" Emefa said quietly.

"I do." Jiffa replied, "But he always gives me the same answers."

"What answers?"

"Oh, I went to this meeting, or that meeting," said Jiffa, imitating her husbands voice.

"Why don't you ask him what time these meetings end?"

"It would make him angry."

"Why?"

"Oh, Emefa! I wish I had a mother and father or a brother and sister to talk to. But I have no one. I'm all on my own."

This outburst alarmed Emefa. "Mum, you have me, and Kobla and Essenam. You can talk to us."

"And I'm grateful. But please go to your room now and leave me alone."

"I 'm not going to leave you: I'll stay with you until Daddy comes."

Shortly afterwards the telephone rang, and Jiffa rushed into the sitting -room.

"Hello? Where are you? Why didn't you tell me this morning?"

Jiffa stood holding the receiver, then she put it down and returned to the bedroom. Emefa was lying on her bed. She sat up when her mother entered.

"Who rang?"

"Your father," said Jiffa quietly.

"Where is he?"

"In Ho"

"What's he doing there?"

"Only God Knows."

"Didn't you ask him?"

"He said he was in a meeting."

Emefa looked at her watch. "But it's almost eleven o'clock."

"Yes."

"So he won't be back tonight?"

"Go to bed, Emefa, please..."

"Mum, let me sleep here with you."

Jiffa looked at her daughter calmly. "Thank you, but I must go and see Essenam."

"Don't bother, Mum. She will be asleep."

"I know, but I want to see her."

They went together to Essenam's room and found her asleep with dried tears on her face.

"Poor child she has been crying," said Jiffa.

"I'm sorry, Mum. I shouldn't have been so hard on her" Emefa whispered. Jiffa kissed her and left.

The night was long for Jiffa. She lay awake thinking of Vincent. Had he really gone to Ho, or was he spending the night with another woman? In the past, he had always apologized for his mistakes; but now his whole attitude had changed. Whatever the reason for this behaviour, she prayed that the good lord should bring it to light. Jiffa turned to look at Emefa, but she was fast asleep.

*C*hapter *T*wo

*N*EXT MORNING, JIFFA WAS STILL ASLEEP when the children had breakfast. Emefa returned to her mother's bedroom after breakfast, and when she saw her still asleep she tiptoed out to the dining room to talk to Kobla and Essenam.

"Kobla what are you doing this morning?" she asked.

"I'm going to see Paul.

"Is he on holidays?"

"Yes, he rang me last night."

"I thought you would be at home. I want to go out, too," said Emefa.

"What's stopping you?"

"I want to talk to you alone," she replied, "Essenam, wait here for me."

Out in the garden, Emefa took her brother's hand.

"Kobla, Mum was crying last night," she whispered. "That's why I don't want her to be left alone."

"Why?"

"It's to do with Dad."

"Oh, God they have been rowing all the time. Where is she?"

"She's asleep."

"Poor Mum, said Kobla. "By the way, where is Dad?"

Emefa didn't answer, because Essenam had come out to talk to her.

"Sister Emefa, I want to go and see Mum."

"No she's asleep. I don't want you to wake her up."

"Can I go and lie beside her?"

"No"

"Can I ask Esi to come for a swim?"

"Yes, but don't go in your dressing-gown."

"I will go and change." Essenam skipped off happily, leaving them alone.

"You asked me a question," said Emefa.

"Yes," Kobla replied. "Where is Dad?"

"He rang last night and told Mum he was in Ho."

"Has he gone to visit grandmama?"

"No. grandmama does not live in Ho. But Kobla, haven't you noticed that Mum and Dad are not getting on well?"

"Yes, that is why I don't stay at home these days. I would much rather go out than watch them quarrelling."

"I know but we can't all go out the whole time, mum needs us," she replied.

"So does Dad," Kobla retorted.

"But he is the one causing all these problems." Emefa buried her head in her hands, fighting back tears.

"Oh, what a miserable house!" said Kobla, "I wish I were at school."

Kobla caught sight of Essenam returning, wearing a swimming-suit.

"Are you going to Esi's house in that?" he asked her.

"Yes."

"Emefa, should she go in her swimming-suit?" Kobla asked.

"No, Essenam, go and put on a dress," Emefa replied.

Essenam went back to her bedroom.

Kobla looked at his watch.

"It's almost lunch time, and Mum has not had her breakfast."

"She needs to sleep. I doubt whether she slept at all last night," Emefa said looking worried.

"How do you know?"

"I slept in her bed."

"I wish I had been with her too."

"Kobla, I hope Dad comes today. If he doesn't, I suggest we all sleep with her tonight. She said some terrible things to me."

"What sort of things?"

"She told me she wished she had brothers and sisters to talk to."

"Can't she talk to us?"

"She doesn't want to unload her problems on us,"

"But we have grown up now and can understand." Kobla said, shaking his head.

"I wish we could find somebody to advise Dad to be nice to Mum." Emefa sighed.

"So do I. Shall we ask Esi's mother to come and talk to them?" Kobla suggested.

"I don't think so. It wouldn't be right to involve her in this. Where is Essenam, by the way?"

"You told her to change out of her swimming-costume."

"Kobla, why don't you go and see Paul?"

"Alright."

"What time will you be back?"

"By tea-time"

"Right see you then."

When Kobla left, Emefa went in to see what Essenam was up to. She met her coming out of her bedroom holding her blue dress.

"What's wrong with it? Emefa asked.

"Nothing."

"Then put it on."

After seeing Essenam off, Emefa checked on her mother and found her still asleep. She gave Ajovi instructions for lunch, and asked her to keep an eye on the house while she went to the library.

Jiffa woke up later in the day and called Ajovi.

"The house is very quiet; where are the children?" she asked.

"Emefa has gone to the library, Madame, and Essenam has gone to Esi's house. I don't know where Kobla has gone to."

"And what are you doing?"

"I am preparing lunch."

Jiffa hesitated. "I have forgotten why I called you," she said.

"Did you want me to lay the table for lunch?" Ajovi asked.

"No, I'm not hungry. Oh yes, I've remembered. I want you to take a chicken out of the freezer."

"Yes, Madame."

Jiffa was getting dressed when she heard Emefa calling her.

"I'm in the bedroom," she replied.

Emefa came in.

"Where have you been?" Jiffa asked.

"Didn't Ajovi tell you?"

"I can't remember."

"I went to the library."

"Oh yes, she did tell me."

"What time did you wake up, Mum?"

"About an hour ago. Why?"

Emefa looked at her watch; it was two o'clock.

"Have you eaten?"

"No, but I'm not hungry."

"You must eat something, otherwise you will be ill."

Jiffa looked at Emefa and saw how worried she was.

"Bring me a glass of tonic water," she said.

She had just finished dressing when Emefa came back.

"I'm going to prepare supper, " Jiffa said. Turning to Emefa to collect her drink.

"Good," Emefa replied, "What are we having?"

"I told Ajovi to take some chicken out of the freezer."

"For stewing or roasting?"

"Roasting," said Jiffa.

"Dad loves roast chicken, doesn't he?"

"Yes."

They went into the kitchen. Jiffa was pleased to see it looking neat and clean.

"Well done, Ajovi," she said. Ajovi smiled cheerfully. "I'll prepare supper myself." "Where is Essenam?" she asked Emefa.

"She has gone to Esi's house to have a swim."

"Good. Oh that reminds me: I have asked your father to get one of his office workmen to change the water in the pool."

"I wish Peter was still here," said Emefa.

"Yes, he was a good houseboy," said Jiffa.

"Are we going to replace him?"

"By all means - I must remind your father,"

Jiffa put the chicken in the oven, washed her hands, and looked at the time. It was four-thirty.

"Come with me into the sitting-room, Emefa," she said. "I'll wait there until the chicken is ready." She walked slowly out of the kitchen, looking exhausted. Emefa knew why her mother was going to the sitting room.

Her father always came in through that door, and she wanted to see him when he arrived.

They sat down on the black leather sofa.

"Have you drunk your tonic water, Mum?"

"No, I left in the bedroom"

"Shall I get it for you?"

"That would be very kind." Emefa ran upstairs and brought down her drink. Jiffa asked her to go and fetch Essenam, because it was getting late.

Just after Emefa left, Jiffa heard Vincent's car in the garage. Her heart sank. Vincent walked briskly into the sitting room, carrying his briefcase. When he saw Jiffa, he passed without greeting her and went upstairs into the bedroom. Jiffa followed him there and found him changing into his dressing gown.

"Vincent," she said quietly. "Why did you ignore me? Am I not a human being? What have I done? What has happened?"

"I would prefer not to talk now, Jiffa - do you mind?" he said angrily. "I'm late for a meeting, and have no time."

Jiffa raised her voice. "You are not going to any meeting until you have answered me. The way you treat me these days needs questioning."

"Why don't you question it yourself?" Vincent sat down on the bed.

"I already have," Jiffa replied, standing in front of the door.

"And what is your answer?" he asked sarcastically.

"Vincent, I'm sure you realize how you have changed"

"You really make me laugh," he said.

"Do I? Well one day your laughter will turn to tears," said Jiffa angrily.

Vincent stood up. "How dare you talk to me like that?" he shouted. "Where would you be without me? I have made you what you are today, and all I get from you are insults."

"I'm not insulting you," Jiffa replied, "So don't point your dirty finger at me."

"How do you expect me to be loving to you when all I get after a hard day's work are insults? I'm fed up, Jiffa, I'm really fed up with you"

"What work? You mean your endless phoney meetings? Where were you last night?"

"I told you, I was in Ho, and if you don't believe me you can jump in the sea and drown. While we are on that subject, I am going to Togo tomorrow, so you won't see me until the week-end."

"I may be gone before you get back," said Jiffa.

"Do you have anywhere to go? Vincent sneered.

"That's none of your business"

"If you don't stop your rudeness I will teach you a lesson you will never forget"

"If you're a man, why don't you try it," Jiffa goaded.

Vincent rushed at her and twisted her arm behind her back.

"Let go of me, you are hurting me!" Jiffa shouted, struggling.

"Good! I want to teach you not to be rude."

"Don't be stupid," Jiffa spluttered.

Vincent slapped her face so hard that she fell on the floor. He stood and watched her as she lay there weeping.

"You are a foolish man!" Jiffa sobbed.

Vincent dragged her onto the bed and slapped her face again. Then he went into the bathroom shaking with rage. Jiffa got up, locked the bedroom door, and removed the key, determined to stop him going to his meeting.

Vincent came out of the bathroom and changed hurriedly, then he went to the bedroom door and tried to open it.

"Where is the key?" he asked, rattling the door angrily.

Jiffa continued to lie on the bed sobbing.

"You will have to cancel your so-called meeting, Vincent and answer my questions."

"Don't be silly, give me the key!" He rushed at her and forced her hand open to get the key, but she threw it across the room. He slapped her face again, picked up the key, opened the door, and left. That night he came home long after midnight, and moved into one of the spare rooms.

At breakfast the following day, Vincent chatted with his children; Essenam was sitting on his lap.

"Where is Mum?" she asked her father. Emefa and Kobla listened attentively,

"She is asleep," Vincent replied.

"Shall I go and wake her up?"

"No she would not like that."

"Are you going to work today, Dad?"

"No today is Saturday."

"So you will be home today?"

"Of course."

After breakfast, they went into the sitting room. Vincent lay on the sofa and Essenam sat on him, while Kobla and Emefa sat in the armchairs. As Vincent listened to what Essenam was saying, his mind was on Jiffa. He had not seen her that morning, and had no wish to. Was he being unkind? Why was he behaving like this towards his wife, whom he had loved ever since she was a child? He looked at Essenam lying on his chest and thought of Jiffa when she was that age. What was the matter with him? Why had he raised his hand to his wife? Was it because of Vera? Why was he giving so much love to Vera and none to Jiffa? Should he move back into their bedroom? As his mind wandered into the past, Essenam called him back to the present.

"Dad - what are we going to do today?"

"What do you want to do?" Vincent replied. Emefa came and sat beside him.

"Shall we go and swim?" he asked. Essenam was about to answer when Emefa interrupted.

"Nobody is to swim in the pool," she said sharply.

"Why?" asked Vincent.

"Mum said the water needs changing. Also, she asked me to remind you - "

"About the houseboy?" Vincent interrupted.

"Yes." Emefa looked at him coldly.

"I had forgotten all about it. What other servants do we need?"

"A gardener," said Kobla.

"And a day -watchman," said Emefa.

"Get me the telephone, Emefa, I'll ring the office straight away."

Emefa did not see why her father could not put down Essenam and go to the telephone. Nevertheless she brought the telephone over to him.

"Hello? This is Mr Agawu. Who am I speaking to? Please make a note of this. I need a houseboy, a gardener, and a day watchman, to start work at my house next week. Line up some good people, and I'll interview then on Monday afternoon.Thank you very much, Bye-bye." Vincent put down the receiver.

Jiffa had sat up all night thinking of how to save her marriage, and had decided to go to Kpetwei and report the matter to her mother-in-law. She looked in the mirror and saw the bruises on her face. It was good to have evidence. She packed a few clothes into a small suitcase, and was just coming downstairs when she heard Vincent on the telephone. She decided to leave the house secretly by the back door, since she did not want him to know where she was going. Ajovi was in the garden; cutting flowers for the bedrooms, and Jiffa went to speak to her quietly.

"I'm going to Kpetwei, Ajovi. Please look after Essenam, put her to bed early and tell her a story. Now, go into the sitting room and fetch Emefa. I don't want her father to know I'm calling her,"

"What shall I say if Emefa asks me why I want her?" asked Ajovi, putting down the flower vase.

"Tell her to come and choose the flowers for her bedroom"

"Alright, Madame."

Vincent was playing with Essenam when Ajovi entered, and did not notice when she called Emefa. They went quietly into the garden. As soon as Emefa saw her mother, she called out," Mum!"

"Ssh!" said Jiffa, putting her finger to her lips. Ajovi went over to continue cutting the flowers and Emefa walked her mother to the gate.

"Where are you going?"

"Listen, I'm going to see your grandmama,"

"Can I come with you?"

"I'd love you to come, but it's better that you stay with Essenam."

"Essenam will be fine. Dad's at home today."

"I'm not so sure about that. He's at home now but do you know whether he will home this evening?"

"Won't you be in this evening?"

"No I'm coming back tomorrow."

"Mum, don't leave Dad, will you?"

"For your sake, I will never leave him."

"Thanks, Mum." Both Jiffa and Emefa were fighting back tears. They hugged each other and stood for a while.

"I must go now," Jiffa turned round to go, then paused, "I have asked Ajovi to tell Essenam a story tonight please don't stop her."

"I would not." Emefa began to cry.

"Don't cry, and please don't tell anybody where I have gone to, especially your father."

"I won't."

Jiffa comforted her daughter, said goodbye, and left.

Chapter Three

EMEFA WENT STRAIGHT TO HER BEDROOM after seeing her mother off. She was still weeping and wondering what was going to happen between her parents. Would they separate? Would her father change his attitude towards her mother if she begged him? Should she ring her boyfriend and ask his advice? No, that would not be right. She heard Essenam laughing and playing with her father. After a while, the telephone rang and she heard Kobla's footsteps. He was hurrying upstairs to their mother's bedroom. Within minutes he ran back to the sitting room shouting, "Daddy! Have you seen Mum?"

"Isn't she in the bedroom?" Vincent asked

"No."

"She's probably in the garden. Who wants her?"

"Her seamstress."

"Let me speak to her."

Kobla handed the telephone over to his father, and stood listening.

"Hello, Jennifer – it's Vincent - can she ring you later? Okay, bye."

Vincent put down the receiver and sent Kobla to ask Emefa whether she had seen her mother. When she said no, Kobla looked round the house, and asked Ajovi, but she also said no. Then he stood in the middle of the compound and shouted. "Mum. Where are you?" There was no reply, so he ran back to his father.

"What? But where has she gone?" Vincent asked. He told Kobla and Essenam to wait while he looked round himself. He went into Jiffa's bedroom, and seeing it was empty he sat on the bed and looked at his watch. It was nearly midday, and he had promised to take Vera out for lunch. If Jiffa was not in, how could he leave the children? Essenam was bound to follow him wherever he went. Should he ring Vera and cancel lunch? No, that would not be possible. Wondering what to do, his thoughts went back to the day he met Vera again. He was on a return flight from Rome to Accra. In the next seat was a glamorous young woman. He wanted to approach her, but she was busily reading. He looked at her expensive outfit and wondered who she was. Her fingernails were an inch long, and painted bright red. The ring on her middle finger was so big; it was a wonder the bone in that finger supported it. Her mauve lipstick matched her blouse and shoes, her white skirt was the same material as her neck scarf, and her hair was straightened.

Vincent admired every bit of her and he decided to get to know her before they touched down. After all they had a long flight ahead and so he would wait for the right moment. And just as they were ready to go on the run way, the captain announced that there would be a delay. Many of the passengers grumbled about the inefficiency of the airline, and Vincent seized the opportunity to talk to the lady.

"You don't seem bothered by the delay," he said.

"I am, but there is nothing we can do," she said quietly

"We could complain to Association of Airlines."

"And what difference would that make? She closed her book and folded her arms.

"A lot," Vincent replied. "By the way, my name's Vincent what's yours?"

The woman looked at him carefully and asked what his second name was.

"Agawu, " he said. She started laughing. "What's funny about my name? he asked, puzzled. But she kept laughing. Eventually she took off her spectacles and asked Vincent whether he recognized her. He looked carefully.

"No," he said.

"Come on: use your Best Brain."

Vincent realized that the girl must know him from their school days. He looked at her closely.

"My name starts with a V," she continued.

"Vera!" shouted Vincent.

They laughed and hugged each other.

"What a small world! After all these years, here we are again," she said.

"Vera, I have missed you."

"Me too."

"What have you been doing with your life?" he asked.

"Nothing much. I have had a lot of disappointments, and I'm still unmarried."

"I'm sorry to hear that," Vincent replied. "Now I feel guilty."

"Don't feel guilty or blame yourself," she said, "But I wish my dream of living with you became a reality."

Vincent put his hand on her thigh and looked into her eyes.

"I still love you," he whispered in her ear.

"Me too," she replied.

"Where do you live?" he asked quietly.

"Osu, near the Castle."

The captain then announced that the plane would take off in a few minutes.

"At last the waiting is over," said Vera.

"I thought you didn't mind," he teased.

"I did, but unlike you I was not going to make a fuss," she replied.

They both laughed. Vincent was enjoying himself.

"You were the fussiest boyfriend I ever had. Are you aware of that?"

"Oh, no. Would you have married me, knowing how fussy I was?"

She looked away. "I won't answer that, because you did not marry me."

"How do you know I'm not going to marry you now?" Vincent asked.

Vera looked at him sharply. "Are you not satisfied with your marriage?" she asked just as the plane took off.

"I am. But nothing stops me from having several wives."

"Don't raise my hopes. We have just met again, after how many years?"

"Eighteen. I think," said Vincent,

"Good Lord! Vincent, do you realise I have nearly doubled in age since we first met?"

"When I saw you just now, I thought you were in your twenties. I was wondering how to approach you."

"If I had known that. I would not have made it easier by admitting I knew you," Vera responded.

"I'm glad you didn't play games with me," He said, sounding pompous.

"Why should I want to play games with the Best Brain?" Vera said, laughing.

"I hate to think of those days. I was under so much pressure."

"You can't complain. I'm sure the fame you had then has paid off now." They helped themselves to some drinks from the air hostess.

"I suppose it has," he replied.

"Where do you work?" she asked quietly.

"Standard Housing Corporation."

"As what?"

"Why do you want to know?" he smiled.

"You can please yourself."

He opened his briefcase, and gave Vera his card.

"Heavens! You are the Assistant Director of SHC!" Vera's heart began to race. She would make him buy her a house. Did he not say that he still loved her? When a man wants a woman, he will do anything she tells him. Vera had been unlucky in love but this time she was determined to make it work.

"What do you do for a living?" he asked her.

"I am a businesswoman."

"What kind of business?"

"I supply boutiques with ladies' fashions."

"Now I see why you're so glamorous. Are you advertising for the boutiques?"

"I suppose so."

They laughed.

"Don't you have your own boutique?" Vincent asked.

"Not at the moment, but I am planning to get one next to the Palm Court restaurant"

"That is a top class area"

"Does that surprise you?"

Vincent was longing to be alone with Vera. He was going to take her back into his life, and this time he would not let her go. He would not listen to anybody, not even his mother, who had put pressure on him to end their friendship years ago. If a man of forty-one could not decide for himself, what was the world coming to? He thought about Jiffa's reaction if she found out, but dismissed it as her problem, and not his.

Vincent chatted with Vera until they touched down. When they left the air craft he asked her whether she would like a lift home.

"Yes please. Did you leave your car at the airport?"

"No. My driver will be there to collect me"

"Oh! Your driver is coming to collect you, that is luxury!"

"Stop joking, and let's go."

Vincent helped her carry her luggage, through customs, and out into the car park. His driver, Frank spotted him and came over.

"Welcome, sir." Frank said. He picked up the luggage and they followed him to the car.

"Mm - a Mercedes!" said Vera. Frank opened the back door for them.

"Frank," Vincent said. "Please take us to Osu, near the Castle."

"Yes, sir."

Frank wondered who the woman was. Vincent and Vera talked softly, touched each other and giggled. Vera directed Frank to her flat and they stopped in front of a four-storey building with balconies on every floor. Frank opened the door and they got out. Then he followed them with the suitcase up to a second floor flat, and came back to the car to wait.

Vera showed Vincent round her two-bedroom flat

"This is wonderful?" he said.

"Do you like it?"

"Very much." They went out on the balcony and gazed out at the Atlantic. "Vera, you are very lucky."

"Am I?"

They could see Frank looking at them, so they went back in.

"Let's have a drink," Vera said, opening the fridge and taking out two bottles of chilled beer. She poured them into glasses and sat next to Vincent on the sofa.

"To your health," they both declared as they clicked their glasses.

"To us as man and wife," said Vincent, laughing. Vera took off her shoes and put her feet up. Vincent admired her long, smooth legs, delicate feet and pretty toes. Then he looked at his watch, emptied his glass and decided to leave. But she brought out another bottle and filled his glass.

"Don't you want any more?" she asked.

"I do." Vincent's voice was shaking. He came closer to Vera, they held each other and kissed. She pushed the table away with her feet, to give her room to press herself against him. After a long kiss, he carried her into her bedroom and they made love.

After a long wait Vincent appeared. From the look on his face, Frank knew he had been up to something. Vera stood on her balcony and waved as they drove off. Vincent felt very happy because this was the kind of excitement he needed to make him feel like a man again. His marriage had become a routine and the all the fun was dead. But as he thought of the present, his mind wandered once more into the past.

Chapter Four

$\mathcal{V}$INCENT AND JIFFA WERE BOTH FROM the Volta Region of Ghana. Jiffa was an only child. Her father was an old man when she was born, her mother in her mid-forties. Jiffa was the prettiest baby ever seen in the village of Adidome, and in her teens her friends called her Beauty. She spent her childhood in Kpetwei with Vincent's parents because her own mother and father could not afford to look after her. Vincent was five when Jiffa came to live with them. She was three years younger and they played happily together as brother and sister. Vincent was the youngest of three children, so he was pleased to have a playmate younger than himself.

Being an old man, Jiffa's father feared he might not live to see his daughter's marriage so he agreed with the Agawu family that Vincent and Jiffa should have an arranged marriage.

When she was six, Jiffa started at Kpetwei Primary School. Vincent was in class three at the same school. It made him feel grown up to take Jiffa to school and bring her home. She enjoyed primary school very much and made many friends, but the one she loved most was Vincent. He left primary school three years after she entered, and went to secondary school. When Jiffa left primary school, Vincent's parents sent her back to her own parents to continue with her secondary education.

Jiffa was like a stranger when she arrived back at Adidome. She knew nobody, and wondered why Mama and Papa Agawu had not kept her. Also, she missed Vincent. However, a couple of years after her return she discovered what her future was going to be.

One evening just after supper, Jiffa's parents summoned her. They were sitting outside in the compound, a dim lantern by her father's side. She was told to bring a kitchen stool and sit down. Then her father spoke to her.

"Now, my daughter" he said in a shaking voice, "your mother and I have enjoyed having you back. You may have wondered why we sent you to stay with to the Agawu family in the first place. As you can see, we are poor, and I am an old man. My health has been bad for years, and recently it has become worst. Your mother has worked on farms to provide for us. I expect you to know that farm labourers earn very little, don't you?"

"Yes, Papa," Jiffa replied waiting to hear what else her father had to say.

"Because of that, the Agawu family decided to help with your upbringing. They have fed you and helped with your primary education, haven't they?"

"Yes, Papa," Jiffa looked at her mother, who was sitting quietly, her chin cradled on her hand.

"Now you have come back here to continue with your education," her father continued. "You probably wonder how we can pay for your secondary schooling, when we could not pay for the primary. Don't you?"

"Yes papa." Actually she did not wonder at all, but she had to say yes.

"I want you to listen carefully, and then ask whatever questions you have on your mind. Is that clear?"

"Yes papa," at last the old tortoise was finally getting to the point.

"A year after you were born, the Agawu and Agbenyo families arranged a marriage between you and your cousin Vincent. He loved you when you were a baby. When he came with his parents to visit us, he would often take you in his arms and play with you. He was only three then, but we thought it a good omen. It became a serious plan when you went to live with them. When you were thirteen, they came to see us and agreed to pay your bride price. They have stood by their word and paid the bride price the day they brought you back. Have they done well, or not?"

"Yes they have" Jiffa was shocked. How could her parents do such a thing? She liked Vincent, but could she love him as a husband? She was disgusted.

"The sum was large, and it enabled your mother to start her trade, roasting plantains by the roadside. It also helped us buy a few things for you. Your school uniform and fees were all part of the money they gave us. Are you still listening?"

"Yes papa," Jiffa could not understand why her mother had kept quiet through out, merely nodding occasionally to show that she agreed with her husband.

"To cut a long story short, I am telling you that from today you have a husband. Is that clear?"

"Yes papa." Jiffa was wondering what an arranged marriage meant. Vincent had been kind to her when they were small but people change. What if he turned out to be horrible person, did she still have to accept him?

"From today, I want you to behave like a responsible woman," her father said. "No playing with boys in the street and no talking to boys in corners. Distance yourself from the boys at school. If you don't, you will bring shame on the family. Do you want to disgrace us your parents who have done so much for you?"

"No papa," Jiffa replied. As far as she could see, her family had done very little for her. It was the Agawu family, not her parents who had brought her up. Her parents had just sold her for a bride price. But how could she tell them that? Vincent was bound to discover that her family was only able to survive because of her bride price

"Now I think your mother would like to add a word or two," said Papa Agbenyo.

"I haven't got much to say," said her mother slowly," since your father has said it all. I'd like to thank him for explaining everything to you. It's very important that you should be told. I beg you, Jiffa, take your father's words seriously or I cannot tell you how terrible the consequences will be"

"Have you anything to say?" her father asked.

"Yes Papa," Jiffa replied. "I would like to thank you both for the many things you've done for me, and for sending me to a secondary school even though you are poor. I'm grateful to know about family matters which I have not been told before." She thanked them again, and went to bed.

Jiffa lay on her mat and tried to sleep. The thought of marrying Vincent was too much to take in. Why was she not allowed to grow up and make her own choice? She loved Vincent's parents dearly, because she had grown up to think of them as her own; but would she like them as her in-laws? She had not seen Vincent for a long time; what would he look like? What if he did not want her? Would the marriage work? Who would take the blame if it did not? As far as she could see, her parents had sold her to ensure their own survival. Why had her mother married an old man with bad health, who couldn't work to support his family? Some women marry blindly, now she had to pay the price of her mother's foolishness, and sacrifice her future so that the crumbs of the rich man's table would reach the poor man's bowl. What a sickening thought! She lay awake for hours.

Jiffa's parents were delighted with the way she took the news because it had been a difficult thing to tell her.

"She has taken it well, hasn't she?" said her mother.

"That's because of the way I approached the subject," said Papa Agbenyo.

"Oh yes," her mother agreed.

"Aah! I can't stop yawning," said Papa Agbenyo. "Let's go to bed: it's late." He got up slowly from his chair and took the lantern, and his wife carried the chairs into the house.

A couple of years after her father's death, Mama Agbenyo made a crucial decision about Jiffa's life. Early one morning, Vincent's parents came to visit them. Shortly after they arrived, her mother called her.

"Jiffa, there is something which I should have told you weeks ago. But since the Agawu family will be part of it, I asked them to be here while I break the news to you."

"Yes, mother," Jiffa replied.

"We have decided that you must give up your education."

Jiffa broke down and wept. She could not believe what she was hearing.

"My daughter," said Mama Agawu, stretching out her hand for Jiffa. "Don't cry. One day you will thank us for taking this decision. It's natural that you should be sad to lose your school friends, but we are thinking of your future happiness. Your father is dead, and as he told you, any man could deceive you and ruin your life."

"Have you heard what your two mothers have said?" Papa Agawu added his voice.

"You have seen unmarried girls in this village with babies, haven't you?"

"Yes, Papa."

"Do you want to be one of them?"

"No papa."

"Then aren't you grateful?"

"Yes Papa." But tears raced down Jiffas cheeks as she thanked her mother and parents-in-law.

Later that day, she was given a letter to take to the headmaster of her school. She wept all the way but dried her tears before she entered the office and handed the letter to the headmaster.

Dear Mr Kpevi,

It is with great regret that we write you this letter. Jiffa Agbenyo has been a student of yours for the past three years. Since her father's death, her family has been forced to take a decision with regard to her education. We can no longer afford the fees, and we have therefore decided that she should give up her schooling as from now.

Jiffa has benefited greatly from the time she has spent at Adidome Secondary School, and we are all grateful for the help you and your staff have given her. It is unfortunate that she has to leave the school before she has completed her education; but we hope you will understand that it is due to circumstances beyond our control.

Once again we thank you for all the help during the last three years.
Yours sincerely,
Mama Shika Agbenyo (widow)

Mr Kpevi lifted his head and looked at Jiffa, there were fresh tears in her eyes.

"I'm very sorry you have to leave," he said sadly. What are you going to do now?"

"I don't know, sir."

"It must be hard on you. I will inform your class. I'm so sorry about this, please take care"

Jiffa thanked Mr Kpevi, left his office, and went to her classroom to see her friends. She knew the real reason for her leaving school was not lack of money, but the fear that she might become pregnant. How could she tell her friends that she was going to get married? Would they laugh at her? Should she tell lies? Fortunately there was only one student in the classroom, the rest were having lunch.

"Hello, Aku," said Jiffa.

"Hmm! Where have you been today?" asked Aku, with a surprised expression.

"I'm leaving school, because my mother can't afford the fees," said Jiffa sadly.

"What? You mean your three years education will be wasted?" asked Aku, shocked.

"Yes," said Jiffa.

"I know your father is dead, but is there nobody in your family who can help with your school fees?

"If there was, I wouldn't be telling you this, would I?"

Jiffa asked Aku to tell the rest of the class when they got back, and promised to write to them. Aku saw her off at the school gate.

"I pray that even at this eleventh hour somebody in your family will wake up and help!" Aku said.

There were tears in Jiffa's eyes as she spoke. Aku was also in tears; they hugged each other and said goodbye.

Chapter Five

*T*HE DAY AFTER JIFFA LEFT SCHOOL, her mother told her to pack all her possessions, because she would be leaving for Kpetwei the following day to live with her parents-in-law. The following morning, she and her mother left Adidome to board the first tro-tro to Kpetwei. Mama Agawu was waiting at the station when they arrived. She welcomed them, and took them home. Jiffa was shown into her bedroom which contained a bed with a mattress made of jute and grass. There were cobwebs all over the ceiling because the room had not been used for a long time. She put down her luggage and joined her mother and Mama Agawu in the sitting-room.

Mama gave them water andtold them that her husband was in a meeting at the palace, but would be home soon. The two women exchanged village gossip while Jiffa sat listening. Shortly after lunch, Mama Agbenyo left. It was difficult to get the tro-tro to Adidome, so she allowed plenty of time. Just before she left, she spoke to Jiffa.

"I hope you will not rude to your in-laws,"

"Yes, Mother," Jiffa replied humbly.

"I don't want to hear bad remarks about you. You must put into practice the training I have given you. I hope you realize that you have now started your married life?"

"Yes, Mother."

"Before I leave, you must promise me that you will be a good and respectable wife and never raise your voice against your husband. When he says something, listen and obey. Finally, give respect to your in-laws, who have helped with your education and upbringing. I'll come and visit you whenever I can."

"I promise to do as you have said," Jiffa replied.

Her mother gave her a hug, "Be a good wife."

Jiffa was no longer the small child she had been when she first lived at Kpetwei. This time she was a grown-up girl living with her future parents-in-law. She woke up every morning to help Mama to prepare shredded cassava for garri. It was a tedious job, but Jiffa was determined to prove that she was not lazy. Who would pay back her bride prize if she was unsuitable for their son?

Vincent was then in his final year at Kpando Secondary Technical School. Since he only came home for the holidays, he did not even know that Jiffa's father had died, let alone that she had come to live with them again. No one knew how he would react when he came home for Christmas and saw Jiffa. He had been kept in the dark about his marriage, because his parents did not think the time was right. But now that Jiffa was to live permanently with them, they decided to tell him as soon as he got home.

Jiffa felt like an orphan in the Agawu household. Sometimes she sat quietly in her bedroom and wondered how her life would be with Vincent. But she consoled herself that she was luckier than some others. Mama and Papa were being kind to her. She might have stayed in her own village and wasted her life having children and no husband to take care of them. Vincent would never do that to her, moreover he was getting a good education, which meant a good job and a bright future.

Late one evening, just before supper, a car stopped in front of the house. Mama Agawu was puzzled, because she was not expecting anybody. She went outside to see who it was. A few seconds later, everybody in the street heard her shouting.

"Wezoloo, Vincent!" She rushed forward and hugged him. Then she helped him take his luggage into the house. As they went in, his mother asked him why he had come home a day early

"My headmaster's driver was coming this way, so he gave me a lift," Vincent replied. They went into the house, and Vincent saw Jiffa.

"What a surprise!" he hugged her. "I haven't seen you for ages."

"I haven't seen you, either," said Jiffa nervously.

"Mama why didn't you write and tell me Jiffa was coming for Christmas?"

"I knew you'd be coming home soon, so there was no point in writing," his mother replied.

Jiffa helped put Vincent's luggage in his bedroom. He was delighted to see her and tried to chat to her, but she was shy, and did everything to avoid him. He had changed, Jiffa thought. He was very tall, with well-cut hair, and bushy eyebrows, which made his eyes seem smaller. The only thing that Jiffa disliked was his goatee beard. As a child he had never stopped asking questions, and it looked as if in this, at least, he had not changed. He was the favourite of the family because he was the last-born and the only son, clever at school and good at games.

Supper was served, and all of them except Papa ate from the same bowl. Mama was so pleased to see her son that she kept talking after very mouthful, and at one point she nearly choked. Jiffa gave her some water.

"Haa! That's better."

"Are you all right, Mama?" asked Vincent.

"Of course," answered his mother. "I'm just so happy to see you."

"I know. We can all have a long talk after supper. Can't we?"

"Yes," said Jiffa. Looking even more nervous.

After supper, Vincent and his mother joined his father in the sitting room. Jiffa was left to wash the saucepans and clean the compound.

"Come and sit with us, Jiffa," said Vincent, standing in the doorway of the sitting room.

"I'll come when I've finished," she said, with a false smile.

"Don't bother her," said Mama, "She will come when she's ready."

Vincent and his parents sat and talked for hours about his end of term exams and college life. He had been selected to represent his college in a quiz competition a week after school re-opened.

"Where will the quiz be held?" asked his father with a proud grin.

"The first round will be held at the examination-centre in Ho. Whoever wins will represent the entire region in the final round at Broadcasting House.

"If you qualify will they publish it in the newspapers?"

"Yes, papa, and I'll be on the radio too. I'm nervous, because I only have a short time to study for the first round."

"That day, I shall tell the whole village to listen to the radio," said his mother clapping her hands and laughing. "What good news! I will pray very hard for you to win."

"So your name will appear in the newspapers?" said Papa Agawu.

"Yes, Papa."

"My name has never been seen anywhere, since I was born. If yours appears then you will be a big man one day."

Vincent noticed that his father was a little envious, so he changed the subject.

"Mama, please ask Jiffa to come and sit down. She can't work while I sit and laugh with you."

"Your father and I would like to talk to you privately before we call Jiffa," his mother replied.

"Have I done something wrong?"

"Of course not, we just want to talk to you," said his father, "I have always been proud of you, and I'm not ashamed to show it. Our love has not spoilt you, quite the opposite. You're a good listener, and when you think it's necessary, you ask questions. Now listen carefully. Your mother and I have decided that it's time we explained certain things to you. How long have you known Jiffa?"

"Since childhood," Vincent replied. "Why?"

"Are you surprised to see her again?"

"Yes. I wish she would come and sit with us so that I can see her properly. She is as beautiful as ever."

"As your mother said, we must finish talking before she comes in. "

"Alright, Papa." Vincent was puzzled, but he remained calm.

"You know Jiffa's parents were very poor, which was the main reason why she came to live with us when she was a child."

"I didn't know that. I thought it was because she was my cousin."

"That was part of it, but the main reason was what I have just told you."

"Poor Jiffa," said Vincent.

"Stop feeling sorry for her and listen carefully. When Jiffa was a child, your mother and I agreed that you should marry her."

"What?" Vincent opened his eyes very wide. "Marry my own cousin? Why? How can I?" He shook his head angrily.

"I'll explain," his father responded.

"Listen to your father" said Mama

"Jiffa's parents lived in terrible poverty. Therefore, to enable her parents to look after her, we agreed on the plan we had discussed years ago and we paid her bride-price"

"Papa, are you telling me that Jiffa is my wife?" asked Vincent in disbelief.

"Listen to your father," said Mama

"I'm listening I just can't believe it." He said raising his voice.

"Yes, she will be your wife after you have completed your education. At the moment your mother and I don't want you to go to her bedroom or for her to come to yours. Did you know her father died two months ago?"

"No," Vincent replied. "Poor Jiffa, is she on holidays now?"

"No she's here because her mother could not pay her school fees after the expenses of her father's funeral."

"You mean she has had to give up her education?"

"Yes," said Papa.

"But that's appalling!"

"The world is never fair," said Mama. So far she had left the talking to her husband, as a mark of respect. "Papa, please continue," Mama added.

"Where did I get to? Oh yes. We don't want you to creep into her room at night. We know this may be difficult for you, but you will have to control yourself. We want to prepare her for marriage, to know what you like and what you don't, especially how to prepare your favourite dishes."

"So what you are saying is that Jiffa is in training to be my wife?"

"Yes," said Papa Agawu quietly.

"Poor girl," said Vincent. "She should not have had to give up her education. Surely we could have helped with her fees, couldn't we?" he asked angrily.

"Your mother and I paid quite a large sum of money as her bride-price. At the moment your mother's business is not doing very well," his father replied.

Vincent did not believe this, but said nothing.

"We know what is best for you" said Papa. Have you seen how a bad woman can ruin her husband's future? And have you seen how women leave their husbands nowadays? You may be angry with our decision today, but tomorrow you will be pleased. Jiffa is the ideal woman for you. Please think carefully about what we have said."

Vincent bowed his head and said nothing.

"Do you have any questions?" his father asked.

"I'm confused, Papa. Give me time to think"

"Alright. But before I finish, I must ask you to end any relationships you have with any other women. Otherwise you will bring shame to the family."

Vincent shook his head. "Papa, I'm extremely tired. May I sleep on this and talk to you tomorrow?"

"Of course," his father replied. "I'm glad you've listened."

As Vincent rose to go, Jiffa came in.

Vincent," she said quietly. I've taken a bucket of water to the bathroom for you."

"For God's sake, Jiffa," he responded, "don't tell me that you've been to the well to get me water?"

"It's not far," she said shyly, turning to go. She could sense that Vincent had been told about their marriage. Would he hate the idea, or like it? He said good night to his parents and left.

Vincent went into his bedroom and was surprised to see that his bed had been made and his things put neatly into his cupboard. He wanted to go to Jiffa's bedroom and thank her, but had been told he was not allowed to.

"Why did Jiffa come into his bedroom, if he was not allowed to go into hers?" he thought. He decided to thank her the next day.

Chapter Six

Vincent lay awake for a long time, pondering over what his parents had told him. How was he to tell Vera that he did not love her anymore? Had Jiffa been told? Was that why she was so tense when he hugged her, and shy when he spoke to her? How could he look her in the face without thinking she was his wife? If he ignored her, would she think he hated her?

After an uncomfortable night, Vincent was up before the first cockcrow. He was worried about Vera and decided to see her that afternoon. Then he recalled the rules his father had laid down the night before. How on earth did his parents expect him to stay in the house to be watched by them? He would only agree to marry Jiffa if he was trusted. His father's rules were for idiots and he was too clever for such nonsense. He would see him in the morning and explain a few things to him.

When Vincent came out of his bedroom, he was surprised to find Jiffa already up. She told him his water was ready in the bathroom.

"Everybody is up, and we have all washed, you're the only one left," she said.

"What you mean is, I'm the only one around without a sweet-smelling body," said Vincent jokingly.

"I don't mean that!" she laughed, and added, "Breakfast will be ready for you and Mama soon. Papa has already gone to the palace".

"Am I looking smart?" asked Vincent as he joined his mother and Jiffa for breakfast.

"Very," said his mother, "Are you going out?"

"Yes. I am seeing a friend later" he replied.

"Which friend?" asked Mama.

"Why do you want to know?"

"Because I am your mother, and I want to know where you are going"

"Patrick," said Vincent sharply.

"I'm sorry if you think I was probing," his mother replied.

"Not at all, I apologise for raising my voice. May I have a word with you after breakfast?" he added.

"Certainly. I'll be in the sitting room," said Mama.

Mama was in the sitting room after breakfast when she called Jiffa. "I want you to supervise the loading of the gari. This morning the driver will be coming to take them to Togo. Be careful when you are counting the sacks. These drivers and aplankeys are all thieves, so keep your eyes open. I'll be waiting here."

"Yes, Mama," said Jiffa, nervously. She was worried by the conversation between Vincent and his mother at breakfast. She cleared away the breakfast and washed the dishes. Then she went into the gari shed, and began counting the sacks and waiting.

On his way to see his mother, Vincent saw Jiffa sitting in the gari shed and wanted to go over and thank her, but he had to see his mother first. "Poor girl," he sighed. "What a life."

Mama was reading her bible when Vincent entered and sat next to her on the sofa.

"I am sorry to keep you waiting, I was making my bed," he said. "I must thank Jiffa for doing it last night."

"I asked her to," his mother replied. "She is here to serve you, and there's no need to thank her for everything she does. But I want you to appreciate it and respect her." After a pause she added, "And I hope you will do nothing to harm her."

"Harm her?" Vincent said, surprised. "Why should I harm Jiffa?"

"Tell me, where are you going?" asked his mother.

Vincent bowed his head for a moment before answering. "To see my girlfriend," he answered quietly.

"Then you now understand why I used the word 'harm.' Can't you sit and talk to Jiffa? Why are you going out and leaving her alone in the house? When you get back, she will have finished cooking for you. You must learn to treat her well."

Vincent felt ashamed.

"Yesterday who brought you water to wash?" his mother continued.

"She did." His head was bowed.

"And what about today?"

"She did."

"And now that you look smart, you are off to see another girl. We have given you a girl, the best wife you could find anywhere. If you think our choice is not good and yours is better, go ahead. Jiffa is sitting in that shed all alone, waiting for nobody. I lied to her in order to be alone with you. She is not your servant, she is going to be your wife. So for heaven's sake get to know her better."

"Mama, I agree with everything you've said. But don't forget that it was only last night that Papa told me why Jiffa was here. I have slept on it, and I wanted to talk to him this morning. But since he is not in, I think you should hear me out."

"Go ahead - I'm listening

"I have a girlfriend whom I love very much. She knows I am coming home today, because I wrote and told her. How can I refuse to see here again? Jiffa is in this house as my future wife, and I've been given so many rules to obey that I don't feel relaxed with her. If you and Papa want me to leave my girlfriend, then you must trust me. If you think I will go to bed with Jiffa, then you are wrong. These rules would drive any man away."

"Vincent," said Mama. "The thought of allowing you to go into Jiffa 's bedroom worries me. How do you think your father and I will feel when you are together? You are a man, not an angel. However, I'll talk to him as soon as he gets back."

"I hate to think that Jiffa is sitting all alone," said Vincent.

"Well why don't you ask her to come and sit with us?" said Mama. Vincent left the room and went slowly out to the shed.

Jiffa was thinking about her mother. How was her business going? The tense heat of the grill at which she stood and roasted plantains was bad for her health. Maybe one day she would be able to help her. Jiffa thought of her father, and this brought tears to her eyes. She lifted her head after drying her eyes with the edge of her cloth, and saw Vincent standing in front of her.

"Why are you crying?" he asked. He knelt down and held her hands. "Has someone upset you?"

"No." More tears ran down her cheeks. "Then why are you crying?" he asked. He helped her to her feet and took her into the sitting-room.

35

"What is wrong?" Mama asked.

"She has been thinking about her mother," Vincent said, acting the part of a caring husband.

"I'm not surprised. She is all on her own in Adidome," Mama replied.

"Stop crying, Jiffa," Vincent said. She dried her tears.

"Come and sit on my lap," said Mama. Jiffa did as she was told. "Now, you are here as my daughter-in-law. I want you to feel at ease with me, and tell me anything that is worrying you."

"Yes, Mama," said Jiffa slowly. She had stopped crying, and was happy to be sitting on Mama's lap. It reminded her of her childhood. Mama had always treated her gently, and she remembered those days vividly.

Sensing that Mama's thighs were tired, Jiffa asked if she could go back to her seat.

"Yes - sit beside Vincent," Then, for the first time, Mama spoke to them about their marriage. "I want both of you to listen carefully. Yesterday was the first time we spoke to Vincent about taking you as his future wife."

Jiffa bowed her head, and Vincent looked at her thoughtfully.

"It won't be the easiest of marriages," Mama continued, "Although you have been brought up in the same way as Vincent, things have changed since the death of your father. Vincent is going ahead with his education, and you are not. That may be a barrier between you in future, but it shouldn't be, because there are many illiterate women who are married to professors and getting on very well. It is the duty of men to help their wives, rather than make them feel inferior. I hope my son will do his best for you. I want you to be at ease with him. You can go to his bedroom whenever you like, and he can come to yours. But, Vincent, I would not forgive you if you make love to her."

Vincent bowed his head.

"You have asked me to trust you," Mama added, "And that is what I'm going to do. I'll talk to your father later, and I'm sure he will agree. Jiffa, I'll arrange for you to go to your mother when Vincent goes back to college, and return when he next comes home. Will that help?"

Vincent raised his head and looked at Jiffa.

"Yes, Mama," Jiffa's voice was soft. What a kind woman Mama is, she thought. She wished she were her real mother

"Vincent, I would like you to stay in today and talk to Jiffa. She is here because of you, and I don't think you should go and visit Patrick. He can come and visit you here if he wants to."

"Alright, Mama," Vincent replied.

"Jiffa, please don't prepare lunch today," Mama said, "There is enough food. Anyway, the chief is having a party for his advisors this evening, and we have been invited."

"Yes Mama."

"Vincent, Papa is going to tell the chief about your quiz this evening."

"Oh, no!" Vincent cried, "Why?"

"You should be proud. The chief is an interesting man, and he will be delighted to know that there is a contestant from Kpetwei. If they put your name in the newspapers, they are bound to mention Kpetwei, aren't they?"

"I suppose so."

"Now, I'm going to spread a mat under the mango tree and stretch my body. It's too hot for me to go anywhere," said Mama, getting up from the chair. Vincent offered her an arm.

"Can I spread the mat for you?" Jiffa asked, eager to please her.

"Yes, my daughter. It's under my bed."

After Jiffa left the room, Mama turned to Vincent.

"I hope you will never treat Jiffa badly. She has gone through many difficulties. And you could be in her position tomorrow."

"I know," said Vincent, pulling on his beard.

"Mama, I've spread the mat with a pillow on it" Jiffa said, before leaving them and going outside.

Mama took her bible and left the sitting room, followed by Vincent.

$\mathcal{C}$hapter $\mathcal{S}$even

$\mathcal{M}$AMA READ HER BIBLE, MAKING IT obvious that she wanted to be left alone. Vincent beckoned Jiffa to follow him, and they went into his bedroom. As she entered Jiffa noticed that Vincent had made his bed, and asked him why.

"Why shouldn't I make my bed?" he replied. "I lie on it, so I must make it, if I lay on it with you, it would be a different matter. I felt guilty last night when I came to find that you have made it beautifully. I then wanted to come and thank you."

"Its good you didn't," Jiffa replied, "Because I wasn't allowed to be alone with you. That was one of Papa's rules."

"So why are we alone now?" Vincenmt asked.

Jiffa was not sure whether she should be sitting in his room or not.

"I talked to Mama this morning and I asked her to trust me not to do anything to jeopardize our future," said Vincent, using the English word, and feeling proud to have done away with his father's silly rules.

"Vincent, have you got a dictionary?" Jiffa's voice was quiet.

"Yes, why?"

"I want to look up the word jeopardize."

"I can tell you the meaning."

"No I want to look it up myself, so that it will stick in my memory." Vincent took the Concise Oxford Dictionary from his bookshelf.

"Shall I help you find it? He asked, giving the book to her.

"No I will find it myself." Jiffa turned the pages of the dictionary. Vincent stood over her as she searched for the word. What a clever girl, he thought. Some beautiful girls are stupid, but Jiffa was as clever as she was beautiful. Her beauty was suddenly irresistible to him, and he no longer saw her as his cousin but as his future wife. He knelt in front of her, and gently took the dictionary from her.

"Jiffa, you'll be mine forever," he said, moving closer to her. She felt shy and uneasy. It was the first time a man had said anything like that to her. Vincent did not give her time to think: he kissed her. Jiffa struggled with him, but she enjoyed it. As for Vincent, he wished he could ignore his parents' wishes and make love to her there and then.

"You should never be shy with me. I have liked you ever since we were children. Now I have to transform that liking into love. I can only do that if you show you love me."

Jiffa bowed her head. "Thank you. Can I look up the word now?" She picked up the dictionary and looked up 'jeopardize'. This time he did not stop her.

"Oh, it means' endanger,' she said. Vincent lay on his bed admiring her. Their eyes met when she looked up. "You've been staring at me, haven't you?" she asked.

"Who wouldn't?" Any man would. Here I am with a beautiful girl in my room, and yet I can't touch her!"

"I'm leaving this room, before I jeopardize your mind," she said and they both laughed. Jiffa stood up.

"Is that the first time you have used that word?" Vincent asked, trying to stop her leaving.

"If I have used it before, would I have to look up the meaning? Or do you think I'm one of those people who will use a long word without knowing the meaning?" She sat back down.

"I was very sad to hear about your father's death," Vincent said.

"Thank you for your sympathy."

"What was wrong with him?"

"He went to the bathroom one morning, lost his balance and fell. My mother was out buying plantations, and I was at school. When my mother arrived later, she found him dead. Nobody was there to help him...." Jiffa looked upset.

"Come and sit beside me, you are too far away."

Jiffa did as Vincent asked. She loved him and there was no need to pretend. He dried her tears, and promised that he would help her continue her education in future.

"Oh, what a kind thought - thank you!" she exclaimed. "I enjoyed school, and I want to study again."

"Was it hard, to say goodbye to your friends?" asked Vincent, longing to touch her, but restraining himself.

"Yes, but what alternative was there? I'm lucky, because your parents have been so kind to me".

"You are a very nice girl, and any family were bound to treat you well. I hope I'll treat you well when we are married."

"The sun has set," Jiffa said. "I must go and wake your mother up, so she can get ready to go. How strange that we haven't even thought about lunch."

"Do you know why?" he asked.

"Tell me."

"Because we are enjoying each other's company. We played together when we were children, and now we are picking up where we left off. So much has changed since then, yet we are here and together again. It is exciting - like a dream."

"Yes," said Jiffa, looking into his eyes.

Vincent realized this, pulled her closer and kissed her.

"I have to go now," she said and ran out.

Mama stretched her limbs and thanked Jiffa for waking her up.

"If it hadn't been for you, I would have slept the whole day. The breeze under this tree is wonderful. Have you tried sleeping her before?" she asked.

"No," said Jiffa, smiling.

"You must try it one day." Mama was pleased that Jiffa looked happy. Being with Vincent had obviously cheered her up. That was what she needed; a kind person who understood her problems.

"Mama, there is water in the barrel. Shall I take some into the bathroom for you?"

"Yes please, Papa hasn't returned, but I think he said we should meet him there. So let's all get ready quickly and go."

Jiffa was getting ready when Mama called. She appeared looking beautifully dressed, in her blue flowered dress with a stiff belt and her best shoes.

"Ooh! Jiffa, you look so pretty! Come and give me a hug." Mama Agawu tried to make Jiffa feel at ease with her compliments. "Where is Vincent?"

"In his room"

"And what is he doing, Please call him, its time to go"

Jiffa walked briskly to Vincent's door and knocked. There was no reply, so she entered. Vincent was fast asleep. She stood and looked at him for a while, and then tapped him gently on the shoulder. He opened his eyes.

"I was dreaming about you," he said.

"What was the dream?" she asked.

"I'll tell you later; meanwhile I want to go on dreaming."

"You can't, it's time to go to the palace. Wake up, Mama is waiting outside."

Jiffa left him and went to the sitting room to be with Mama.

"There you are at last," said Mama when Vincent appeared

"I don't know why you are in such a hurry," Vincent retorted. "It's only six o'clock."

"I have no watch," Mama replied. "I use the sun to tell the time. Anyway, it's better to be early than late."

Mama was sandwiched between Jiffa and Vincent. They held hands and strolled along the dusty road to the palace.

"I had a lovely sleep under the mango tree," said Mama.

"That's good, the breeze cools every part of your body." Vincent replied.

"I'll try it, one day," said Jiffa.

"Maybe we could try it together," Vincent said. "On separate mats, I mean."

"Do you have to put it like that?" said his mother.

"I'm sorry, Mama. I did not mean to embarrass Jiffa."

"Let me tell you about this party," said Mama. "The chief organizes these parties three times a year. This one is to celebrate the end of the year. He does it to thank his advisors and all those who work for him."

"How many people will be there?" Vincent asked.

"It varies. Why?"

"I wondered whether it would be obvious if we left early."

"You can leave at any time you want, but I have to stay on with your father. Jiffa, will you stay on with us, or come back with Vincent?"

"I will do whatever you think is right" said Jiffa quietly. She wanted to return with Vincent, but was too shy to say so.

"No, Jiffa, the choice is yours," said Vincent sharply. He too wanted Jiffa to come with him.

"I think you will be too tired to wait for Papa and me, so come back with Vincent. We will follow later." Mama realized that Vincent would feel he was not being trusted if she told Jiffa to stay and wait for them.

"So I'm to bring Jiffa home with me. Is that right?" Vincent wanted to be absolutely sure.

"How many times do I have to say it?"

"Oh Mama, don't raise your voice. I'm just pleased that I'll be able to get away early."

The drumming from the palace could be heard miles away. There was a crowd when they arrived. Papa's position as a chief advisor, meant that his family were special guests. Mama introduced Jiffa to the chief as her future daughter-in-law. They all greeted the chief and the important guest.

The chief had arranged for Vincent to sit next to him, so that he could ask him about the quiz. Anything that would bring Kpetwei into the public eye had to be taken seriously. The drumming and dancing stopped and libation was poured to declare the party officially opened. Then the music started again, and all the guests helped themselves to food and drinks. Jiffa enjoyed herself tremendously - for the first time in her life she was meeting important people. All thanks Mama and Papa.

The only person who was not enjoying himself was Vincent. He was sitting next to the chief, and could not get away as early as he had hoped. Even if he could, he felt that Jiffa would not follow him because he could see her chatting gaily to people at he other end of the table.

"Your father told me that you will soon be in the newspapers. When will it be?" asked Chief Kushieto.

"After the Christmas holidays." Oh, what a bore thought Vincent. What has his quiz got to do with this chief? How he wished he had not come. He was not coming to any of these parties ever again.

"And will you be chosen?" asked the chief, with a broad smile. If Vincent won the quiz, he would organize a party like this for him.

"I don't yet know. The first round will be held in Ho, and the finals in Accra."

"If you are chosen, please let me know, because I'd like one of my advisors to accompany you to Accra."

"Alright, sir." Why on earth should an advisor go with him to Accra? Vincent asked himself. This chief is either drunk or mad, or both. His advisors should advise him better.

The news that Vincent's name might appear in the newspapers spread very fast around the table. It was the first thing his father had told the chief when he came to see him that morning. Everyone showed great admiration for Vincent's brilliance. His mother kept talking about it, as if nothing else mattered in the world. One of the guests turned to Jiffa and asked if she was proud of her future husband.

"Yes," she said shyly. She had no idea what they were all talking about since Vincent had not mentioned the quiz to her. But she did not want to look ignorant, so she joined in. Later on, when nobody was listening, she asked Mama about it. Oh so this was what it was all about, thought Jiffa. A competition which had not even taken place, and yet these people talk as if Vincent has won.

It was getting late, and because Papa Agawu had to stay behind for yet another meeting, Mama asked permission to leave. She walked home with Jiffa and Vincent, and talked about the party on the way.

"It was fun, wasn't it?" said Mama.

"Yes, it was nice," answered Jiffa. She had really enjoyed herself.

"What about you?" Mama asked Vincent.

"Not very much," he replied.

"Why not?" But she knew perfectly well why Vincent was sulking.

"I was sitting next to the chief, and he kept talking about my quiz. Why did Papa tell him? Supposing I don't win, then what will he do?"

"There's no need to take your anger on your father. As far as I can see you are annoyed because you were not able to go home with Jiffa, It was not our fault that we were given a seat with the important guests. I want you to bury your anger on the road before we get home."

"I'm sorry," said Vincent.

They hurried home, because the wind was blowing very fast.

"Mama, can Jiffa come into my bedroom and chat for a while?" asked Vincent when they got to the gate.

"Ask Jiffa, not me," Mama knew that Vincent could not take Jiffa into his bedroom so late in the evening without her approval. Poor Vincent, A man looks strong, but he can so easily be brought to his knees by a woman.

"Why were you so gloomy?" Jiffa asked, watching him undress. "Please wait till I am gone before you undress."

"Why? I'm yours, so you may as well as see everything now"

"I'm not ready, so please leave your pants on!"

Vincent sat on his bed. "There's nothing to be shy of. I hope you are not going to behave like a child when we get married."

"I came into your room to cheer you up. If you are going to be rude then I am leaving" Jiffa stood up, but he stopped her.

"Please don't go. I'm sorry. I'm frustrated. Come and sit beside me, I will tell you about my dream." His voice was shaking.

"Why are you unhappy? This afternoon we were chatting nicely, what is wrong now?" She sat beside him to cheer him up.

"This afternoon I dreamt I was making love to you, and when I woke up there was a semen in my bed."

Jiffa turned and faced him. " You dreamt you were having sex with me?" She stood up.

"Is that surprising?" he asked.

"I can't answer that." Jiffa's voice was hoarse. "You must understand something. Until we get married, I want you to concentrate on your books. Think how lucky you are to be at college! Forget I exist for the moment. My future and our children's future are in your hands. Can't you see how terrible it would be if you threw it all away? I beg you, control yourself. If your parents see that I'm distracting your concentration by being here, they will send me back to Adidome. Do you want that?"

"No," Vincent replied. He sat with his head bowed and listened carefully. For the first time he realized that his parents had chosen a good woman for him.

"Look at me. Your parents have been very kind to me, and I'm not going to disobey them just to satisfy your sexual desire. So if you want me to stay in this house, behave yourself. Goodnight."

Jiffa went to her bedroom and locked the door. Minutes later she heard Papa's voice chatting to one of the neighbours. How lucky that he had not seen her coming out of Vincent's room at that late hour!

Vincent thought about what Jiffa had said. She was right, he had to control himself. Where would she go if his parents turned her out? Poor girl! She had talked this evening as if she were his mother.

Chapter Eight

*V*INCENT'S HOLIDAYS PASSED QUICKLY AND BEFORE he knew it there was only a day left. Even after Jiffa had told him to control himself, he still longed for her; but she refused to give in. The only satisfaction he had was the occasional kiss when she came into his room.

The day before he went back to school, his parents talked to them.

"I hope you have enjoyed your holidays," his father said.

"Yes, Papa, I have."

"What about you, Jiffa?" asked Mama. "Have you enjoyed your stay?"

"Very much, Mama."

"Vincent will be going back to college tomorrow," said Mama.

"The day after, I want you to go and visit your mother and come back whenever you want to. But I would like you to be here whenever Vincent is on holidays. To be honest I wish you were not going, because we will miss you very much. But you have left your mother alone for too a long."

"Yes, it's time you went back to see her," Papa agreed emphatically.

"I can't thank you enough for your kindness," said Jiffa. I'll miss you too..." Choked by weeping, she could not finish her sentence.

Vincent put his arm around her," Don't cry,"

"We know how you feel," said Mama. "I love you just as I love Vincent. Why don't you take her to your room and talk to her, Vincent? After all, she won't be seeing you for some time. The two of you should have this evening on your own. Don't you agree, Papa?"

"Certainly."

Vincent and Jiffa walked slowly to his room and sat on the bed.

"I'll write to you when I get back to college. You must trust me not to let you down. Please don't cry," he said.

Jiffa dried her tears and turned to him.

"Anybody in my position would cry. You're going back to school. The day after tomorrow I will also leave for Adidome. All my friends will be back in school, and I will be selling roasted plantains by the roadside to help my mother."

"I know how badly you want to continue with your education," Vincent said. "I can not help you now, but I promise that as soon as I get a job I shall help you to continue from where you left off. Does that cheer you up?"

"Yes," she said. "I know you'll keep your promise. Meanwhile, I'll read my books whenever I have time to keep my mind sharp for the future."

"I'm glad you've cheered up," Vincent pulled her gently towards him and kissed her.

"Why don't I help you pack your things? You'll be leaving early tomorrow."

"Yes that is a good idea," but his mind was elsewhere.

"What are you thinking about?" she asked, touching him gently.

"I have had a wonderful idea,"

"What?"

"Since it's my last night, why don't you sleep here?"

"Vincent!" Her eyes were wide open. "No, that is exactly what your parents don't want.

"I know but I'll ask their permission."

"Do you really want me to sleep here?" she said, looking into his eyes.

"Don't you?" He was reading her mind.

"Yes provided you..."

Vincent laughed, and did not hear what Jiffa said.

"Have you finished laughing ?" she said strenly.

"Yes."

"Then may I continue?"

"Yes, Mama."

"Please don't call me Mama, I'm not your mother."

"But you behave like her."

"Does that surprise you?"

"Yes and no. After all she brought you up."

48

"May I finish what I was saying? I will sleep in your room, provided you leave me in peace."

"What were you thinking of?"

"Keep your promise to your mother. So that she can trust you forever"

When Vincent left the room, Jiffa got out his suitcase and packed his things. Having unpacked for him when he arrived, she knew what he needed to take back. Vincent's promise consoled her and increased her confidence. While she was waiting she took his dictionary and looked up a few words.

Vincent's parents were discussing his future when he entered. His mother commented. "There is a saying that if you mention someone's name and you don't see the person then he or she is dead. You entered just as your name was mentioned"

"That is just one of those African beliefs," Vincent replied. His father agreed and they laughed.

"Why is it funny?" Vincent was pleased. If his parents were in a good mood, there was a chance they would agree to his proposal.

"We have too many unexplained beliefs, Mama," he said, excited at the prospect of a discussion.

"Give me an example," she said.

"One is not supposed to whistle after dark, in case a ghost comes and takes you away. What ghost?" he asked.

"Is that all?" Since it was Vincent's last evening, it was great to be having a chat.

"No, Mama, you know there are plenty of them but I can't think of any more now." His thoughts were on Jiffa, he did not want to stay too long, or she would be asleep by the time he returned. But he did not want his parents to think he was in a hurry to leave so he told his mother to give him a minute to think.

"Mm... what about the belief that nobody should sweep at night, otherwise poverty will take over the house?"

"Who told you that?" asked Mama.

"You did. I remember it vividly. When I was a child, you warned me never to sweep at night. And you said the same thing to Jiffa."

Papa was laughing at them - he would side with the winner because he could never be bothered to argue himself. He had always shown great love and respect for Vincent ever since he had been a child. They had often sat knee-to-knee and discussed problems. Vincent's ideas sometimes made more sense than his own. How could he tell his son that he was cleverer than his father? The only way was to treat him as an equal. Vincent's future looked bright. The only danger was in his marriage. Marrying a selfish woman who did not understand him would ruin his position and he would lose his self-respect. Women could reduce the most powerful man on earth to nothing. A woman is born with natural powers. She does not need to prove it.

"Where is Jiffa?" asked Papa.

"In my room," Vincent replied.

"Why didn't she come with you?" His father looked suspicious.

"She is fine, Papa." Vincent was about to ask permission for Jiffa to stay in his room when his mother began talking again.

"I will miss Jiffa so much when she goes. Not because she is my daughter-in-law, but because of her character. She is so gentle. Her manners and behaviour make me love her even more. How many girls of her age could face what she has gone through? Papa and I feel guilty for allowing her mother to take her away from school. It must be terrible for her to see you still studying and we are the ones who agreed that she should stop. But I'm afraid it's more complicated than that..."

"Everything's complicated," interrupted Papa. "Nobody understands the world we live in; not even those Europeans, who claim to. Some people are lucky, others are not. One part of the world is dying of hunger, the other from over-eating. You could simplify matters, and say that if the 'haves' gave to the 'have-nots' hunger and diseases would be wiped out. But nothing is simple, and we must accept that we are in world we don't understand. Nobody will ever understand it, otherwise our forefathers would have understood it before us. I'm sure Vincent could argue against that, but it's too late now, so he can take this challenge next time."

Vincent thought about what his father had said. Why was it that Jiffa had to stop her education, while he was able to go on with his? It might not be simple, but it was totally unfair.

"I have promised to pay for Jiffa to complete her education when I get a job," said Vincent.

"That must have cheered her up," said Mama.

"It did."

"You are good for her. Neither your father nor I could have cheered her up so quickly, but you have given her the right medicine. I think you should go and be with her now, or she will feel neglected."

All this time, Vincent had been thinking how to approach his parents about Jiffa sleeping in his room. Now he came straight to the point.

"I want Jiffa to sleep in my room tonight," he said, looking at his mother, It was no use asking his father, because he would just tell him to ask his mother. Mama Agawu did not dominate her husband, but her views carried weight.

"I thought she was sleeping there anyway," came his mother's reply. Vincent realised suddenly that his mother had read his mind as soon as he came in. She had deliberately not asked after Jiffa, and had waited all this time for him to say why he had come. Thank God he had not dressed it up, because she would have made him look a complete fool. He hoped Jiffa would not follow in his mother's footsteps. One clever woman in the house was bad enough, with two, life would be unbearable.

"Mama, you know very well that Jiffa will not sleep in my room without your permission."

And I shall not allow it unless you keep your promise," said Mama with a wicked grin.

"I promise," said Vincent. Earlier, he had won the argument about African beliefs, and had laughed at his mother, but now she was having the last laugh. He said goodnight.

"Sleep well, and see you tomorrow," said his mother.

Chapter Nine

VINCENT LEFT, AND WENT HURRIEDLY BACK to his room.

"Poor boy!" said Papa. You are very good to him. He loves you, yet you tease him."

"I had been watching him since he came in. I knew he had something on his mind," said Mama. "He just didn't know how to express it."

"He was longing to leave, and we held him back" Papa said, laughing.

"I wish he was not leaving tomorrow," said Mama. "These holidays have passed too quickly, and I am so happy that he has accepted Jiffa really well. I thought the arrangement would disturb him, but things have worked out beautifully."

"I think they were born for each other. Do you remember when they were young?" asked her husband.

"Yes" said Mama. "He was always amusing Jiffa and playing little tricks on her. Oh, I can't wait to see them marry."

Vincent got to his room, but it was too late, Jiffa was fast asleep! He was delighted to see that she had packed his suitcase. What a treasure! He stood and looked at her, imagining what kind of life they would have together . A beautiful wife, a nice house and happy children. What more could a man ask for? He changed quickly and got into bed. When he drew back the bedspread he saw his dictionary with a letter in it.

Dearest Vincent,
I've waited for hours, but since you did not come I decided to leave this note, in case I'm asleep when you come in. As you can see, I've packed your

suitcase. *The things I've put in it are those I unpacked on the night of your arrival. Maybe there are certain things you don't want to take with you this term. Please repack if you want to.*

Vincent, I'd like us to see your parents first thing tomorrow morning, so that I can thank them for all they have done for me. They have not only cared for me when I was a child; they are thinking of my future. Few people can be as lucky as I am. Also, I beg you to concentrate on your books. Don't worry about me: I'll be all right. It would pain me to learn that your studies have suffered because of me. I will pull through whatever problems I meet, by the grace of God.

The only thing I ask of you is to answer my letters.

My address is C/o Togbi, P. O. Box 87, Adidome, Volta Region.

Finally, I wish you luck for this term, and success in your quiz competition.

I remain yours forever.

Jiffa

I have two powerful women in my life, Vincent thought as he read the letter for the second time. How could Jiffa say she was lucky? He opened his suitcase and filed her letter away.

Jiffa woke up at dawn, and saw Vincent fast asleep. She crept out of bed quietly so as not to disturb him, and went outside to clean the compound. Then she took a bath, prepared breakfast, and knocked on Mama's door to wake her up. Vincent woke up suddenly and looked puzzled. Did he dream that Jiffa had slept in his room, or was it real? He could not remember.

Later that morning, he got up hurriedly and went for his breakfast.

"Mm! you do look smart," said his mother.

"Mama, you always say that, whenever I wear anything"

His parents might think he had a nice time with Jiffa last night. If only they knew.

"I won't comment on your appearance ever again," said Mama.

"I'm only joking." He turned to Jiffa. "Thank you for packing my suitcase last night."

"What time did you come to bed?" asked Jiffa.

"And what time did you leave the room this morning?" Vincent asked.

"Why are you answering my question with a question?"

Mama listened carefully and agreed with Jiffa.

"Well quite late, you were fast asleep, and I did not want to wake you up. I put the dictionary back on the shelf." He wanted her to know that he had got her letter.

"You must have fallen asleep very early," said Mama.

"I was very tired," said Jiffa shyly. What would Mama be thinking?

"You were tired because you wept for such a long time," said Papa. "Crying is exhausting." Jiffa wished they would change the subject.

"Vincent," said Papa, "Finish your breakfast quickly. I will be in my room waiting"

"Here are your school fees and pocket money." Papa gave him two envelopes." Do you want to give Jiffa a present before you leave?"

"I was going to give her some of my pocket-money," said Vincent quietly.

"No, have this extra money. Isn't that better?" said Papa.

"Yes, but you have given me enough money, and it wouldn't hurt to give her part of mine." Vincent felt sorry for his father. How could he repay his parents for their kindness? He just hoped he would never have to go against them. He thanked Papa and promised to let them know the results of the quiz. Then he went out and called Jiffa into his bedroom.

"Thank you for the letter you wrote last night. I'll take your advice seriously, and I shall keep that letter all of my life."

"What is so special about it?"

"It's your first letter to me. Just like having your first girl friend. No matter how many others you have later, you never forget the first." He waited to hear what she would say to this tactless remark.

"So who was your first girl-friend?

"You, of course." Vincent kissed her. "I hope you will reply promptly to my letters. Take this, it's a present from me." He gave her the money.

"Thank you," Jiffa replied. It's very kind of you to do this."

The taxi was on time and took them to the station. Papa sat in front and talked to the driver while Mama gave Vincent last-minute advice. The coach was almost full and he had to rush to get his luggage on board. Vincent shook hands with his father, hugged his mother and Jiffa together, and boarded the coach.

Surprisingly enough, Jiffa did not cry when the coach left. She was thinking of her own journey back to her mother. Would her mother be happy to have her back, or would she see her as a burden?

They went back in the same taxi and she decided to show Mama the present Vincent had given her.

They reached home and went into the sitting room. Jiffa asked whether she should bring them some water.

"Yes, my daughter, I'm dying of thirst. I'm sure Papa would also like some."

Jiffa brought the water and Mama drank it without a break. Aaa!" she said. "Water is the best wine on earth."

Papa was ready to leave when he suddenly turned to Mama "We are having supper with the chief this evening. I should have told you earlier, but Vincent's departure distracted me. I will be waiting for you and Jiffa"

"Are there going to be a lot of people?"

"No, it will be just them and us" said Papa, talking as he left.

"Jiffa, put two chairs under the mango-tree so that we can get some fresh air." Mama was missing Vincent already. The two women sat knee-to-knee, chatting.

"I wanted Vincent to come with me this morning to thank you and Papa for all you have done for me."

"You should never thank me. If anything, I ought to thank you. You are my treasure".

"This is what Vincent gave me before he left." Jiffa took an envelope out of her pocket and gave it to Mama.

"Oh, Vincent, how generous of him." Mama and her husband had agreed that Vincent should give Jiffa a present, but she pretended not to know about it. When she counted the money, she realized that her son had added part of his own pocket money to it. She was pleased. After what she had seen of these two, she knew that their marriage would be a success. There is no such thing as a marriage without problems, but when two people genuinely love each other nothing can drive them apart.

"I wish Vincent was here," said Jiffa. It was the first time she had been able to talk like that to Mama. She was quiet for a moment then she started to fight back tears.

"Don't cry, my dear, I know how you feel about him, but it won't be long before you get married. Vincent is missing you too, I'm sure of that." She gave the envelope back to Jiffa.

Young love always began like this. Mama hoped she could trust Vincent not to let Jiffa down in future. You could never trust a man completely with women. But as long as you didn't see or hear anything, it did not matter too much.

Chapter Ten

*V*INCENT'S JOURNEY BACK TO KPANDO WAS not comfortable. The coach moved slowly from pothole to pothole, and the passengers wondered when they were going to reach their destination.

"What is the future for a country if all of its roads are full of holes?" said a passenger in the back row. The other passengers turned and looked at him. Most of them agreed, and a debate began about what the government was doing with the country's resources.

"Oh yes," said another passenger. "It looks as if our backsides will be broken to bits by the time we arrive, if we ever do!" The other passengers cheered and clapped loudly.

"You are right!" said a group of women sitting in the row opposite Vincent. They were all dressed in white. There was peace for sometime, than a haggard middle-aged man next to Vincent broke the silence.

"Things were not like this in the olden days. Our forefathers walked everywhere, but now we want to copy the white man.

"Why don't you set an example by walking, then?" said one of the women. "How can we go back in time?"

"Then this is how we shall suffer," replied the man. "We feed off the white man's leftovers. Why can't we build our own roads, instead of paying for results like this?"

"I agree with you," said a woman. She was sitting behind Vincent, so they both started talking.

"I have worked for over six years in a company at Kpando, said the lady. The work in the office was meant for two people, but I did it alone: typing, meeting clients, booking hotels for overseas visitors, attending meetings - you name it, I did it. One day my boss called me and said he was going to advertise the post of a personal secretary. Since I'd been doing the job anyway, I wondered why he didn't promote me instead."

"Who was your boss?" interrupted the man sitting next to Vincent.

"I don't think you will know him," answered the woman. He used to be the assistant director of Volta Lake Authority"

"So what happened?. Vincent was listening intently. The woman's voice was soft, and with so much noise going on, it was hard to hear.

"Early one morning, my boss called me into his office. I thought I was going to take shorthand, so I took my pad and pencil with me. When I entered, I saw him with a white lady. He introduced her as Emily Lancaster. "From now on," he said "Miss Lancaster will be your superior. Please show her how things work in this office."

"Why should you?" asked the man sitting next to Vincent." "She was only your superior because she had a white skin. I'm sick of my countrymen. I was in Britain three years ago, you know. By the way, what's your name?"

"Helena Okulu" said the woman, who was wearing a green skirt and white blouse. "What's yours?" she asked

"Kwashie." They shook hands.

"Were you really in Britain?" asked Helena. She was amazed, because Kwashie looked worn out. One would not think he had ever left his village, let alone travelled to Britain.

"You don't believe it, do you?"

"I can't say that, because I don't know you." But Helena did not believe him. At that point Vincent turned and looked at Kwahie, and shook his head.

"Yes I was there"

"Why did you come back?" she asked.

"It's a long story. What's the time?" Kwashie asked Helena.

"Twenty to one,"

"Oh! We have time for part of the story. Who knows, maybe we'll meet again to continue it."

"Let's hope so," She felt sorry for him.

"After university I went to Britain to pursue my career as an architect," said Kwashie, looking at Helena. She was surprised, so was Vincent, who was now longing to join the conversation. "Yes, I was at University of Science and Technology."

"Looking at you, nobody would believe you," said Helena.

"Don't worry: I realize that myself. It's painful to know that one's life has been wasted. I didn't go to Britain on a government scholarship. I went to visit, with the intention of staying on to do a part-time course in architecture."

"Did you do it?" Helena was now beginning to believe Kwashie. He was speaking in his own language; but whenever he had to explain something to Helena in English she noticed that he spoke it very well.

"No. I arrived in Britain sometime in December. It was winter, and I was wearing jeans and a cotton shirt. I cannot describe the cold. It was like walking into a deep-freezer and not being able to get out. Steam came out of my mouth as if I was smoking a cigarette."

"Didn't you have anything warm to wear?" asked Helena.

"No but that was just the beginning of my difficulties. My brother had promised to meet me on arrival, but he wasn't there. With the help of a friend I got through immigration and took a taxi to his address. He had told me all would be well when I came over." He turned round to look at one of the ladies who had attacked him earlier on. She was asleep and snoring so loudly that Kwashie could not concentrate.

"My brother was at home when I arrived. The taxi-driver told me my fare was twelve pounds. I left my suitcase in the taxi and ran up to my brother's flat to get two pounds from him. I only had ten pounds to pay the driver."

"Why did you leave your suitcase in the taxi?" asked Helena" Your possessions must have been worth more than two pounds. If the taxi driver had driven away, what would you have done?"

"It doesn't work like that. A British taxi-driver would not allow you to get away with a penny. To start with, all the taxis have meters, that tell you how much you have to pay. Anyway, I rang my brother's doorbell, and he came out. I was shocked by the way he greeted me, but I ignored that and asked him to give me two pounds to pay for my taxi. 'I have no money,' Those were his exact words. Then he went up and got money from his wife."

"Did you know the wife?"

"No I had never met her before. She was a Jamaican born in Britain. When I entered my brother's flat, I realised that my coming had been a very big mistake."

"Why?"

"The problem was that his wife had not given him permission for me to stay with them".

"What!" said Vincent. Kwashie and Helena turned and looked at him.

"So you have been listening to our conversation," said Kwashie, with a smile.

"Yes."

"What made you join in?" asked Kwashie.

"I will not tolerate my wife giving me orders," Vincent replied.

"Are you married?" asked Kwashie, knowing perfectly well that Vincent was too young to be married.

"Yes and no,"

"What is your name?" asked Kwashie.

'Vincent Agawu"

"Now, Vincent, what did you mean by yes and no?"

Helena was watching them with interest.

"At the moment I'm a student."

"What college?"

"Kpando Secondary Technical School," said Vincent.

"Oh, Kpantec," said Kwashie. "Do you know Mr Apaloo?"

"Yes," said Vincent smiling, "He's our English teacher. Such a nice man. How do you know him?"

"He was my contemporary at UST," said Kwashie proudly.

"I see," said Vincent. 'But Mr Apaloo is in his thirties, how can he be your contemporary?"

"I look older than my age."

Helena felt sorry for him. His premature gray hair and haggard unshaven features made him look much older.

"Don't be sorry - I know it myself, and I feel bitter, bitter!" His shouts woke up the snoring lady.

"Why do you have to shout like that. Mr Bitter? Do you think you're in your own house? Why don't you face up to those who have made you feel bitter, instead of waking me up like this?" Many of the passengers turned round to see who the woman was talking to but Kwashie did not reply.

"Please continue, Kwashie," said Helena. She was longing to hear what had happened to Kwashie to make him so bitter.

"What's the time, Vincent?" asked Kwashie. He knew Helena wanted to hear the rest of his story, but he did not want to make a fool of himself, in case they arrived at the station before he had time to finish it. Instead, he asked Vincent what his 'yes and no' had meant.

"I have a cousin who my parents want me to marry."

"An arranged marriage?" asked Kwashie, smiling.

"Yes," said Vincent.

"Shake my hand. Vincent you are a lucky man. If my parents had arranged a marriage for me, I would be a much happier man today. As it is, I have failed in every way. I have no wife and children. Just look at me, do you think any woman would want me? I envy you, Vincent, I hope you make the best out of your marriage."

He patted Vincent on the shoulder, fighting back tears. "You have a future; I only have a past." Vincent took his hand and told him to pray and hope.

"Don't be upset, Kwashie," said Helena.

"We are almost in Kpando, so let's hope we meet again one day to continue from where we have left off."

"I live in Kpando with my grandmother" said Helena. Let me give you my address so you can visit me any time you come here. She opened her handbag and took out a pen and pad.

"Are you going to write shorthand?" said Kwashie, laughing.

Oh, don't remind me of those days, I was a bitter person, too," said Helena, wrinkling her forehead.

"There we are," he said, "I have found a companion - Mr and Mrs Bitter."

She wrote the address down and gave it to him.

"Vincent" he said "Give my regards to Mr Apaloo."

"Please, what is your second name?" Vincent asked.

"Amevor,"

"I will do that. And I hope you'll come and visit him one day, so that I'll see you again."

"I'll try," said Kwashie.

Kpando station was in sight, so Kwashie shook hands with Helena and Vincent, as they all prepared to alight.

"I've enjoyed meeting you two," said Vincent. He wished he could spend the whole day talking to Kwashie. He would ask Mr Apaloo for Kwashie's address and write him a letter. That would give him a nice surprise.

"It's been nice to meet you, too, Kwashie," said Helena. "I haven't noticed the journey at all, in fact, I could go back with you now, and listen to the rest of the story.'"

"Me, too," said Kwashie. "I would have loved to hear about your boss and Miss Lancaster"

The coach stopped at the station and the passengers alighted. Vincent said goodbye to Kwashie and Helena, and went off in a taxi. He could still see them chatting in the distance. How could three strangers enjoy each other's conversation so much that they longed to stay together, he wondered.

*C*hapter *E*leven

*J*IFFA WAS IN THE KITCHEN PREPARING lunch when Papa Agawu left hurriedly to see the chief.

"I don't know about you, but I am very hungry. Mama was tasting the soup in the kitchen.

"Let me lay the table now," said Jiffa getting everything ready. As they sat down to eat Mama could not help praising her.

"Mm! what lovely akpene! It slides so smoothly down my throat. You make cooking look so easy. I really wish you were not going tomorrow, because I will miss you."

"I will miss you too. But don't worry, time goes quickly, and before you know it I will be back." Jiffa was enjoying all the praise and love. Suddenly Mama looked sad, Jiffa noticed and asked her why.

"I was thinking about Vincent, he promised to write as soon as he arrived"

"I'm sure he will," said Jiffa. "He's such a kind person"

"I am so happy the two of you will get married one day and I know you will be very good for him. Vincent behaves like a child sometimes. You will have to be a wife and mother to him. Not every woman has the gift to do that. Did he tell you what I said last night?" She was trying to find out what had happened in the bedroom when Vincent went back to her.

"I was asleep so I didn't even hear him come back" said Jiffa apologetically.

"I'm glad, it serves him right for arguing with me all evening",

They finished eating, and Jiffa brought Mama soap and water to wash her hands.

"Thank you Jiffa, and now why don't you bring the two mats and spread them under the mango-tree? It's your last afternoon here, so let's enjoy the breeze." They chatted for a while, then fell asleep.

When Vincent got back to school, his friends helped him take his luggage to his dormitory. The other boys talked about their holidays, but he kept his arranged marriage to himself, in case they teased him. Some of them would think he was too intelligent to have his marriage arranged for him. It was his own life, and he did not want to discuss it. He made his bed and lay down because his back ached. How he wished Jiffa was around to give him a massage. Anyway it would not be long before they were married.

Mama Agawu and Jiffa woke up just in time to get to the palace. They had no time to wash, so they just changed and rushed out.

"We shouldn't have slept under that tree," said Mama, as they hurried out of the house. "It has nearly made us late."

"We have just enough time to get there," said Jiffa. Mama was panting for breath, so Jiffa slowed down. "Shall I run ahead and tell them you're on your way?"

"What a good idea. Please run along, if I keep hurrying like this, I'll be dead before I arrive."

When Jiffa arrived she was met at the gate by a young man.

"Can I help you?" he asked.

"I have come to see Papa Agawu," said Jiffa.

"He's in a meeting with my father," said the man.

"Who is your father?" asked Jiffa.

"Oh, you don't live in this village, do you?"

"No, I'm just visiting" she said. She was longing to get away from him before Mama arrived.

"Where do you live, if I may ask?" He knew Jiffa wanted to get away, but he was not going to let her go.

"Adidome," said Jiffa. She wanted to walk away, but that would be rude. She did not even know who he was.

"Ah! I know it well," said the man, smiling.

"May I see Papa Agawu, or could you tell Chief Kushieto that Mama Agawu is on her way?" This man would go on talking all night unless she stopped him.

"You mean, tell my father, "said the man pompously.

"Is the chief your father?" asked Jiffa.

"Yes. Please come with me," Jiffa followed him into the sitting room, and he offered her a chair.

"My name is Mawusi Kushieto. What is yours?"

"Jiffa Agbenyo" Why was he asking her so many questions?

"You have a beautiful name, has anyone told you that before? Wait, I'll be back in a minute, I'm going to inform my father."

After he left the room, Jiffa thanked God she had not been rude to him. That would have brought shame to the Agawus.

Mawusi came back shortly. "My father will be with you soon. What can I offer you to drink?"

"Coca-cola" Jiffa felt shy.

"Fine," said Mawusi, and went out to get it.

Where was Mama, wondered Jiffa. It had been some time since she left her.

Mawusi came in with a glass of coca-cola and gave it to her.

"Mama Agawu just asked me where you were, and I told her you were here," said Mawusi.

"Where is she?"

"In the kitchen, talking to my mother."

"Oh good. I was worried about her."

"Now you can relax and enjoy your drink," said Mawusi. Jiffa smiled and Mawusi was happy that he could talk to her until supper was ready.

"Which part of Adidome do you live in?"

"Near the tro-tro station," said Jiffa, without going into details. If only this man would stop asking questions, she would enjoy his company much more.

"My mother tells me you visited us recently," said Mawusi.

"Yes. I came with Vincent and his mother," said Jiffa. "It was wonderful." She felt like telling him that the evening had been enjoyable mainly because he was not around asking questions!

"I was sorry to miss it. I expect my absence was felt, because on such occasions I am always around. Unfortunately I had to go to Segakope to carry out some business transactions for my father," said Mawusi.

What a pompous man, thought Jiffa, talking about carrying out business transactions, he was probably just buying a few goats. Mawusi wished he had been at home. He was certain that Jiffa would have been his girl-friend by now.

"How often do you have parties like that?" she asked. She pitied Mawusi for thinking his absence had been felt. In fact nobody had mentioned his name.

"Mawusi!" a voice called from the kitchen. He got up and left. A moment later he came back and politely asked Jiffa to follow him.

All eyes were on Mawusi and Jiffa as they walked into the dinning room. She curtsied to the chief while Mawusi waited to offer her a chair.

"Please help yourselves," said the chief. Mawusi offered to help Jiffa, but she refused.

"You will not know what I like, so I'll do it myself," While the others chatted about village affairs, Mawusi tried to woo her.

"Jiffa," he said quietly" "Are you still at school?"

"No," she answered abruptly. She was fed up with him and his questions. Why couldn't he leave her in peace to eat her food? Just before she swallowed another mouthful he continued.

"Why is that?"

"I can't explain because it's too complicated," said Jiffa. She hoped that would put him off, but it did not.

"I shall not insist if you don't want to tell me. But perhaps you'll tell me one day," said Mawusi, with a false smile. "Can I get you some more?" he added, seeing Jiffa's plate was almost empty.

"Yes, please," At least that would give him something to do. As she sat waiting, Mama Agawu called her attention.

"I'd like you to thank Chief Kushieto before we leave, he has given you a nice present."

Mawusi came back with the food.

"Yes, Mama," said Jiffa, wondering what the present might be.

"When will you come back to Kpetwei? asked Mawusi.

"I don't know." She was irritated and wanted to get away as quickly as possible. Should she tell him about Vincent? No, it would be foolish to put ideas in his head.

The Agawus asked permission to leave just before mid-night as Jiffa was to travel early the following morning. She thanked the chief and shook hands with everyone there. When she said goodnight to Mawusi, he looked her in the eyes and squeezed her hand gently. She knew what he was up to, but she was not going to play his game. Anyway, she was going to Adidome and would probably never see him again.

It was drizzling when they left. Flashes of lightning and the loud sound of thunder frightened both Mama and Jiffa. Papa paid no attention to them. After they had walked halfway home, they heard a loud rush of rain and they were drenched. At home they dried up quickly and went to bed.

Chief Kushieto and Mawusi were still drinking when Mama Kushieto cleared up and went to bed. The chief had kept a close watch on his son all evening and could not help noticing that his son was developing something for Jiffa. He may not know who Jiffa was, so it was about time he put him in the picture.

"Jiffa is nice girl isn't she?" said the chief. They helped themselves to more drinks.

"Very. I had a long and interesting talk with her," said Mawusi. He could not wait to tell his father.

"That's good. Mama Agawu has just been telling me about her. Her father died only recently," said the chief.

"I 'm sorry to hear that. She didn't mention it to me. How do Mama and Papa Agawu know her?" he asked.

"She's their niece and they brought her up. It was only three years ago that she went back to her parents at Adidome," said the chief.

"Oh she didn't mention that, either" said Mawusi.

"But you just told me you had and interesting conversation with her. If she has not told you any of this, what did you talk about?" he said, looking at his son carefully.

"Oh, other things, Papa," He felt a complete fool.

"Then I hope she told you that she's going to marry Vincent," said the chief.

"No, she didn't," said Mawusi sadly

"It's an arranged marriage. As soon as Vincent finishes his course they will get married," The chief hoped he had made it clear to his son to keep away from Jiffa, so that he would not create difficulties between the two families.

"What a silly idea," said Mawusi. "Why can't Jiffa, make up her own mind as to whom she wants to marry? Supposing she does not love Vincent, what a waste of her life. She is a very beautiful girl, and men will go down on their knees for her. Why is her future being decided for her" Mawusi was angry at the very thought of it.

"You may think it's silly, but her parents are doing what they think is best for her." Chief Kushieto was now tired and he wanted to go to bed.

"I don't think she is in love with Vincent. I talked to her all evening and I did not get that impression,"

"That was what I have been told." He felt sorry for his son.

"She is still too young to know what she wants. She should be allowed time to choose her own husband," said Mawusi.

"Well, I'm off to bed now," said Chief Kushieto, "I hope I've made Jiffa's situation clear."

"Yes, Papa," but he was actually thinking, "No Papa." They said good night.

In bed that night Mawusi made up his mind to go and see Jiffa in Adidome. He was not going to allow Vincent to marry her. He was going to try very hard to convince Jiffa. It was going to be a straight fight between himself and Vincent. Yes two men, but they had nothing in common. Unlike Vincent, Mawusi had never been to secondary school. After his elementary education he had trained as a motor mechanic and a driver. He was keen to learn the trade, and in less than six months he was able to mend his father's ancient Volkswagen van. His skills became useful when his father opened a poultry-farm in Segakope. Mawusi drove miles to buy the chicken feed. His part-time mechanic job kept him alive whilst he worked for nothing on his father's farm. It was therefore not surprising that Chief Kushieto asked him to manage the farm when he inherited the Kpetwei chieftaincy on his own father's death. He had kept the poultry business in Segakope, and Mawusi agreed to go once a week to supervise the workers and collect the weekly takings. His hard work had paid off, and he was now able to pay himself a good salary from the farm.

Chapter Twelve

IFFA WENT TO BED AND WAS soon fast asleep, but the she was woken up by a loud crash of thunder. Frightened and unable to sleep again, she thought of Mawusi. Why had she not told him about Vincent? Was she being unkind? Maybe he only wanted to be her friend? Why did he irritate her? How would she have behaved if she had been alone with him? She tried in vain to dismiss those thoughts. She even wondered whether Vincent was as faithful, as he seemed. She could not go back to sleep, so she decided to get up and pack; it would keep her busy and help get Mawusi out of her mind. Soon she heard the first cockcrow, so she went out and cleaned the compound, took her bath and prepared breakfast. After breakfast Papa left for the palace.

Later that morning, Mama Agawu gave Jiffa a big parcel to take to her mother and a smaller one for herself. By late morning a taxi pulled up at the gate to take her to the station. Mama accompanied her and advised her throughout the short journey.

"Please write to us when you get to Adidome."

"I will."

"Lord! I nearly forgot," said Mama. She untied the knot in her cloth and gave some money to Jiffa. "I meant to give this to you before we left, but I forgot. Vincent calls me the forgetful old woman. Today I've proved him wrong. I hope you will back me up."

"I will, Mama." Jiffa took the money and thanked her.

The Adidome tro-tro bore the inscription 'WHY WORRY.' It was empty, when Mama and Jiffa got there and the aplankey was shouting for passengers. Jiffa chatted with Mama until it was time for her to board. Then they hugged each other and said a tearful goodbye.

"Oh, I will miss you terribly," said Mama as she let go of her. With the engine revving Jiffa boarded the tro-tro and was gone.

"My greetings to your mother," Mama called out as the tro-tro drove off. The taxi-driver waited and then took Mama back home.

Mawusi woke up late that morning and drove to the station, hoping to catch a glimpse of Jiffa before she left. His father's green Volkswagen was old, but very strong. There were deep puddles on the road, and the car went in and out of them, splashing muddy water over the windscreen. It was too thick for the windscreen wipers, so he got out and wiped it off with a rag. He was furious, as he was racing against time and drove very fast to the station. He saw an aplankey busily calling for passengers so he parked the car and walked over to him.

"Is this the first tro-tro to leave for Adidome?" asked Mawusi.

"No the first one just left a few minutes ago," said the aplankey.

"Oh dear." Mawusi looked worried.

"If you want to get to Adidome, you can come with us we'll be leaving very soon," he said.

"No I came to see someone. Do you know Adidome well?" Mawusi asked.

"Yes!" said the aplankey, laughing.

"What's funny?" asked Mawusi.

"I was born and bred there."

"How was I supposed to know where you come from?"

"Anyway, why did you ask?" said the aplankey. Passengers had begun boarding his tro-tro, and he was in a hurry to get away.

"I'm looking for someone in Adidome. She lives near the tro-tro station," said Mawusi.

"Do you know her name?" he asked.

"Her first name is Jiffa". The aplankey turned away and shouted for more passengers then came back.

"It will be very hard to help you if you don't know her second name. But I know someone in Adidome who knows almost everybody. He is Togbi, a carpenter. The workshop at the station named Togbi and Sons belongs to him. Then he rushed away, called for passengers and left.

Mawusi drove home slowly and thoughtful. He had not liked the way his father talked the previous night. All he cared about was avoiding family quarrels. What a coward! It made him angry that Vincent was to marry Jiffa, and he was determined it would not happen. He had always been jealous of Vincent. Chief Kushieto talked about Vincent with such pride. What Mawusi disliked most was the way Vincent sat with older men and talked to them as equals. He was just a schoolboy, yet he behaved as if he knew everything. He had been born to a ready-made life: a good education, a happy home, doting parents, and now a beautiful wife. That was too much. It would be a battle between both of them and the winner would take Jiffa.

Chief Kushieto was with his advisers when Mawusi arrived so he went to talk to his mother, who was in the kitchen preparing lunch.

"Where have you been?" she asked.

"To the station, said Mawusi.

"What for?"

"To send a message to a friend". He was not going to tell his mother about his plan, he did not trust her to keep it secret.

"Your father was looking for you just now."

"Did he say why?"

"He wants you to order some drinks for collection next week."

"Aren't there enough drinks in the palace?" he asked, making himself comfortable on a kitchen stool.

"Not for what they are planning," she said as she stirred her stew.

"And what exactly are they planning?"

"The village will hold big party for Vincent if he wins the competition," she said.

"What competition?" he looked surprised.

"Haven't you heard? Vincent is taking part in an all school quiz competition next week at Ho. If he wins, he will represent the entire Volta Region."

"What kind of competition is it?"

"It's to choose the cleverest student in the country to go and study in Britain," said his mother. If Vincent wins, he will bring prestige to the village. That is what your father is discussing with his advisors."

"Who will pay for him to go to Britain?" he asked.

"The government. He will get an allowance while studying and when he gets back he will be given a house and a car"

Mawusi shook his head in disgust.

"You don't seem to be pleased for Vincent."

"Of course I am pleased." How could he say he was not? His mother would think he envied him. But he did envy him - who would not? Yet another piece of good luck for that spoilt boy. Mawusi could not say this, because his mother adored Vincent. But what would happen if Vincent won the scholarship? Would Jiffa go to Britain with him?

Mawusi felt sorry for himself as he went to his bedroom. Then he had an idea. He would give Jiffa a few days to settled down, then pay her a surprise visit. This idea cheered him up. He took an overnight bag from under his bed and packed a few things.

Days after Jiffa left, Mawusi was ready to ask permission from his father to use the car, but he did not want to tell him where he was going. Was he not old enough to do what he liked? He heard his mother calling him, and went to the kitchen.

"Your father wants you in the sitting room, she said.

Mawusi found his father chatting with a few of his advisors.

"I've forgotten why I want you" he said, "I'll call you again when I remember." It was the right moment to ask for his favour.

"I'd like to borrow your car tomorrow," he said.

"Where are you going?" his father asked.

"To visit a friend."

"Alright."

"Thank you, I'll be in my room"

Jiffa's tro-tro left Kpetwei with mountain of luggage on the roof. She was sandwiched between two fat women. The one on the right had a baby sleeping on her back, the one on her left was dressed in black, presumably she was going to a funeral. Shortly after they left, the baby woke up and began to cry. Her mother put her to her breast. The baby smiled at Jiffa.

"She likes you," said the fat lady.

"How old is she?" She knew the baby was a girl because she had earrings.

"Just over a year." Jiffa found it hard to believe, because the baby was very small. The fat woman saw the change on Jiffa's face, and she added. "She is very small for her age."

"Why?"

"She's sick."

Suddenly there was a loud bang, and the lorry ran into a ditch. Everyone screamed, but fortunately no-one was hurt. The passengers climbed out, with the help of the driver and the aplankey. Some of them turned their anger on the driver, warning him that if he went on overloading his tro-tro he would one day lose everything. Others praised God for delivering them from danger. A few collected their luggage and left, refusing to pay. Jiffa stood beside the fat lady and her baby while the driver and aplankey changed the wheel.

"It's strange your baby didn't cry," said Jiffa, who was shocked and frightened.

"Yes, I am taking her to see a herbalist in Adidome to get some medicine for her."

"What's wrong with her?" she was being inquisitive, but the fat lady did not seem to mind.

"She is epileptic," I have spent a lot of money on her, and I hope she gets cured."

"Why don't you take her to the hospital?"

"I started by taking her to hospital, but the tablets were so expensive that I could not afford them any longer."

"Have you been to this herbalist before?" asked Jiffa. The way she was asking so many questions reminded her of Mawusi.

"No, a friend has just recommended him to me."

"I hope you get good results," Jiffa felt sorry for the baby and her mother.

"So do I."

They left as soon as the tro-tro was ready. There were free seats so the fat lady decided to sit in front. Jiffa sat alone with her thoughts. How was her mother coping with her business? Should she have left her alone? If Vincent visited her in Adidome where would he sleep? Their small mud house had only one big room and a very small one for Jiffa. It was too small to take a bed, so she slept on a mat. She did not mind that. Her mind was elsewhere when she heard the aplankey call, "Fares, please." Jiffa was startled.

"How much?" She noticed his rotten teeth.

"Have you got luggage?" he asked.

"Yes."

"Then it's double," said the aplankey

"Why?" she asked.

"Because passengers is one price, and luggage is another price," he said.

"How can one small suitcase be the same price as a human being?" asked Jiffa angrily. She was supported by some of the other passengers.

"Lady," said the aplankey, "That is the normal charge. You're lucky I'm only charging you double, some aplankeys would charge double and a half."

"Double and a half!" What does that mean?" shouted one of the women in the middle row. The aplankey turned round to answer.

"Don't you know?" he asked.

"If I did, would I ask?" said the woman. "What a fool! All you aplankeys do is cheat us. I doubt whether you give all the money to the driver anyway, let me tell you, none of us will pay double. Your driver nearly killed all of us, you're lucky we're not taking you to the police station." The other passengers cheered loudly and refused to pay the double fare.

"I will report you to the driver when we get to the station," said the aplankey.

"Both of you can go to hell!" said the woman.

"If you report me to him, I will report you both to the police. Are the documents on this tro-tro up to date? If you don't want problems shut your stinking mouth and sit down." The aplankey did not answer, and there was silence until they arrived at Adidome.

Chapter Thirteen

$\mathcal{J}$IFFA ALIGHTED AND COLLECTED HER SUITCASE from the aplankey. Then she said good-bye to the fat lady and left. She soon spotted her mother in the distance looking tattered and thin with her head-tie undone. Her blouse originally white, was now a dirty grey. She was busily turning plantains on an open fire with sweat racing down her face. My poor mother, Jiffa thought. If I had money, I would make her stop this job - it's not good for her health standing all day in the scorching sun. She walked up and tapped her on the shoulder.

"Wezoloo!" Jiffa! You look beautiful," her mother cried and they hugged each other. "Oh, I'm glad to see you again" she said, speaking and laughing at the same time.

"I've missed you, too," Jiffa said, putting down her luggage. "How is everyone at Kpetwei?" Her mother was still admiring her.

"They all send their regards." Her mother turned the plantains as Jiffa spoke to her. "Mama, why don't you sit down, and let me take over? You look tired."

"Thank you very much. I haven't been feeling well for the past few days," said Mama Agbenyo.

"What's wrong with you?" Jiffa took charge.

"I feel shivery in the evenings, I've lost my appetite, and my whole body aches."

"Have you been to see the doctor?" Jiffa asked, serving plantains and peanuts to two passers-by.

"No, how can I stop work?" she asked.

"If you are not well, then you should not come to work," Jiffa raised her voice.

"If I don't work, how can I live? I make very little profit, and if I had to stay at home I will soon be living on my capital. That would be the end me. Who will help me back on my feet? If that happens, I'll starve."

Jiffa felt really sad for her mother. She realised that poverty was the worst thing that could happen to any human being.

"I know. But standing in the sun by an open fire is very bad for you,"

"What alternative do I have?" she asked, opening her palm to emphasize the point.

"When I finish selling this batch I think we should stop for the day. I'll help you carry everything home,"

"I've done some shopping. Will you prepare me some soup when we get home? I feel like having some soup".

Jiffa carried the remaining raw plantains and picked up her suitcase. Walking side by side they left. As they walked through the crowd, Jiffa told her mother how well Mama and Papa Agawu had treated her, and what a nice person Vincent was. She told her about the party at the palace, but did not mention Mawusi.

They were almost home when their next-door neighbour saw them.

"Jiffa! Where have you been?" he called out.

"I've been to Kpetwei to visit my relations."

Togbi offered a helping hand.

"Good heavens you really look beautiful!"

Mama Agbenyo walked ahead as Jiffa chatted with Togbi.

"Your mother is working herself to death. Please talk to her. If she goes on like this, I fear for the future," said Togbi.

"What can I do?" said Jiffa sadly.

"You must stop her. All the neighbours are worried. Since your father's death, she has become a recluse. She leaves home before dawn to buy plantains, carries them all the way from market to the station, and stands in the sun all day roasting them. Is she trying to destroy herself? She is too old to be working this hard" Togbi looked worried.

They arrived home and Togbi left, promising to come back later.

Mama Agbenyo brought two kitchen stools from under her bed. They sat and discussed family matters. Jiffa gave her mother the parcel from Mama Agawu and she opened it excitedly.

"Look!" she shouted. There were three printed cloths and a pair of slippers.

"How beautiful," said Jiffa, touching the cloth to feel the quality.

"How can I thank these people? I wish there was something I could do for them in return," said her mother.

"I don't think you should worry about that. Mama Agawu does not expect anything. We have enough problems without thinking of what to give to people who already have everything." Jiffa was angry. Her mother had sold her only asset to the Agawu family. And now she was thinking of giving them something again.

"I wasn't thinking of giving them anything expensive, but in this world you can't always receive, you must also give".

"I'm sorry I raised my voice," said Jiffa, seeing her mother's sad face. "Shall I open my parcel, too?" she asked.

"So you have also been given a present, oh, it makes us look like beggars," said Mama Agbenyo.

"If we are beggars, so be it," said Jiffa. "You cannot work any harder than you do. We have to face the fact that we are poor. A poor person cannot afford to be ashamed when receiving anything."

"I've forgotten to ask why you have come. I thought you were going to stay in Kpetwei."

"I came because Vincent had gone back to school. Besides, Mama Agawu thought you would need help."

"I hope you're not thinking I don't want you here. I'm delighted you've come. I only asked because Mama Agawu told me you would stay with her until Vincent was ready to marry you."

"She didn't want you to be left on your own for too long. Don't worry about me, because Vincent gave me some money, and so did Mama and Papa Agawu. I can start a little trade with that, and live off the profit. That will make things easier for us," she said.

"I love you dearly, Jiffa. You may have wondered sometimes why I married an old man who could not look after me."

"Yes, Mama, I have." Jiffa had gained confidence since she had been living with the Agawu family - she could not have said this in the past.

"I was once married to a man who made my life miserable. Your father was a neighbour and he saved me. He was a widower, because his first wife died in a road accident shortly after they got married. I have never told you this before, but I think it's time you realized what I have been through. Your father and I got married and moved into this house. It may look small, but it was all he could afford to rent. I'm sorry you have to mop up this mess, and I pray that everything you do may prosper." Tears ran down Mama Agbenyo's face as she finished speaking, Jiffa bowed her head and wept, too.

"Thank you for telling me this." She got up and embraced her mother. "You look tired, so go and have a rest and I'll prepare you some soup."

Jiffa had listened to Togbi's advice and decided that her mother should rest for a few days before going back to work.

Late one evening, Jiffa was preparing supper when Togbi appeared, holding a small basket of smoked fish.

"It's yours," he said, giving the fish to Jiffa. "I want you to prepare some soup for your mother. By the way, how is she?"

"Fine. I have told her to rest."

Togbi sat down. "Quite right It was good you came back. None of the neighbours could have persuaded her to rest."

"I'm not going to let her go to work for some time. I have planned to go myself," said Jiffa.

"Is it true you've stopped schooling?" asked Togbi.

"Yes. Who told you?" Jiffa was surprised Togbi had heard about it.

"One of the neighbours,"

"Who?" She asked.

"I can't remember,"

Jiffa heard her mother calling her, so she left the cooking and ran to the bedroom. "What can I do for you, Mama?" she asked.

"I'm shivering again. Please cover me with that blanket," Jiffa covered her up and went out to tell Togbi.

"What should we do" he asked.

"I think we should take her to the hospital," said Jiffa.

"My car has broken down, so let me get a taxi while you help her to change."

"Will you come with us?" Jiffa looked worried, but Togbi reassured her.

Jiffa took the soup off the stove and dashed to the bedroom to help her mother change. Then she covered her with a blanket to keep her warm. Mama Agbenyo's teeth were chattering and her hands were very cold. Minutes later, Togbi appeared with the taxi, and he carried Mama Agbenyo into it. Jiffa sat with her mother at the back, while Togbi sat in front and directed the driver.

Chapter Fourteen

ADIDOME GENERAL HOSPITAL WAS NOT TOO far from the house, and the driver managed to get there in a short time. Togbi helped Mama Agbenyo into the waiting room, and called one of the nurses.

"What's wrong?" the nurse asked. Mama Agbenyo could not speak because her teeth were chattering so much.

"She has been shivering," said Togbi. Jiffa was rubbing Mama's cold hands.

"Can she walk?" the nurse asked.

Mama shook her head, so the nurse fetched a trolley. She was then wheeled into another room, where her temperature was taken.

"She has a very high temperature," said the nurse. "What is your relationship with her?" she asked Jiffa.

"She is my mother."

"Has she been here before?"

"No."

"Is he your brother?" the nurse asked, pointing at Togbi.

"No, a neighbour," She turned to look at Togbi who was gazing at Mama Agbenyo. Her eyes were firmly shut.

The nurse began making notes on Mama's history.

"What is her name?"

"Shika Agbenyo," said Jiffa.

"Age?"

"Sixty-one."

"What are her symptoms?"

"She has been shivering, and her hands are very cold. Also she has lost her appetite," said Jiffa. She tried to think of her mother's other symptoms.

"And she has pains all over her body," added Togbi. Jiffa was grateful because she was confused.

"Anything else?" asked the nurse.

"No," said Jiffa.

"Please follow me to the doctor's office."

The doctors' block was outside the main building. They pushed past other patients who were waiting to be examined. The nurses wore neat green uniforms and stiffly starched aprons. Their caps were firmly pinned to their hair; not even a hurricane could blow them off. They pushed the trolley along the corridor and just before they reached the end, Mama Agbenyo woke up with a start.

"Where am I?" she asked. The nurse stopped the trolley and spoke to her.

"You are not well, and the doctor is going to examine you. Please lie down quietly." Mama looked terrified.

"You will be fine" said Jiffa, reassuring her mother. "Togbi is here with me, so don't worry."

"Thank you. I'm happy you are both here," and she shut her eyes again.

They pushed the trolley to the door of the doctor's office, and the nurse informed the him.

"Bring the patient in, " the doctor said. Togbi wheeled the trolley into the room, and Jiffa followed closely behind.

The doctor had very dark skin, his white coat made him look even darker. His hair was neatly brushed, and his moustache trimmed. He was sitting behind a big mahogany desk covered with files and papers. His name, Dr. A .A Appiah was pinned to his left breast pocket. The nurse gave Mama's notes to him, and he studied them carefully. Then he got up from behind his desk to examine Mama Agbenyo. He removed the blanket from her skinny body and touched her forehead. He sent for another nurse then he turned to Jiffa and Togbi.

"Your mother's condition is not good and she will be admitted for more tests. I will go over to the ward. Please wait for me here."

When the doctor left, Jiffa started crying. Togbi put his arm around her.

"Please don't cry. Your mother needs good treatment and then she will be fine."

"Togbi, my whole life is one big problem!" Jiffa exclaimed. "I wish I had someone to help me, because this is too much for me. I'm only sixteen."

The doctor entered with a nurse and told them to go with the her. "She will take you to the ward. Paulina, can you let me know when you have finished?"

"Yes, doctor."

They left. Togbi helped the nurse wheel the trolley back down the corridor. Just before they reached the waiting room the nurse told them to turn right, and walked along another corridor through some double doors and into the ward. Togbi and the nurse pushed the trolley to the far end of the left row. With the help of another nurse, Mama Agbenyo's was given a drip. They all watched closely.

The nurse left and came back with Dr. Appiah, who looked at the drip to check whether it was working properly. He touched Mama's forehead again; it was still hot. He made a few notes, then he turned to Jiffa and Togbi.

"Since she's asleep I advise you to go home and come back tomorrow. The visiting hours are from four to eight in the evening." He saw tears in Jiffa's eyes, and patted her gently. "Don't worry, your mother will be fine."

Jiffa took her mother's hand and whispered something in her ear, then they thanked the doctor and the nurses and left.

When they reached the main road, Togbi decided they should walk back and they took a short cut through the bush. Jiffa was upset so Togbi stopped and took her hand.

"I know your difficulties, but weeping will not solve them. I will come with you every day to visit your mother. Will that help?" he asked.

"Thank you very much," Jiffa dried her tears. "What would have happened to my mother if you have not been there? Who would I have turned to? Togbi, am I going to be an orphan?"

"For God's sake, Jiffa, stop crying. If you don't take care you will be ill. And what good will it do your mother if you join her in hospital? Listen, I don't think you should be alone tonight. Would you like to stay at my house? My wife has taken the children to Togo to see their grandmother, so the house is empty."

"Thank you very much. I will go home and collect a few things," said Jiffa.

I'll come with you," said Togbi, with a friendly smile. He had hoped Jiffa would smile back, but she did not.

The only brick house in the neighbourhood belonged to Togbi'. It had a veranda and three small bedrooms, and slept seven. His two grown-up daughters lived in one room, and his three boys shared another. Togbi was a well-known carpenter. His workshop was near the tro-tro station, but he often worked at home in his tool shed. He had begun training his three sons so that they could carry on the business when he grew old. His eldest son, who was eight, had almost finished making a small stool. Togbi had wanted a son as a first-born, but he was disappointed. His second child was also a girl, which caused difficulties between him and his wife. Then, luckily, his dream came true; his next three children were all boys.

They arrived home exhausted. Jiffa collected her things, and remembered the soup.

"Can I bring it ?"

"Of course , but I have enough food at home."

"I want to finish cooking it in your house," said Jiffa. Togbi picked up her small suitcase and parcel, Jiffa collected the soup, locked up and left.

Togbi opened his bedroom so that Jiffa could sit down. Then he lit the lantern and brought her some water to drink. Togbi and his wife had the biggest of the bedrooms. There was a double bed under the window. Opposite the bed stood a wardrobe. To the left was an armchair with two straw-filled cushions covered with plastic. To the right of the door was a long showcase cupboard, where a few glasses and plates were displayed. A lantern stood on a small table in the middle of the room. There was a kerosene stove and a water-cooler behind the door, and a piece of old linoleum on the floor.

Jiffa's eyes took in every inch of Togbi's room. How nice to be a carpenter, she thought: you can make all your furniture from other people's leftover wood.

"Your room is ready - bring in your things!" Togbi took her into his daughter's bedroom.

"What a neat room!" said Jiffa, as she entered.

"I can't stand children who don't clean their bedrooms. I have warned my daughters that if I see their room in a mess I'll make them sleep outside.'

82

"Isn't that rather harsh ?" said Jiffa, arranging her things.

"They will be lazy if I'm soft on them."

"Which bed shall I use?"

"I've changed the sheets on the right one. Let me show you the bathroom."

They came outside and he pointed to a small corrugated iron enclosure behind his tool shed.

"Thank you." Jiffa went back to finish unpacking.

"Come into my room and have some supper when you are ready".

Togbi lit the kerosene stove, and warmed up some stew, then he soaked some gari with cold water, and laid the table. Soon afterwards Jiffa reappeared, and they ate from the same bowl.

"Delicious stew, who made it?"

"I made it myself," said Togbi proudly.

"Have you always been a good cook?"

"I love cooking for my family."

"Does Mama Togbi enjoy your food?" asked Jiffa.

"She longs for more!" said Togbi laughing." Now, Jiffa, I'd like to know why you have to stop schooling. I promise not to tell anybody." Jiffa paused for a moment.

"After Papa's death, there was no-one to pay my fees," she said quietly.

"Couldn't your mother borrow? There would have been no boarding fees, only tuition."

"Don't you realize that she would have to pay it back with interest?"

"I wouldn't have let her pay interest if she had borrowed from me," said Togbi.

"Togbi you're very kind, but it's more complicated than that."

Jiffa cleared the table and brought her parcel into Togbi's room and opened it. He was pouring some water from the water-cooler when Jiffa called his attention.

"Oh, what a beautiful cloth! And that gold chain! Who gave them to you?" He was happy that Jiffa had cheered up.

"Someone at Kpetwei."

"The person must be very rich."

"She is my aunt," Togbi touched the cloth and asked Jiffa to wrap it around her body.

"They suit you wonderfully. But Jiffa, if you have a rich aunt, why couldn't she pay your fees?"

Jiffa decided to tell Togbi the truth. "A marriage has been arranged for me."

"For you?" He was surprised

"Yes."

"Who is the lucky man?"

"My cousin."

"So his mother gave you all these things?"

"Yes."

"What is your cousin's name?"

"Vincent."

"Do you love him?"

"Yes. But even if I didn't, do I have a choice? My mother will not be able to pay back my bride-price, and that will be a problem."

"Oh, Jiffa I wish you had been allowed to make your own choice."

"I never will, Togbi, so I don't even wish it."

"A niece of mine had an arranged marriage about four years ago. It did not work out, because they were not suited to each other," said Togbi sadly.

"I was brought up with Vincent, so I know him very well."

"When are you getting married?"

"After Vincent has finished his course."

"Oh, so he is a student. Does he have a girlfriend?"

"I have not asked him."

"That is the first thing you should have asked him."

"What school is he at?"

"Kpando Secondary Technical School."

"A boy in boys' school thinks of nothing but girls. I would be surprised if he has no girl-friend."

"Oh, Togbi! Do you think he would let me down?"

"I can't say. But you have to ask him. What are his parents like?"

"They are nice. I like his mother because she is very warm."

"I would love to meet them."

"One day I'll introduce you."

Jiffa began to think about her mother, and became quiet.

"What's wrong? Togbi asked, noticing her mood had changed.

"Do you think my mother will be alright?"

"I'm sure she will. She just needs rest. Please don't start crying again."

"I'm not going to." She wrapped up her parcel and said good night to Togbi.

"Promise me you won't go into that room and start crying."

Jiffa promised. She said goodnight and left.

Togbi lay awake and thought about Jiffa. How could her parents have arranged a marriage for her? Vincent sounded like a nice boy, but what would a schoolboy do for her? Instead of marrying her to someone who could look after her, she had been thrown away on a schoolboy with no experience. Worse still: if he had a girl friend, he would use Jiffa and leave her to rot. He lay awake for a long time before he fell asleep. Then he was woken up by screams from Jiffa's room. He rushed out and banged on her door. She was weeping as she opened it.

"What's wrong?" he asked.

"I dreamt that Mama was dead!"

"You are having a nightmare," he said. Come and sleep in my room.

"I'm sorry to be so difficult, Togbi."

"You're not. Dry your tears and get some sleep. Tomorrow afternoon we'll go to the hospital and see your mother."

Togbi offered his bed to Jiffa, and he slept on a mat. She was soon asleep, but Togbi just lay on his back and stared at the ceiling.

Chapter Fifteen

MAWUSI HAD DECIDED TO LEAVE FOR Adidome early the next morning. He was in his room when his mother called him for supper. His father was busily shovelling food into his mouth when he came in to the dinning room.

"Where have you been?" asked his father.

"Nowhere."

"Didn't you tell me you were going out?"

"No." Mawusi sat down and helped himself. "I asked if I could use the car tomorrow."

"Oh, I thought it was today. I must be growing old. I forget everything these days."

"How can you call yourself old?" asked Mama Kushieto.

"Look, I will be sixty-six next month, and to me that is an achievement."

"Didn't your father live to be over hundred?" asked Mama Kushieto. "You're only sixty-six and you're boasting about it."

"May be, but what about you?"

"I wasn't the one who started this competition," said Mama Kushieto. Suddenly the chief stopped eating.

"Mawusi, you remember I called you this afternoon and forgot why I wanted you?"

"Yes Papa."

"I have just remembered. It was to do with Vincent's quiz competition"

"What about it?" asked Mawusi.

"You know, Vincent is extremely clever, and there is a chance he may win. If he does, I want you to drive me to his school."

"What are you going to do there?" asked Mawusi, with a false smile. He was trying not to get angry; if he did, his father would stop him using his car tomorrow.

"I want to make a speech at the school. Since Vincent is from Kpetwei, it is only right that I, as chief, should see his headmaster and teachers."

"That is a very good idea," said Mama Kushieto. "When is the competition?"

"The day after tomorrow. The village is planning a big celebration for him."

Mawusi stopped eating and looked at his father. "Papa, the competition will be in two stages. The first is to choose someone to represent the region, so even if Vincent wins, he still has to enter the final round. Why don't you wait until he has won the overall competition before the village celebrates?"

"No, if he wins the final round he will be going to Britain. That will be a celebration for the entire region. This is our chance to show that Vincent is a product of Kpetwei. The name of this village will be published in the newspapers all over the country. It will be a big thing for us all."

"Anyway, let me know when the competition is, so that I will be ready to drive you there."

"Mawusi, help yourself to some more," said his mother.

"No, Mama, I'm full. I'm going to bed,"

"But you have only just woken up," she said.

"I'm quite tired; besides, I shall be leaving early tomorrow morning." He left the room quickly, before his father could ask him where he was going.

Mawusi lay on his bed, planning how to get away from the village during this so-called celebration for Vincent. How could his father be so insensitive as to give him a description of it? Left to Mawusi, the quiz would pass unnoticed. His main concern was how to handle Jiffa the following day. Will she make him feel unwanted? If she did, he would leave immediately but if she welcomed him he would spend the day with her.

Jiffa was fast asleep when Togbi woke up. He cleaned the compound and washed. Then he took some water into the bathroom for her. He had already made up his mind to stay at home and work on the twenty chairs for a local day nursery, a job which he was supposed to have finished last year. After breakfast of gari and beans, he started work. He whistled merrily and planed the wood, sharpened his chisel and hammered the nails. Two of his chairs were almost ready when Jiffa woke up. It was quite late in the morning, and the sun was already hot.

"Did you sleep well?" Togbi asked, when Jiffa came into the shed.

"Very. I didn't even dream." She washed her face from the plastic bucket of water under Togbi's bench.

"There is water for you in the bathroom,"

"Did you take it there?"

"Yes."

"Oh Togbi! You remind me of the way I served my aunt and uncle when I was in Kpetwei."

"Do you take water into the bathroom every day for them?"

"Yes"

"Why can't your future husband do it?"

"He isn't used to doing things like that," said Jiffa.

"What do you mean, things like that?"

"I can't explain. I feel sticky. Let's talk later." Jiffa went to the bathroom and Togbi went on whistling and hammering. Then he stopped for a short rest.

"Ooh, after washing my body, I feel good!" Jiffa said.

"Were you expecting to feel bad?"

"You know what I mean, Togbi."

"No I don't, I want you to explain it properly."

She rushed into the room to get dressed. He was pleased that she had forgotten her nightmare, and as he whistled a familiar tune, Jiffa joined in and sang the words. They sang it over and over. Togbi was pleased that Jiffa was enjoying it. When she finally came out from the room, he could not help commenting, "You look like a doll in a shop-window."

"What do you mean?"

"I mean, you are richly dressed." They laughed. "Your breakfast is in my cupboard," he said.

"I'm not very hungry." She stood beside Togbi and watched as he made a chair.

"I've just had breakfast," said Togbi, "but I'm hungry again."

"There must be something in your stomach which swallows the food,"

"I think you're right." He stopped hammering and looked at her.

"Why don't you go and see the doctor?" Then Jiffa remembered the nightmare and became quiet.

"Is anything wrong?" asked Togbi. "Look, there is no need to cry. Your mother will be alright. At four o'clock we'll go to the hospital and see her. Meanwhile I will be staying here with you."

"Are you staying at home just because of me?"

"Yes, I don't want to leave you here alone."

Jiffa hugged Togbi and thanked him. "I'll leave you to work, and I will write my letters in your bedroom. After that I will prepare some lunch."

"Hurry up so that I can have some lunch immediately."

"Togbi you will have to wait for me to finish writing my letters, then we can have the soup for lunch"

"Are you going to write to schoolboy?"

"His name is not school boy, so I don't know who you're talking about. I'm going to write to my aunt and uncle"

"Jiffa, my tummy is rumbling!"

"Stop thinking about your stomach." She laughed, and went into the house. Then she shouted from the bedroom. "Do you have a pen and a writing pad?"

"Look in my drawer, and you will see a pen and a paper," he replied.

What an angel Togbi is, thought Jiffa. She opened the drawer and took out the pen and paper, wiped Togbi's small table with a piece of cloth, and sat down in the chair ready to write.

Dearest Mama Agawu.

I am writing to thank you for treating me so well during my stay with you. How are you and Papa? I hope not too bad. I am also fine. I had an accident on my way back, so I arrived at Adidome an hour and half late. Fortunately, nobody was hurt, but we were all shaken. The driver changed the burst tyre and we arrived safely.

Mama, I also thank you very much for the lovely presents. I want to start trading with the money you gave me. It is kind of you to do all this for me. I also thank Papa. Without you, I don't know what would have happened to me. I hope one day I will be in the position to repay you. I enjoyed seeing Vincent again after such a long time. He had not changed at all.

Before I sign off. I want you to know that my mother has not been well, and was admitted to Adidome General Hospital yesterday. One of our neighbours helped me to take her there. I will be going to see her this evening. I shall let you know what her condition is later.

I miss you both very much.

All my love,

Jiffa

*C*hapter *S*ixteen

---

*M*AWUSI LEFT KPETWEI BEFORE HIS PARENTS woke up. He wanted to get to Adidome as early as possible. By sunrise he was miles away. After a while he stopped at a small village and had some breakfast. It was many years since he had been to Adidome, and he missed the turning. Eventually he passed an old farmer and stopped to ask the way. The man had his hoe on his shoulder, with his son carrying a big basket behind him.

"Good morning, Papa."

"Can I help you?"

"Yes, I'm going to Adidome, but I can't find the turning."

"You passed it long ago."

"How far back is it?"

"Quite a distance. You will see a sign post, if not, then the wind has blown it over."

"So how will I see the turning?"

"Keep asking and you will find it. Don't give up!"

"Thank you," Mawusi turned the car round and drove back more slowly, so as not to miss the turn. He thought of what the farmer had said - "Don't give up!" And he decided he would follow that advice, and never give up in life.

After Mawusi had driven some distance he stopped at a palm-wine bar.

"Can I help you?" the owner asked, coming over to serve him.

"Sorry I'm not buying palm-wine. I came to ask the way to Adidome."

Thinking that Mawusi was going to buy palm wine, the woman had already taken a calabash to serve him. She was disappointed.

"Turn right at the first junction and go straight. You will see the tro-tro station" Mawusi thanked her and bought a small calabash of palm-wine to cheer her up.

"It's good," said Mawusi looking happy.

"Yes it's fresh, the village boys delivered it a few minutes ago."

"You can tell from the froth."

Mawusi paid the woman and drove off. When he came to the turning he saw that the signpost had fallen over. He followed the instructions and got to the tro-tro station. Parking the car by the roadside, he got out and walked across to one of the drivers, who was dozing behind his steering wheel.

"Excuse me, can you tell me where Togbi and Son's carpentry workshop is?"

"Over there on the right," the driver replied. "But it's shut"

"I must see him." Mawusi looked worried.

"Does he know you are coming?"

"No."

"Do you know his house?"

"No. But I was told that Togbi was well-known, and that somebody could give me the directions to his house."

"If you wait a moment, my aplankey may be able to help you. He has just gone to buy some food."

"Thank you very much." Mawusi stood beside the tro-tro and watched the people going to and fro. The place was dusty and noisy. All the aplankeys were shouting for passengers and there were quite a few beggars, singing for alms. Mawusi gave one of them the change from his palm-wine, and the beggar sang for him. He waited a long time before the aplankey arrived,. He then recognized him as the man he talked to at Kpetwei tro-tro station.

"You!" said Mawusi. "Don't you remember me?"

The aplankey looked at him blankly.

"I was the person who asked you whether you knew Adidome."

"Oh! So you got here."

"The driver told me you might be able to help me find Togbi."

"His workshop is over there."

"It's closed. So I would be grateful if you could show me the way to his house."

The aplankey put his food down and gave him the directions.

Mawusi tried to drive off quickly, but with pedestrians crossing and impatient tro-tro drivers wanting to get on with business, it was not easy for him. Soon he was out of the crowd and on to the road leading to Togbi's house. Mawusi looked carefully at every house as he passed. Eventually he spotted the house in the distance and parked in front of it. When he entered the compound he saw the carpenter in the shed and went up to him. Togbi stopped work and his eyes were fixed on Mawusi as he approached.

"Good afternoon," Mawusi said.

"Can I help you?"

"I'm looking for someone called Togbi."

"You are speaking to Togbi." They smiled.

"I have been directed to you because I'm looking for a girl called Jiffa."

"What is her second name?"

"I don't know, but I have come all the way from Kpetwei to see her."

"I know someone by that name, but I don't know whether she is the one you are looking for. Wait here, I will be back" Togbi went quickly into his bedroom and told Jiffa.

"What's his name?" she asked.

"I did not ask, but I think it's Vincent. Come and see."

"Wait, I'll put my letter away." Jiffa had just finished writing a letter to Vincent and hurriedly put it away before she came out with Togbi.

Her jaw dropped when she saw Mawusi.

"Mawusi, what are you doing here?" She asked, coming out to the shed to talk to him. Togbi followed and he was surprised, because Jiffa had not mentioned the name Mawusi.

"I've come to visit you," Mawusi replied.

"Visit me? What a surprise! This is Togbi, a very good friend of mine."

"Hello my name is Mawusi." The men shook hands.

Jiffa stood like a statue. Who had asked Mawusi to come here? What had she to say to him?

"Jiffa, why don't you take Mawusi inside and give him some water?" Togbi said. "He must be tired after his journey."

Mawusi followed Jiffa into Togbi's room. She offered him a chair and looked at him shyly.

"How are you?" he asked. He was pleased she had not told him to go away.

"I'm fine. How did you get here?" Jiffa brought Mawusi a glass of water.

"In my father's car."

"Who gave you my address?"

Mawusi drank the water before answering.

"You told me you lived near the tro-tro station."

"I know, but I did not give you the address."

"I went to Kpetwei tro-tro station and asked one of the aplankey." Mawusi smiled, seeing that Jiffa was amazed by his arrival.

"Jiffa!" Togbi called from the shed.

"I'm coming." She left.

"Who is he? whispered Togbi.

"He's from Kpetwei."

"How do you know him?"

"He's the son of the chief."

"Ooh! Jiffa - a chief's son! You mean royalty. That is serious."

"Listen, he is not my friend, so I don't know why he has come to visit me."

"How did he get here?"

"In his father's car."

"Hhm! I must come and talk to him. He's more of a man than a schoolboy."

"Are you coming to talk to him because of his father's car?"

"That's only part of it. He is a bold man to come here even though he is not wanted."

"We must go and talk to him, or he will feel unwelcome."

"You just said he's unwanted, so does it matter if we don't speak to him?"

"I'm feeling faint from hunger, Jiffa. Could you reheat the soup and prepare akpene for us? Please, do it now."

Jiffa followed Togbi into the house, and took the stove and the soup into the kitchen, leaving Mawusi and Togbi to have a chat.

"Did Jiffa know you were coming?" asked Togbi.

"No: I wanted to give her a surprise."

"She just told me your father is the chief of Kpetwei."

"Yes, he is," said Mawusi shyly.

"Does that mean you are a future chief?"

"I don't know." What a nice man, thought Mawusi.

"Has Jiffa told you her mother is in the hospital?"

"No, what's wrong with her?" Mawusi wanted to hear everything.

"The doctor didn't say. She has lost weight, and needs rest." Mawusi excused himself from Togbi and went to his car.

When he had left the room, Togbi stood up and peeped through the window.

What a smart car! he said to himself. Hearing Mawusi's footsteps, he sat down quickly.

He came back in and gave Togbi a bottle of gin.

"Is that for Jiffa's mother?"

"Yes, but since she is not well I want you to keep it."

"Togbi got up and shook hands with him "I haven't drunk gin for a long time. I normally drink akpeteshie. That's rough stuff, but this..." Togbi raised the bottle. "... is the best! Thank you very much."

"Don't thank me, it should be the other way round. I was worried, because I did not know how Jiffa would react when she saw me. The way you have welcomed me has made it much easier." Mawusi genuinely liked Togbi. Besides, he might help him woo Jiffa.

"What do you do for a living?" Togbi asked. Mawusi was smartly dressed in a sea blue shirt, grey trousers, and shiny brown shoes.

"I have two jobs," he smiled. "I trained as a motor mechanic - "

"A motor mechanic?" shouted Togbi.

"Yes, and a good one, too."

"You've been sent here by God!"

"Why?"

"I have to drive Jiffa to the hospital this evening to see her mother, but my car has broken down. It's too far for her to walk." Togbi was cunningly mentioning Jiffa's name to get his car fixed.

"Can I look at it for you?"

"Let's have some food first," said Togbi. His stomach was rumbling non-stop, and he could not concentrate on anything like his old ramshackle car.

"What's wrong with your car?" Mawusi was pleased to be needed.

"Just about everything. That car has given me problems ever since I bought it. Sometimes I feel like throwing it in the dustbin."

"What sort of car is it?"

"A Morris Minor. By the way, what is your second job?" he asked. Mawusi was about to answer when Jiffa entered.

"Lunch is ready, could you help me bring it in?"

"Of course." Togbi stood up quickly and followed Jiffa into the kitchen.

"Mawusi is a great man," he said to her.

"Why?"

"Do you know what he does for a living?"

"How could I, when I don't even know him?" Jiffa poured the soup into a big bowl and put the akpene on one of Togbi's china plates, which was used only when there were visitors.

"Don't be like that: this man will be a great help to us."

"Maybe to you, but not to me. I don't want him here. After lunch I shall tell him to leave."

"After lunch he's going to repair my car, so there is no question of him leaving."

"Is he a mechanic?"

"Yes."

"Do you know how good he is?"

"He says he's good."

"And you believe him?"

"Why not? He looks honest. Do you know he has given me a present?"

"Ah, Togbi! You only like that boy because of what you will get out of him."

"He's not a boy, he's a man, and you must respect him."

"I'm not going to say any more. If you want to eat, please follow me." She laid the table and offered Mawusi water to wash his hands. Togbi had already washed his hands in the kitchen. They all ate together. .

"Mm! Jiffa, your soup is very good," said Togbi, after he had swallowed some akpene and okro soup.

"Thank you. My aunt said the same thing when I was in Kpetwei."

"You mean Vincent's mother?" asked Togbi. Mawusi's face changed as soon as Vincent's name was mentioned.

"You know already, so why ask?" said Jiffa.

"Mawusi, how long have you stayed in Kpetwei?" asked Togbi. He had not known why Mawusi had come but he had given the game away by squeezing his face when Vincent's name was mentioned.

"Not long. I used to visit when my grandfather was the chief, but I did not live there."

"Where did you live?" asked Togbi.

"Segakope."

"Was that where you went during that party?" asked Jiffa. "It was first question she had asked Mawusi since lunch.

"Yes," Mawusi answered eagerly. I had to go and pay my father's workers."

"I thought your father was a chief," said Togbi.

"So did I," said Jiffa.

"He also has a poultry farm in Segakope."

"How can he be in two places at the same time?" asked Togbi

"My father doesn't run the farm any more, I'm in charge."

"So you're a businessman?" said Togbi with a broad smile.

"In a way."

Jiffa looked at him quietly. Was Mawusi speaking the truth? First he said he was a fitting mechanic, and now a businessman. How could both things be true?

"Who wants some more to eat?" she asked.

"Don't ask that kind of question, just bring it, and it will be consumed," Togbi said.

"I thought you were satisfied," said Jiffa going out to the kitchen.

"Me, satisfied! You must be joking. What I have just eaten is just the preface. I'm now going to start chapter one."

Mawusi laughed. How right, he thought. Togbi was one of the nicest people he had met, no wonder he was popular in Adidome. Jiffa came back shortly with more food.

"Togbi, where is the present Mawusi gave to you?"

"In my cupboard. Do you want to see it?"

"Yes."

"You can't give Togbi a present, because you don't know him"

"Jiffa keep out of this. It is between two men, nothing to do with you".

"I have to give the present to Togbi, because he helped me to find you."

"I thought you got the directions from one of the aplankeys at the station. Why didn't you give the gin to him?

It's none of your business, Jiffa," said Togbi. "Your business now is to wash the dishes. Then you must go home and get a few things for your mother, then we can go to the hospital."

"What things" She looked worried when her mother's name was mentioned.

A towel, some slippers, whatever she may need. Use your brain."

"You've reminded me," said Jiffa, smiling." I must write to Vincent and ask him whether he is ready for the Best Brain Competition."

"Are you still talking about that schoolboy" said Togbi.

"Are schoolboys not human beings?"

"Of course, but they lack experience."

"Experience of what?"

"Ask Mawusi," said Togbi.

"Why?" said Jiffa angrily. He looked at her.

"Mawusi is a man with experience," said Togbi .

Mawusi was grateful to be called as an experienced man.

Jiffa left the room, to wash the plates and collect her mother's things.

She behaves like a child," said Togbi.

Mawusi agreed, but said nothing. "Togbi, can I look at your car now?"

"Yes, come with me."

"Oh, you've covered it"

"Yes, I don't want the colour to fade"

They took off the tarpaulin. The car was bright red.

"Why did you paint it with a brush, instead of spraying it?"

"This was how it was when I bought it."

Mawusi examined the car carefully, checking every part of it; then he made a list of spare parts for Togbi to buy.

"More money to be spent on this thing," said Togbi - he really regretted buying it.

"I will be going to Segakope next week. I'll try and get some of these spare parts from a friend of mine."

"Do you want to go back to Kpetwei tonight?" asked Togbi.

"Not really: I'm quite tired. Besides, I haven't had the chance to talk to Jiffa properly."

"You are welcome to sleep in my son's room."

"Thank you very much." Mawusi smiled happily. "Shall I drive you to the hospital to visit Jiffa's mother?"

"That's a good idea. What's the time?" Mawusi looked at his watch.

"Ten to four."

"We should leave now"

Chapter Seventeen

$\mathcal{J}$IFFA SAT IN HER MOTHER'S BEDROOM and thought about Mawusi. Why did she dislike him? He had driven all the way from Kpetwei to see her and the least she could do was to be polite to him. She got ready and then remembered Mama Agawu's letter. It had to be posted today, but she had no envelopes, she would ask Togbi.

"I haven't got any, he said. "I have given you paper, find your own envelope."

Mawusi's eyes were fixed on Jiffa. What a beauty, he thought, and his desire for her increased.

"Togbi if you give me a sheet of paper, some glue, and a pair of scissors, I'll make Jiffa some envelopes" said Mawusi in a quiet voice. Togbi had noticed the look in his eyes when Jiffa entered. He gave him the items and left.

"How many envelopes do you need?"

"One - oh no, two,"

"Who are you writing to?

"Someone in Kpetwei."

"Why do you want two envelopes?"

"I'm sending the other letter to somebody else." Jiffa did not mention Vincent's name, because she knew it would hurt Mawusi.

"You're writing to Vincent, aren't you? I know you are supposed to marry him but it's not your choice, is it? Jiffa, I've come all the way from Kpetwei to see you. I love you."

"It's impossible," she said, throwing her arms into the air angrily.

"Nothing is impossible"

"It's easy to say that. I love Vincent so please, let's not talk about it again."

"You don't really know what you want, do you?" he said

"Yes, I do," Jiffa replied sharply.

"No you don't." But Mawusi did not want to upset her so he apologized for contradicting her.

"Don't apologize. You may be right"

"You need an experienced man. Didn't you hear what Togbi said?"

"He would say that, wouldn't he? If you brought me a bottle of gin, I would probably call you an experienced man."

"It's nothing to do with the gin. I am much more experienced than Vincent .Look at me, I can marry you today, not when I have completed my education."

Mawusi put out his hand to give Jiffa the envelopes, and he pulled her closer.

"Leave me, or I will scream," she said.

"Scream for what?"

"For Togbi to come and kick you out." Mawusi let go her hand.

"He wouldn't do that. By the way, he has offered me a room to spend the night."

"It's not true,"

"It is true" said Togbi, over hearing their conversation. "Jiffa, have you collected the things for your mother?"

"Yes. They're in that basket on the veranda."

"Then let's go."

They left the house and went out to the car. Togbi sat in the back like a chief. Jiffa reluctantly sat in front beside Mawusi, and they set off along the dusty road. Mawusi drove slowly, his mind on Jiffa.

"Can you direct me, Togbi?" said Mawusi, as they turned on to the main road.

"Go straight, until I tell you."

"I hope you will not forget to direct him. Otherwise we will end up in Kpetwei," said Jiffa. Mawusi smiled. Was Jiffa joking, or being rude? Her voice sounded friendly, so perhaps she was beginning to like him.

"And if I don't, I hope you can direct him yourself." Togbi was watching Jiffa carefully.

"I won't, because he hasn't asked me to." She turned round and looked at Togbi. Jiffa was torn apart. She was beginning to love Mawusi but was terrified of the consequences.

"Can you direct me, Jiffa?" asked Mawusi. As he turned to look at her, their eyes met. Waves of desire filled him, and his hands shook on the steering wheel.

"Alright, I'll tell you where to turn."

Mawusi wished he could take Jiffa in his arms and kiss her.

"Turn right at this T-junction,"

Togbi knew exactly what Mawusi was going through, he was a man, and he knew what it was like to love a woman and not be able to get her. Jiffa was so beautiful that even he sometimes found it hard not to desire her.

"Turn right again," said Jiffa. She looked at Mawusi's profile, and liked it.

"Should I go straight after that" Mawusi's voice was so quiet that Togbi could not hear what he said.

"Turn right again soon," Jiffa, said, in an even quieter voice.

"Is it right turn all the way? Jiffa did not reply. Instead their eyes met again, and she bowed her head.

"Turn right at that building on the left, that is the hospital," Jiffa pointed at the building.

Mawusi parked the car and they went in through the main entrance. They were almost at the ward when Jiffa realized that she had left the soup in the car.

"I'll get it," Mawusi sais. Jiffa and Togbi waited in the corridor.

"You must admit, Mawusi is a treasure," Togbi said.

"Treasure is too strong a word. I will say kind," Jiffa replied.

Mawusi came back with the basket, and Jiffa thanked him. They continued along the corridor and went through the double doors into the ward. Dr. Appiah was at Mama Agbenyo's bedside when they got there. She was breathing heavily, and there were tubes in her nose.

Jiffa was terrified when she saw the tubes. Mawusi noticed, and quickly took her hand.

"How is she?" Togbi asked the doctor.

"Much the same, I'm afraid. She has not opened her eyes since you left," said the doctor.

"Will she be alright?" asked Jiffa, with tears in her eyes.

"Yes" he said. "But at the moment she is very ill. Could you come with me?"

They followed the doctor to his office. Mawusi tried to comfort Jiffa.

"Your mother will be alright. Stop crying, it's bad luck to cry when someone is ill." Jiffa stopped sobbing.

When they got to the office, Mawusi waited outside in the corridor. Poor Jiffa, he thought, her father died recently, and now her mother looked seriously ill. What would she do if her mother died? Where would she live? Vincent 's parents were her only hope. What an advantage it would give Vincent to keep Jiffa with them permanently...

Jiffa was weeping when they emerged from the doctor's office. Togbi tried to cheer her up. Outside Mawusi rushed to her side, held her and comforted her.

"What did the doctor say?" Mawusi asked as they walked to the car.

"He wanted to see the other members of the family," said Togbi. Jiffa dried her tears.

"Where do they live?" Mawusi was hoping there were other relatives apart from those he knew.

"Kpetwei," said Togbi.

"Are they her only relatives?"

"Yes" she said.

"Do you want me to drive you to Kpetwei now?"

"No," said Togbi. Let's go tomorrow morning. Do you agree?"

Jiffa nodded

They drove back to Togbi's house in silence, broken by the occasional sob from Jiffa. Mawusi was wondering how he could help her without making her feel he was taking advantage of the situation. She needed cuddling.

Jiffa's weeping had two sides to it. She genuinely loved Vincent but Mawusi's kindness was making her wonder whether her parents had been right to choose her future husband. Vincent had been kind too. He had even promised to pay her school fees when he got a job. But Togbi was right: he was still a schoolboy. Would he be faithful or reject her later? If so, where would she go? She might have had children by then, and no man would marry a second hand woman. Was she refusing Mawusi today, only to regret it tomorrow? Would her mother recover, or not? Oh, what an uncertain future! The more she thought, the worse she became. Her mind was so muddled she began wailing loudly.

Mawusi pulled off the road and stopped. Then he turned to her "Please don't cry, your mother will be fine," he said. Then he held her gently and took a handkerchief out of his pocket to wipe her tears.

Chapter Eighteen

WHEN THEY REACHED THE HOUSE, MAWUSI parked the car and they all went into Togbi's room. Jiffa lay face down on the bed. The thought of Mama Agbenyo dying flashed through Togbi's mind, reminding him of Jiffa's nightmare the previous night. Then he turned to Mawusi.

"I'm going to get supper ready, please make sure she doesn't weep again"

"I'll do my best," Mawusi replied, at last he had a chance to be alone with Jiffa. He sat beside her and gently rubbed her back. "Stop feeling sorry for yourself. Your mother will be alright." He could imagine a wonderful life with her.

"I'm feeling sorry about everything, not just for myself,"

"Such as?" he asked.

"I can't tell you," she sobbed.

"Why? I love you and the least you could do is to share your thoughts with me. I have never felt the same since the moment I first saw you, and I am sure you know it."

"You must understand that apart from Vincent and his parents I have nobody. Can you imagine what will happen if I don't marry him?" Jiffa turned to look at him.

"Nothing will happen. Anyway, how do you know Vincent doesn't have another woman?" This was Mawusi's chance to persuade Jiffa to change her mind.

"No woman visited him all the time I was in Kpetwei," she said, drying her tears.

"Did you ask him?"

"No, but I trust him."

"May I advise you?"

"If you want to," she said.

Mawusi had managed to take her mind off her sick mother and also stopped her crying. She was even beginning to enjoy the conversation.

"Never trust a man."

"Are you one of the men I should never trust?"

"I'll only answer that if you agree to marry me."

"No, I will agree to marry you if you answer me." Jiffa realized that Mawusi would do everything she asked, so she waited for him to speak. Mawusi saw a smile on her face, and that gladdened his heart. He sat silent for a moment, then he spoke in a very soft voice.

"Jiffa, you can trust me to never let you down. My heart is burning for you to accept me. Please tell me you love me."

Mawusi did not wait for Jiffa's reply, as he could see from her eyes that she wanted to say yes. He brought his lips close to hers, and kissed her. Jiffa responded, and Mawusi pulled her gently towards him. He did not let go of her lips until they were both satisfied. From the way Jiffa responded, he knew that she had been longing for him.

"Supper will soon be ready" Togbi announced with a smile. He noticed a change on Mawusi's face, and realised that he had been having some fun at last.

"Do you want any help?" asked Jiffa.

"No. I want you to stop crying," said Togbi, sitting down.

"She stopped crying long ago," Mawusi said. He wanted Togbi to know that he was a responsible person.

"I saw that when I came in. Well done. I couldn't have calmed her down like you have. I failed completely, the last time I tried." Togbi opened the cupboard and brought out the gin. "Supper is going to be delicious, so we should have an aperitif." He took some glasses out of his showcase, and served Mawusi.

"Do you want something to drink?" he asked Jiffa.

"What have you got?"

"Fanta," I keep it under my bed, he began searching for it.

"Why do you hide it under the bed?" asked Jiffa. She got off the bed and sat beside Mawusi.

"Wouldn't you hide Fanta if you had children in the house?" Togbi asked.

"No," answered Jiffa.

"That's because you will marry a rich man, but I'm poor."

Mawusi looked at Jiffa, but neither of them said anything.

Togbi offered Jiffa the drink, then he had an idea. "I want to pour libation to our ancestors and ask them to protect Mama Agbenyo." He poured some gin and recited the prayers.

"Agoo! Fathers and Mothers of our clan! Accept this offering for the healing of our sick mother, Mama Agbenyo, We call on you to send herbal medicine for the purification and cure of Mama Agbenyo. If she has brought this suffering upon herself, we call on you to forgive her and heal her affliction."

Jiffa and Mawusi watched as he prayed. Then the men clinked their glasses and drank the gin. Supper was served soon afterwards but Jiffa was feeling guilty for allowing Mawusi to kiss her. How could she have done such a thing? Was Mawusi not the person she disliked so much? If Vincent heard about it, would he reject her?

Togbi was only too pleased to see that something had happened in his absence. If Jiffa had been his daughter, he would marry her off immediately. Every parent's dream is to see his child married to a responsible person. Mawusi qualified in every way, a future chief, a businessman, a fitting mechanic and above all a kind person. He could sense that even Jiffa was beginning to fall in love.

"Togbi, your praying was excellent," said Mawusi suddenly. He couldn't bear the silence any more.

"I'm flattered, because as a chief's son you must have heard a thousand and one prayers," Togbi replied, trying to remind Jiffa that Mawusi was from a royal family.

"Yes, libation is poured anytime there is a function, whether it's a big festival or a small party." The party which was being arranged for Vincent suddenly came into his mind.

"What did you say your father's name is?" asked Togbi.

"Chief Kushieto."

"Is he the first or the second?"

"The second."

"So you will be the third."

"I don't know." Mawusi smiled. "All I know is my father gives me lessons on pouring libations."

Jiffa turned and looked at him.

"So he's already preparing you to take up the throne?" asked Togbi.

"I wish I knew, as I said, nobody has told me."

"When will you know?"

"Probably after his death"

"How old is he?" Togbi wanted to know everything.

"Sixty-two or sixty-three. I can't remember."

"He doesn't look sixty -two," said Jiffa.

"Do you know him?" Togbi asked, knowing perfectly well that Jiffa had met Mawusi's father.

"I've met him twice. Once at a big party and the second time at a dinner. He even gave me a present. You can ask Mawusi." Jiffa was proud to have had such a close contact with royalty.

"Its true," said Mawusi, eagerly backing her up.

"What was the present?" Mawusi asked Jiffa. Togbi watched them with interest.

"Why do you want to know?"" Jiffa said quietly.

"Please tell me," his voice was quiet. It amused Togbi to watch them flirting.

"You will have to guess," she said smiling.

"Money?" asked Mawusi. "Am I right?"

"Yes," Jiffa replied shyly.

"Oh Jiffa! I'm very pleased to have guessed right," said Mawusi, touching her gently.

"Heavens! I haven't written to thank him," Jiffa exclaimed.

"I thought you were going to use the second envelope for his letter," said Mawusi.

"No," said Jiffa.

"Who were you writing to?" asked Togbi.

"A friend called Aku. I hope you won't ask me any more questions."

"I don't believe you," Togbi said. "I've never heard you mention that name before. Where did you dig it up from?"

"What do you mean, dig it up from? Do you think I'm a farmer, digging worms from the soil?"

"You're not a farmer, but you can dig," said Togbi.

Jiffa wanted to change the subject. "Have you finished?" she asked Mawusi, seeing him lick his fingers.

"Yes."

Togbi was still eating, and did not raise his head.

"Do you want to wash your hands in the kitchen, or shall I bring you a bowl of water?"

Mawusi followed Jiffa to the kitchen. He washed his hands quickly and then he kissed her. They were both relaxed as they were alone. There was no danger of Togbi walking into the kitchen because he had enough food on his plate to keep him busy for some time.

"My love for you is growing every second," Mawusi whispered. "Please think again."

"I love you, too," Jiffa replied, "but I can not marry you."

"I don't think Vincent is the right person for you. He is too clever. You need a man who will love and care for you." He kissed her again, and held her tight against his body so that they could feel each other's heartbeats.

"I love you," said Mawusi over and over again. They were dead in each other's arms, and did not hear footsteps approaching. Togbi came suddenly into the kitchen and they pulled away from each other.

"I'm sorry, I didn't mean to take you by surprise," Togbi said. Jiffa was embarrassed, but Mawusi was pleased.

"There's no need to be sorry," said Mawusi.

Togbi smiled, he was now confident that Mawusi would win, Only a fool would come all this way for nothing.

"What time are we going to leave tomorrow?" Mawusi asked when they came into the bedroom.

"About eight o'clock. I'll get up early and do some work before leaving."

"What are you making?" asked Mawusi.

"Some chairs for a nursery school," said Togbi, gesturing with his hands.

"What kind of jobs do you like?"

"Anything except nursery school chairs." They all laughed.

"Togbi, you're lucky to be asked to make those chairs," said Jiffa. "I remember when you got that contract, it was before I went to Kpetwei. If it was boring, why did you accept it?"

"It was because of the money," answered Togbi.

"If the money is good, why are you complaining?" asked Jiffa.

"He wasn't complaining?" said Mawusi. "He was explaining something to us."

"I knew you would side with him," Jiffa retorted, "Men always stick together, don't they?" For once, Jiffa did not look at Mawusi's face, as she raised her voice slightly.

"I'm sorry if you think I was supporting Togbi. I didn't mean it like that," Mawusi replied. But why should he apologize? A sixteen year-old girl had made the royal feel like a doormat.

"Jiffa, will you stay the night when you go to Kpetwei tomorrow?" asked Mawusi.

"Why do you want to know?"

"I was thinking of Togbi. He could stay in the palace."

"May be he would like to stay in my aunt's house," Jiffa looked at Togbi.

"I will not stay under the same roof as that schoolboy," Togbi retorted, "I'd rather stay with Mawusi,"

"You only want to stay in the palace"

"And why not? It's not every day that I get asked to stay in a grand house"

"Will you come and have supper with us tomorrow?" Mawusi asked Jiffa.

"I don't think so, my aunt may have arranged something and I don't want to spoil her plans,"

"Do you have freedom in your aunt's house?" asked Togbi, wondering what kind of life Jiffa had in Kpetwei.

"What sort of freedom?" asked Jiffa.

"Freedom to do what you like. I hope you're not restricted there, as your parents restricted you here,"

"I'm not restricted, but I don't go out unnecessarily."

"Your life must be limited," said Togbi. Mawusi nodded.

"No it's just different." She said. Mawusi was scratching his body, so Togbi asked him whether he wanted to wash before going bed.

"Yes, please: otherwise I won't sleep properly."

"Jiffa, please take a bucket of water into the bathroom for Mawusi." He knew that Jiffa would not like this idea, but if she had been doing it for Vincent, a commoner, then surely she could do it for Mawusi, a royal.

"I'll take it myself," said Mawusi. "Please show me where the water is." He stood up.

"You are my visitor. If I come to the palace, I hope I shall not have to carry water into the bathroom." Togbi replied.

"Where is the bathroom?" Mawusi asked.

"Come with me - I'll show you," Jiffa said, so he followed her outside.

"What a nice man Mawusi is" said Togbi, when Jiffa came back.

"I know, but don't rub it in," she said.

"I'm not rubbing anything in. But he is the kindest young man I have ever met. You saw how he wanted to carry the water into the bathroom himself?"

"That doesn't make him kind - if a man wants to have a bath, I think he should carry his own water."

"Who carries water into the bathroom for Vincent?" asked Togbi.

"I do," Jiffa replied, flatly. "Togbi, stop telling me that Mawusi is better than Vincent. Why don't you wait and meet Vincent before you make your judgement?"

"I'm not saying Mawusi is better. All I said was, I have never met anyone so noble. I feel I have known him for a long time. In fact I feel as if I could live with him"

"Then why don't you go and live in the palace?"

"When he becomes chief, I shall do so. I hope you will be his queen so we can all remember this day,"

"Don't hope for anything,"

"Make up your mind, Jiffa - which of these men do you love?"

"Togbi, we have gone over this subject about fifty times. The saliva in my mouth will dry up if we talk about it again"

"If you don't love Mawusi, then don't lead him on,"

"Did he tell you I was leading him on," Jiffa said angrily.

"No, but I'm not a child, and I have eyes to see."

"Seeing is not enough. You must try and understand, too. I only allowed him to kiss me because I felt sorry for him. That's not leading him on,"

"So you feel sorry for him now, and hurt him later?"

"I'm tired, and I want to go to bed," Jiffa said sharply.

"Then make Mawusi's bed, and you can have my bed"

"Thank you. I really enjoyed your bed last night. Give me the sheet".

She finished making the bed hurriedly and was about to leave when Mawusi came in.

"What were you doing here?" He said, seeing that Jiffa was about to rush out.

"I came to make your bed."

"Did Togbi ask you to make it?"

"Why do you want to know?"

"I want to know whether you care about me so much as to make my bed without being told to."

"Togbi asked me to make it"

"So you would not have made it if he hadn't said so." Mawusi stood in her way. "Why couldn't you cheer me up by saying you made this bed because you love me?" he said softly.

"I don't want to lead you on, only to hurt you in future. So please, let's be friends, and nothing more."

"But Jiffa, you told me a few minutes ago that you loved me. How can you change your tune so suddenly?"

"I'm confused, please let me think about it".

Mawusi gave her a goodnight kiss.

"I hope you get some sleep," said Jiffa.

"See you tomorrow," he said.

"Are you sleep?" Jiffa asked Togbi, who was already lying on his mat when she returned to the bedroom.

"No: I was praying."

"Do you often pray?"

"I pray when I want something good to happen."

"What are you praying for at the moment?"

"Why do you want to know?" he asked.

"Because I'm an inquisitive lady."

"I'm praying that the caring gentleman will marry the inquisitive lady," said Togbi.

"Well, I won't comment on that. Goodnight, Togbi."

"Sleep well, inquisitive lady."

Mawusi lay awake, wondering what to do next. Had he gained anything by coming to Adidome? Would Jiffa give up the idea of marrying Vincent? What else could he do to make her realize that he loved her? Then he remembered something dreadful: Vincent's competition was on the following day, and the party was being given in the evening. Oh, how he wished Vincent would not win! If he did Togbi would have to stay on for the party. On the other hand, maybe that would be a good thing: he would see what the schoolboy was really like. Mawusi decided he would do all he could to make Togbi welcome in his father's house; his influence might even make Jiffa change her mind.

Chapter Nineteen

WHEN HIS CLASSES HAD BEGUN, VINCENT realized the extent of the task ahead of him. As well as his schoolwork, he had a week to prepare for the competition. The headmaster had asked him to move into his house for extra help. He had his own shower room, and for Vincent that was a luxury.

"Don't hesitate to ask me for anything you need," the headmaster told him, "I have my own library downstairs so please use it. My wife will give you supper, so relax and concentrate."

"Thank you very much, sir,"

Vincent felt like a different person in the headmaster's house. His concentration was better, and he studied from early morning to late evening. He planned to rest on the last evening and go early to bed and so he would feel fresh in the morning.

Vincent had not forgotten Kwashie's message to Mr. Apaloo, and after school he went over to see him.

"Have I come at an awkward time, sir?" Vincent asked, seeing that Mr Apaloo looked puzzled.

"Of course not. I was just coming over to see you myself." He offered him Vincent a chair.

"Why were you coming to see, sir?" he asked, accepting a glass of beer.

"Only to see if you need any help before tomorrow," said Mr. Apaloo. He was sitting on the sofa, his legs crossed, enjoying his beer.

"I'm not going to revise this evening, sir, but I'd appreciate any last minute tips." He was pleased that Mr Apaloo treated him like an equal.

"I used to do the same at university: I always rested on the day before my exams, and it helped me. Now, why have you come to see me?"

"I have a message for you, sir?"

"And what could that be".

"From one of your university contemporaries,"

Mr Apaloo looked surprised. "Who?"

"His first name is Kwashie. I have forgotten his second name." Vincent put his hand to his forehead, and tried to remember the name of the man he had met on the coach.

"I know many Kwashies," said Mr. Apaloo. "So unless you describe him I shall not know who it was."

"I don't think you will recognize him from my description. He told me he had not seen you for a long time," He did not want to describe Kwashie, because it might upset Mr. Apaloo. "Could you tell me the surnames of the Kwashies you know?"

"What a task!" said Mr. Apaloo. "Why can't you remember the surname yourself?"

"I should have written it down, but I did not. I am sorry sir, I've stored too much information these few days, and I just can't remember."

"I hope you'll be able to retrieve whatever is in your brain tomorrow." If Vincent could not even remember the surname of someone he had just met, how could he win this quiz? Had the school made the right choice?

Vincent saw the disappointment in Mr Apaloo's eyes, and asked him again to mention some surnames,

"Alright. Number one: Kwashie Ahiabre. Two: Kwashie Nyamasikpu. Three: Kwashie Amevor..."

"Aha, that's it, sir - Kwashie Amevor!" shouted Vincent.

"Where on earth did you meet him?" asked Mr. Apaloo, in astonishment.

"On the coach from Kpetwei to Kpando."

"It does not add up because I know he is in Britain."

"Do you know him very well?"

"Yes, he was a great friend. He even promised to invite me over. Then suddenly he stopped answering my letters, so I assumed he couldn't be bothered."

"What was he like at university?" asked Vincent.

"One of the cleverest people I knew. He was top in everything and he also enjoyed fooling about. He was head of the Students' Union for a while, and was respected by us all because he stood firm on every issue."

"Did he have difficulties being a union leader?"

"No he was a natural leader, and he played his cards well. Most of the lecturers were his friends, so he got away with many things that others would have been punished for. I wish I could see him again and have a good laugh."

"Do you know where he lives, sir?" Vincent asked, wanting to know about Kwashie's background.

"Not at the moment. His father was the Navy Commander and they lived in a big house at Cantonment. Shortly after he left for Britain, his father died in a car accident. I remember going to see his mother to sympathize with her. She left that house soon afterwards, because it belonged to the government."

"I could sense that you were really good friends" Vincent was intrigued.

"Yes, we were. Did he give you his address?" asked Mr. Apaloo. Vincent had probably forgotten that too, he said to himself.

"No, sir" Vincent could not remember whether Kwashie had given him his address or not.

"Don't worry, I will try and get it from another friend"

The grandfather clock in Mr. Apaloo's sitting room began to strike seven, and Vincent got up to leave, because it was supper time at the headmaster's house.

"Good luck for tomorrow," Mr. Apaloo said, shaking hands with him. I hope it goes well. My advice is to read each question carefully and understand it before answering"

"Thank you, sir," Vincent replied.

Amavi, the headmaster's house help was laying the table when Vincent came in.

"Where have you been? Mr Degbe has been looking for you." She spoke as if Vincent had escaped from a prison-cell.

Mr. and Mrs. Degbe were in the sitting room. He went over to see them.

"Let's meet in my study after supper" said Mr Degbe. At table, they drank to Vincent's success, before enjoying the beef and mushrooms in brown sauce with yam. Nobody talked about the competition, which was a relief to Vincent.

The Ministry of Education had arranged that the competition should begin simultaneously in all the nine regions to prevent misunderstanding and malpractice. All participants should arrive half an hour before the time. In his study that evening, Mr Degbe gave Vincent an alarm clock.

"Thank you, sir,"

"Do you have any questions?"

"No sir"

"Then sleep well, and good luck."

Vincent had a shower before going to bed, and to put the competition out of his mind he thought about Jiffa. He also thought about Vera, whom he had seen secretly a few times during the holidays. He had not yet told her about his arranged marriage. Should he write to her after the quiz? His mind drifted to Kwashie Amevor. What a sad life! After such a bright start, no wonder he felt bitter.

Then his thoughts turned to the competition. It frightened him to think that the reputation of the school depended on him. Would he make it? And how clever were the other students? He tossed and turned before finally sleeping.

Chapter Twenty

$\mathcal{V}$INCENT WAS UP BEFORE THE ALARM went off. He got ready and went downstairs. Mr. Degbe was in his study, putting some letters in his briefcase when he heard a knock.

"Good morning, sir,"

"Is that the new uniform?" asked Mr. Degbe.

"Yes, sir."

"Have a pen," He took one out of his desk drawer and handed it to Vincent.

"Thank you, sir, but I've got one already,"

"One is not enough, it could go wrong, and then what will you do?" They went into the dining room to have breakfast.

The driver came in just as they had finished, to say he was ready. Mrs. Degbe came downstairs to wish Vincent luck before they left. Mr. Degbe read the newspapers, while Vincent thought of what awaited him. Examination halls throughout the country had been prepared for the occasion. A travel bursary to Britain was worth a great deal of money, and would give enormous prestige to the college that produced the winner; so the police had been on guard throughout the night, to make sure there was no possibility of cheating.

Mr. Degbe and Vincent arrived with plenty of time to spare, but they were by no means the first. Some of the contestants were already there and getting to know each other. Mr Degbe chatted with some of the teachers, while Vincent sat quietly and prepared his mind. Gradually all thirty contestants arrived, each representing a school in the Volta Region.

Shortly after they all arrived a lady came into the waiting room and introduced herself as Mrs. Kluvi, the chief invigilator. She called out the names of the candidates in alphabetical order and gave them numbers. They were then taken into the examination hall. There was a policeman at the door who searched everyone thoroughly. Each desk was labelled with the name of the contestant and an examination paper. As soon as they were seated, Mrs. Kluvi. addressed them.

"Ladies and Gentlemen, welcome to Ho examination centre. Before I distribute the examination papers, I would like to say a few words. I am here to attend to any problems you may encounter. Do you all have pens? If not please raise you hands. That means you are all ready. Every question must be answered in full. Nobody must turn the examination paper over until I tell you to do so. Finally, it is my duty to warn you that any student caught cheating will be immediately disqualified. And now ladies and gentlemen, you have an hour to finish. Please turn over your papers and start work. Good luck."

Vincent read the first questions and his heart sank.

What was the name of the Carthaginian aviator who explored the West Coast of Africa in the sixth century BC? He read through the other questions quickly. How was he going to answer them all? Then he remembered Mr. Apaloo's advice, and read the questions again slowly, then he started writing. Just before the hour was up, he had answered forty-five questions out of fifty. The ones he left unanswered were:-

Of what afro-Ashanti linguistic group is Hausa the most widespread language?

Who, in 1783, made the first flight in a hot-air balloon over Paris?

Which member of the royal family of Portugal was largely responsible for the European exploration of West Africa in the fifteenth century?

On what famous date of the calendar was Julius Caesar assassinated?

What was the Gettysburg Address, and when was it made?

"Get ready to stop work," said Mrs. Kluvi. Vincent had stopped already. Even if he had the whole day he would not be able to answer the remaining questions. All the same, he was pleased to have answered forty-five tough questions.

"Stop work, put down your pens, and fold your arms." Mrs Kluvi went round and collected the papers. Vincent looked round at the other contestants, and saw a mixture of relief and disappointment on their faces.

"Please remain seated until I come back," she said.

It was an uncomfortable experience waiting in silence, but she came back shortly and continued.

"Ladies and gentlemen, your papers are being marked. I shall now call ten students to come with me for the oral examination."

The students were shown into another room, the examiner welcomed them warmly and explained the rules.

"You will each be asked ten questions in one minute. Don't waste time: if you can't answer say, "Pass." Vincent took a deep breath to stop his heart racing, and waited for his turn. The oral was just as hard as the written paper, if not harder, all the same, he managed to answer nine out of the ten questions. He was then told to go into the examination hall. There were a few students in the hall when he entered and he sat next to one of the them.

"How did you find it?" he asked the girl.

"Terrible! I would have never gone through such an ordeal if I had known what it was going to be like."

"My name is Vincent Agawu from Kpando secondary technical school. What is yours?" he asked.

"Leticia Armah,"

"Oh, you are not an Ewe," said Vincent.

"No, I'm a Ga," representing Anloga secondary school"

"Do you know a girl called Vera Mensah?"

"Which form?"

"Three," said Vincent, thinking of sending Vera a message.

"I don't know her. I'm very new."

"Where were you before Anloga?"

"Tema Secondary," said Leticia.

"Why didn't you go to a sixth form school in Accra?" asked Vincent.

"Achimota was my first choice, but I wasn't accepted, so I had to take my second choice, which was Anloga," said Leticia.

"Have you regretted leaving Accra?" he asked.

"At first I was lonely, but now its alright"

By now all thirty contestants were chatting, laughing, and waiting for their results.

Then, at lunch time, Mrs Kluvi came back into the hall.

"Ladies and Gentlemen, the results are ready. But before they are announced you will go into the dining room and have lunch. You must all be back in this hall at two o'clock. Is that clear?"

"Yes, Madame," they all chorused.

The tables had been laid for thirty, and the students were supposed to help themselves. Some had second and third helpings. There was laughing and talking but everybody's mind was on the results. At two o'clock Mrs Kluvi announced it.

"Ladies and Gentlemen, I am honoured to announce the names of the winners. Before I do so, I want to inform you that the Press will be interviewing the winner, and that the results will be announced on the radio this evening. I also wish to thank you all. For the effort you have put into this competition there can only be one winner. I'll announce the names of the first three, in reverse order. As you are aware the one who comes first will represent the whole region in a fortnight. I'd like the winners to stand up when I call their names. Third place goes to Leticia Armah, representing Angola Secondary School. Second place goes to Mawuli Klevor, representing Keta Secondary School. But the overall winner of today's competition, and the student who will represent this region is Vincent Agawu of Kpando Secondary Technical School."

There were cheers as Vincent stood up. What a relief, he thought, at last the agony was over. He shook hands with the other two winners, and all three went with the invigilator into another room.

The results had been already announced to the headmasters and teachers who had accompanied the students. Mr. Degbe wanted to jump for joy, but felt it would not be proper. All the other teachers shook hands and congratulated him.

"You must be very proud today," said the headmaster of Keta Secondary School.

"I am. I have always been proud of Vincent," said Mr. Degbe. He left the other teachers in the waiting room, and went outside to phone his school.

Within minutes of hearing the news from Mr. Degbe. Mr. Apaloo had assembled the whole school. The boys shouted and cheered.

"Vincent is our saviour!" they shouted. "Kpantec! Forwards forever, backwards never!" The teachers also celebrated the glory Vincent had brought to the school, and they shared in his achievement. Mr. Apaloo sent a telegram to Vincent's parents, telling them to listen to the radio because their son's name was would be mentioned on the news.

There were three journalists from the Daily Graphic, Daily Times and The Volta Voice waiting to interview Vincent. There were also several photographers taking pictures of him.

"What was the hardest bit of this competition" one reporter asked him.

"Every bit of the exams was difficult, but the hardest bit of it was waiting for the results," said Vincent, enjoying his new found success.

"So what will you do now?" asked another journalist.

"I'm now going to start studying for the final round in two weeks," Vincent said proudly.

Mr. Degbe was waiting for him outside the examination hall.

"Congratulations!" he shouted. Never before had Vincent seen his headmaster display so many teeth in a single smile.

"Thank you, sir," he replied, shaking hands with him. The car was ready, and they left.

"Vincent, well done," Mr. Degbe said over and over again. "Were the questions difficult?"

"Yes, sir," he said. "I left five questions unanswered."

Mr Degbe could not wait to get to school.

Chapter Twenty-one

*M*AWUSI HAD A BAD NIGHT, HE tossed and turned and felt exhausted and unable to sleep. He wrapped himself in a cloth to keep off the mosquitoes, then he started sweating. He was very relieved when he heard Togbi's footsteps on the verandah so he opened his door and came out.

"Why are you up so early?" Togbi asked.

"I couldn't sleep,"

"I am sorry about that. Is there anything I can do? Before going to the well"

"No, I will come with you" They were just about to leave when Mawusi called Togbi's attention. "I forgot to tell you something last night,"

"What is it?" asked Togbi

"I want to leave Adidome before breakfast"

"Why?"

"My father wants me to drive him to Kpando to collect Vincent."

"Which Vincent?" asked Togbi.

"The school boy,"

"I thought you did not like him."

"I don't, but my father does," said Mawusi.

"Couldn't Vincent come home himself?"

"He has been chosen as an entrant for the so-called "Best Brains" competition, If he wins today's contest, in two weeks he will represent the Volta Region at the finals in Accra."

"My God!" said Togbi, his mouth open. "Is he that clever?"

"He seems to be. I just hope he doesn't win," said Mawusi

"Why?"

"He is very spoilt. It's bad enough even now. Heaven knows what will happen if he wins." Mawusi shook his head in disgust.

"And what exactly do you think will happen if he wins?" Togbi was fascinated.

"My father will organize a party for him in the village."

"You mean your father the chief? How come?"

"My father loves him very much. Listen" They stopped for a moment. "On the one hand I don't want Vincent to win," Mawusi continued. "But on the other hand, if he wins the final round, the prize is a scholarship to Britain. And since he will not take Jiffa, I will marry her. So now you see how complicated it is."

"A scholarship to Britain!" shouted Togbi. "Does Jiffa know about this?"

"I don't think so. I heard about it after she left Kpetwei."

"That boy sounds clever. If his school have chosen him they must really believe in him."

"Don't worry, that boy believes in himself. But will that be good for Jiffa? A boy who thinks he's the centre of everything?"

They walked slowly, chatting as if they had known each other for years and came back with three buckets of water; Mawusi carried one, Togbi two.

"Please don't remind Jiffa about Vincent's competition. I don't want her mind to be on him all day," said Mawusi.

"I'll try not to." Togbi said, before going into the bathroom to wash.

Mawusi went back to his bedroom and lay down. He was very tempted to go into Togbi's bedroom to see Jiffa.

"I've finished," said Togbi from outside. "Do you want a bath before we go?"

"Yes," Mawusi replied.

"I'll wake Jiffa, so that she can have her bath when you finish." Togbi went and woke her up and told her they had to leave earlier than planned, because Mawusi had to do a job for his father.

"What job?" asked Jiffa, still half-asleep and stretching.

"I don't know. But if he's giving us a lift to Kpetwei, we must do what he wants."

"Mawusi was with us all day yesterday. Why didn't he mention it?" she asked.

"You don't need to come if you don't want to. You could easily get a tro-tro at the station, and Mawusi and I could go together."

"I don't think Mawusi would leave me behind. No matter what, he will wait for me," she said.

"Jiffa don't take advantage of the fact that Mawusi loves you."

"I'm not taking any advantage"

"Yes you are. Go and have your bath now. I can hear Mawusi's footsteps."

She left the room, and bumped into Mawusi on the verandah.

"Jiffa, I have taken your water to the bathroom," said Mawusi

They left Adidome very early. Jiffa was sitting in the front, and complained of feeling tired.

"Why?" asked Mawusi, feeling pretty tired himself.

"I don't know, because I slept well, so I don't understand why I am tired."

Togbi was listening.

"I didn't sleep well at all, " said Mawusi.

"Really? Jiffa said, looking surprised

"I wish I could rest when I get home"

"Why can't you?" she asked.

"I have to drive my father somewhere.'

"Poor you, I'm sorry you feel so pushed around," said Jiffa.

"Who told you that?" asked Mawusi.

"I can sense it. You have to go to Segakope, you have to pour libations and you do almost everything for your parents, don't you?"

"I suppose it is the price you pay for being the eldest."

"Mawusi, what is your mother like?" Togbi asked.

"She is one of those women who supports her husband in every thing. I think she takes too many orders from my father, and she has to share every problem with him, instead of solving it herself."

"Do you share ideas with her?" he asked.

"Yes. But she tells my father everything."

"So who do you confide in?"

"Nobody. If my brothers were around, it would be easier," said Mawusi.

"Where are they?" Jiffa asked.

"They live with my uncle in Keta."

When they had covered about half the journey, Mawusi stopped for petrol. Togbi offered to pay, but Mawusi refused. When he got out of the car .Jiffa turned to Togbi.

"What a kind man he is," she said.

"Jiffa, he is doing all this to show how much he loves you. I hope your parents have done the right thing by arranging your marriage to someone you don't know."

Jiffa agreed, but said nothing.

Mawusi drove off thinking about the next few days. Would Vincent win the competition? His parents would be angry if they heard he had been to Adidome to visit Jiffa. Will Jiffa tell Vincent? He glimpsed Kpetwei junction in the distance. Jiffa was sleeping, so he woke her up.

"I'm sorry, Jiffa, but I can't take you to your house. Where do you want to alight?"

"The tro-tro station will be good for us." She turned and looked Togbi.

"I thought of driving you home, but if the neighbours see my father's car they will start gossiping."

"Gossip is the main activity in every village," said Jiffa. "Togbi can tell you what it's like in Adidome."

"Is it that bad in Adidome?"

"I promise you that Adidome could win a gossip competition," said Togbi.

Mawusi stopped at the station and they alighted.

"You've been wonderful," said Togbi, shaking hands with Mawusi. "Are we going to see you this afternoon?" he asked.

"Yes, I'll be home. Jiffa can bring you to the palace after you have delivered your message."

"Will you take me there, Jiffa?" asked Togbi.

"Yes," Jiffa thanked Mawusi for his help, and they shook hands Mawusi looked into her eyes and squeezed her hand gently; it was the second time he had done that. The first time, Jiffa had been angry, but this time she smiled. Mawusi told them repeatedly to come and see him and drove off.

Chapter Twenty-two

$\mathcal{M}$AMA AND PAPA AGAWU WERE UP very early. Papa went to see the chief to put some finishing touches to the arrangements for the party. Mama was busy making gari when Jiffa and Togbi arrived.

"Wezoloo! cried Mama. She embraced Jiffa. "How are you?"

"I'm very well. Mama, this is Togbi, he is our next door neighbour."

Mama shook hands with Togbi , offered them water and took them into the sitting room.

"Jiffa, I have missed you so much Only this morning I was thinking that if you were here I would have finished preparing my gari"

Togbi looked at Mama with interest. "I hope you haven't been working too hard?"

"I used to have help from my daughters until they got married. Vincent helps me sometimes when he is on holidays."

Jiffa knew that was not true because she had never seen Vincent helping Mama.

"I will soon be coming back to help you again."

"I'm sorry Papa is not here to see you. He has gone to see Chief Kushieto about the party."

"What party?" asked Jiffa.

"The party for Vincent if he wins today's competition. I thought that was why you have come."

"No, it's just a coincidence."

"Then you must stay for the party, it's going to be big. We're all confident that he will win."

"Then I'm glad I came. I hope Togbi won't mind staying the night too?" said Jiffa. Togbi smiled and nodded.

"So what brought you here in then?" Mama asked.

"It's about my mother."

"What about her?"

"She's very ill, and has been admitted in hospital. I don't know what I would have done without Togbi's help."

Mama got up and shook hands with Togbi and thanked him.

"So how is she?"

"She is not well. When Togbi and I went to see her yesterday evening she had tubes up her nostrils, and her eyes were firmly shut."

"What!" Mama leapt up, "Then she's very ill. Oh dear, what shall we do now?" I must go and see Papa immediately."

"Mama. Can I go instead?" asked Jiffa.

"That would be good. I expect he will be in a meeting, but wait for him."

'I want to show Togbi the palace so I'll take him with me," said Jiffa.

"That's a good idea. I'll see you later".

"What a good excuse to go and see Mawusi," said Togbi as they walked briskly along the dusty road. "That was clever, Jiffa."

"I hope you don't think I'm going to see Mawusi. Vincent's father is there, what do you think would happen if he sees me in Mawusi's room?"

"How can he see you if he's in a meeting?"

"I know, but I can't go into Mawusi's room."

"Then I will go and see Mawusi alone, but you must understand that he has given you so much help, the least you can do is make him happy."

"How can I make him happy without hurting his feelings later? Aren't you the one who warned me against that?"

"Yes but give him a chance.,Jiffa, Shall I tell you a secret that Mawusi told me this morning?"

"If it is a secret, why are you going to tell me?" Jiffa knew that Togbi could never keep secrets.

"It concerns you. Mawusi thinks you don't know, but maybe you do. I'll tell you all the same. Do you know what will happen if Vincent wins the final round of the competition?"

"No,what?" asked Jiffa, eagerly.

"He will be sent to Britain on a government scholarship for several years."

"Oh my God! Will he leave me here?" Jiffa was surprised that Vincent had not told her about it.

"It looks like it, doesn't it?" said Togbi.

"What will happen to me?" she asked. "I wonder whether my aunt knows about this. If she does, why hasn't she said anything? I'm glad you told me. I'll ask Mawusi about it."

"About what? I've told you what will happen."

"I want to know who told him."

"I don't want you to ask Mawusi anything. Otherwise, next time I hear something about you, I will not tell you."

"What shall I do if Vincent goes to Britain?" she asked.

"He may even marry a European," said Togbi.

"Don't say that because whatever we say can come true!" she said angrily.

"If Vincent goes to Britain, it will be a blessing in disguise," Togbi said. "I feel it in my bones that he is not the right man for you. Mawusi has shown himself to be very kind,"

"But that is just the surface. Do you know his real character?" Jiffa asked.

"No more than you know Vincent's," Togbi laughed. "Now we ought to stop this conversation because we're almost there."

Mawusi was in the kitchen with his mother when he heard a knock at the gate. He went to open it.

"Hello! Come in and join me, I am having lunch." He shook hands with Togbi and Jiffa.

"No, thank you. We are here to see Papa Agawu." Jiffa said.

So Mawusi took them to wait in the sitting room. When Mawusi left the room, Togbi turned to Jiffa.

"My tummy is rumbling. Why did you refuse lunch?"

"We're not here to eat,"

"Maybe you're not, but I am. If I wait any longer I may die of starvation."

"Can't you wait until we get home?" asked Jiffa.

"No, Jiffa, no."

Mawusi came to tell them that the meeting would be over in an hour's time and insisted that they have lunch.

"Alright," said Togbi quickly.

Mawusi went to the kitchen and returned with a large bowl of okro stew and akpene.

"Would you like to eat in the dinning room or my bedroom"

"Your bedroom," said Togbi. He was not at ease in the sitting room. Mawusi's room would be better. Jiffa got up quietly and followed them.

Mawusi's room was three doors away from the sitting room. It was much bigger than Togbi's room. He had almost the same things in it, but unlike Togbi, Mawusi had a radio. He put the food on his centre-table, and offered Togbi a chair. Then he asked Jiffa to sit beside him on the double bed.

"Oh sorry - I haven't offered you any drinks." He left the room and came back with three bottles of chilled beer.

"I don't think I could drink a whole bottle," said Jiffa.

"Why not?" asked Mawusi. He was sitting so close to Jiffa that their bodies touched.

"I don't want to be drunk."

Togbi was too hungry to talk. He left the talking to them.

"One bottle of beer will not make you drunk."

"You must be joking, even half a bottle will. Besides, I don't want my breath to smell of alcohol when I speak to Papa Agawu."

"Is that your reason for not drinking?" Mawusi asked.

"Yes," Mawusi looked at Jiffa and whispered, "Please drink." Then he tickled her and wished they were alone.

Chapter Twenty-three

MAMA AGAWU WENT ON BAGGING HER gari after Jiffa and Togbi had left. She thought of Mama Agbenyo and her illness. What could be wrong with her? Maybe her husband's death was part of the problem. The tubes in her nostrils sounded alarming. She made up her mind to go back with Jiffa and Togbi to see her. Mama Agawu was deep in thought, when a young man in khaki uniform arrived at the gate.

"Good afternoon, Mama."

"Oh, you startled me - I didn't hear your footsteps,"

"I'm sorry," said the young man.

"It's alright. Can I help you?"

"I'm looking for Mama or Papa Agawu.

"I am Mama Agawu, Papa is not in."

"I've been sent from the post office to tell you that your son Vincent has won the first round of the competition, and it will be announced on the six o'clock news."

Mama was jumping, clapping and dancing even before the messenger had finished speaking.

"Thank you very much!" she cried.

The messenger congratulated Mama and left. The noise brought the neighbours to her compound .Everybody wanted to know what had happened. Mama said it over and over again, then she hurried of to the palace to tell the chief. Wonders would never cease! Jiffa had come just in time to share Vincent's joy.

Mama Kushieto was laying the table for lunch after she had finished serving Togbi and Jiffa when she heard Mama Agawu shouting.

"Victory, victory! I have just heard that Vincent has won!" Mama's shouting brought all the elders outside of the meeting.

"I had always known Vincent would make it right to the top," said Chief Kushieto. He was very happy. "I have never doubted his ability to win this competition."

"Thanks to the gods of Kpetwei, for the help they have given him," said Papa Agawu.

"I must go to his school immediately," said the chief and he left his advisors and went to get ready.

Mawusi heard the shouting and came out to see what was happening. When he heard that Vincent had won, he went back to his bedroom and told Jiffa and Togbi. Jiffa ran out to join in the jubilation.

"What happens now?" asked Togbi.

"I have to drive my father to Kpando," Mawusi replied, "But I'm exhausted and all I want to do is sleep."

"That's because you drove us back from Adidome," said Togbi.

"Not at all, I would have driven back anyway," said Mawusi.

"Then why are you so tired?"

"Last night was the worst nightI have had for ages: I couldn't sleep at all. I thought about Jiffa till daybreak."

"Do you think she loves you?" asked Togbi.

"Yes, she told me in your house."

Togbi's mind went back to the scene in the kitchen. "I'm sure it's true; but she's trapped,"

"How can I release her?" asked Mawusi.

Mawusi cleared up after lunch while Togbi sat back and finished his beer. He retuned with more drinks because he had noticed that Togbi's bottle was empty.

"I'm going to Kpando now with my father," he said, "Make yourself at home. I don't know when I'll be back but mother knows you are here, and when supper is ready she will come and call you."

"Thank you for looking after me so well," said Togbi.

"What I am doing is nothing compared to the love you have shown for me"

"I'm glad you appreciate small things. Drive safely."

Mawusi was about to leave when Jiffa ran in. He stopped her at the door and stole a quick kiss, then Jiffa told him she was feeling tipsy.

"Why don't you lie on my bed until I get back?" What a stupid time to be going to Kpando! Mawusi thought. Here was Jiffa in his bedroom feeling tipsy, a perfect opportunity. But there was nothing he could do.

There was drumming and dancing on the school compound as the students awaited for Vincent's arrival. When they saw the headmaster's car, they began clapping. The driver slowed down so that Vincent could wave to the cheering students.

The car pulled up in front of the office and they got out. The whole school was called into the assembly-hall

The song 'When the Saints go Marching In' was being sung when the headmaster and Vincent walked in.

"Staff and boys of Kpando Technical College," the headmaster began his address, "You all know why we are gathered here. I am very proud to be the headmaster of one of the best schools in this country. Vincent Agawu's performance today has underlined what most people already say about us. The excellent teaching has resulted in this great achievement. Out of the thirty students who participated in today's competition, Vincent Agawu came first. The results will be announced on the six o'clock news this evening, so those of you who have access to radios can listen to it. I would like the whole school to say three big cheers for Vincent Agawu. Hip hip!"

"HURRAY!"

"Hip hip!"

"HURRAY!"

"Hip hip!"

"HURRAY!"

"I hope there will be many others like Vincent in this school," continued the headmaster. "In a fortnight he will represent the entire Volta Region in the final round of the competition, which will be held in Accra. We all wish him success in his endeavours. Thank you all."

The boys clapped, cheered and sang as everyone left the hall.

At the first stroke of six everyone gathered round their wireless sets for the news:

"Here is the six o'clock news. First the headlines. The first motorway has been opened by the President, Dr. Kwame Nkrumah. The OAU is to have an emergency meeting at Addis Ababa next week. The Prime Minister of Nigeria will begin a two-day official visit to Ghana tomorrow. And finally, the Best Brain Competition, held today throughout the country, has chosen its nine finalists.

Osagyefo Dr. Kwame Nkrumah opened the first motorway in Accra this morning. The eighteen-mile motorway links Accra and Tema. Thousands of people lined the streets to welcome the President. After declaring the motorway officially opened, the President was the first to be driven along it in his limousine. Others who followed later were the Ministers of Works and Housing, Transport and Communications, and Lands and Mineral Resources. Other dignitaries were also there to grace the occasion.

The OAU is to have an emergency meeting in Addis Ababa next week. All thirty African States are expected to be represented. Among various important issues for discussion are trade-links with former colonial powers, and to support the freedom fighters in Southern Africa.

The Nigerian Prime Minister, Alhaji Sir Abubakar Tafawa-Balewa is to begin a two-day visit to Ghana from tomorrow. The President and other members of his cabinet will be at the airport to welcome him. During his visit, he will address parliament and hold talks with the President at the State House.

The Best Brain competition held in Ghana's Secondary Schools has chosen its nine contestants for the final round due to be held in Accra in a fortnight. The competition was started simultaneously in all nine regions of the country. The names of the winners and their schools are as follows: -
Greater Accra Region - Henry Oku, of Achimota Secondary School;
Eastern Region - Mary Evans, of Aburi Girls Secondary School; -
Ashanti Region - Osei Nti, of Prempeh College;
Central Region - Percival Acquah, of Adisadel College;
Brong-Ahafo Region - Vivian Osafo, of Sunyani Secondary School;
Western Region - Reginald Offei, of Fijai Secondary school;
Northern Region - Isa Dorsaah, of Tamale Secondary school;
Upper Regions- Ali Baaba, of Navrongo Secondary School;
Volta Region - Vincent Agawu, of Kpando Secondary Technical.

And now, sport..."
The school cheered when Vincent's name was mentioned. Mr. Degbe turned off the radio, and he and his wife congratulated Vincent again.
"What do you want to do now?" Mr. Degbe asked him.
"I would like to go and see my friends," Vincent replied.

$\mathscr{C}$hapter $\mathscr{T}$wenty-four

$\mathscr{T}$HE JUBILATION IN THE PALACE WAS deafening when Vincent's name was announced on the news. The crowd danced to some beautiful tunes from the drummers. There was eating and drinking as the Agawus accompanied the chief to his school. There was so much praise for Vincent as they drove off. Mawusi switched off. When would his father realize that being clever is not the only thing on earth?

"How far have we to go?" Chief Kushieto asked after they had taken a break in their praises for Vincent.

"Not far," Mawusi replied.

"Thank you so much for your help," said Mama.

"It's my pleasure," replied Mawusi. All I get is the crumbs, he thought, now that they have finished worshipping their hero, Mawusi was left with a few words like thank you.

When they reached Kpando town centre, Mawusi found his way to the school. He stopped at the gate to ask a passing student where he could find Vincent Agawu.

"He is in the headmaster's house. Turn left at the main block and follow the sign."

Mawusi drove off slowly, admiring the large, well-maintained school buildings. He pulled up in front of the headmaster's house and waited.

"Don't you want to come in?" asked Papa Agawu, seeing that Mawusi had not switched off the engine.

"I'll lock the car, " Mawusi said , he could not face seeing Vincent talking pompously to grown-ups, he would have much preferred to wait in the car.

The gate of the headmaster's house was open and they went into the hall, Chief Kushieto leading the way in his white damask robe.

"Can I help you?" Amavi asked politely.

"Yes," said Papa Agawu. "We are looking for the headmaster."

"Please come into the sitting room." She offered them a chair and went upstairs to call Mr Degbe.

"Did they give you their names?"

"I did not ask, sir," said Amavi feeling foolish.

"How many times have you been told you to ask the names of visitors?"

"Sorry, sir, I forgot."

"Tell them I will be with them shortly"

Amavi went down to the sitting-room and offered the visitors water. Mawusi had joined them by the time the headmaster came down.

"Oh hello!" he said when he saw Mama and Papa Agawu. "So sorry to keep you waiting."

They all shook hands.

"This is Chief Kushieto of Kpetwei, and his son Mawusi," said Papa Agawu.

"Can I offer you something to drink?"

"No, we are here to ask your permission to take Vincent home. Chief Kushieto has organized a big party to celebrate his success."

Mr. Degbe was disappointed as he was organizing a small party for Vincent. But how could he say no if a bigger one had been arranged in his village?

"Alright I will call him down."

Vincent was getting ready to go back and see his friends when he was called to the sitting room. Everyone got up and embraced him The headmaster was now ready to shower more praises.

"Vincent did marvellously well coming first out of thirty contestants. He has brought glory to the school and we have every hope that he will win the finals."

"He's very popular in the village and with his brains he could even be a future president of this country," said Chief Kushieto. They all laughed and clapped. Mawusi just looked at them with interest.

"You are being taken home for a celebration," said the headmaster.

"That's wonderful!" said Vincent. He went back to his room and returned with a small overnight bag. They all went out to the car, and said goodbye.

"Have a good time," said Mr. Degbe. "You certainly deserve it."

Jiffa slept well on Mawusi's bed after he left for Kpando. Even the drumming and dancing did not stop her. Togbi joined in the celebrations and he was really happy to be at Kpetwei at just the right time. Food and drink were flowing. Then he thought of Jiffa - how many other girls would refuse to marry a man like Mawusi, a future chief? And yet here she was treating Mawusi the way she liked. He went into the bedroom to wake her up.

On the way back to Kpetwei, Vincent was sandwiched between the chief and his mother, and Papa Agawu sat in front with Mawusi. Everyone in the car was asking Vincent about the competition; then Mama told Vincent that Jiffa was in Kpetwei.

"Why? I thought she was going to stay with her mother for a while."

Mawusi listened carefully.

"Her mother is ill, so she came all the way to tell me."

Mawusi wanted to shout that it was he who had driven Jiffa to Kpetwei, and that he loved her.

"What's wrong with her mother?" asked Vincent.

"Exhaustion, I think. She has been admitted to hospital for some rest."

"Is Jiffa at home?"

"She was at Chief Kushieto's house when we left."

Yes, and she's lying on my bed, thought Mawusi.

"I can't wait to see her,"

"One of their neighbours is with her - a man called Togbi. He helped her take her mother to the hospital."

"I've seen his name somewhere," said Vincent. "Oh, yes, she uses his postal address."

Mawusi drove faster, to get home quickly. As they neared the house, they heard drumming and singing. Chief Kushieto told Mawusi to blow the horn when he got near the palace, to signal their arrival. Mawusi disliked the idea, but if that was what the chief wanted he could have his way. The crowd mobbed the car when he drove in.

Chief Kushieto and Vincent walked side-by-side into the sitting room, and everybody cheered. One fat lady rushed in front of them and spread her cloth on the floor for them to walk over. Vincent's parents followed behind, also receiving praises. Mawusi parked the car, and went to his bedroom to see whether Jiffa and Togbi were still there; but his room was empty. He went into the sitting room, and saw Jiffa sitting next to Vincent, surrounded by the chief's advisors and friends. Mawusi searched for Togbi, and spotted him in the crowd. He went up and tapped him.

"Oh! I saw you arrive," said Togbi. "Is that Vincent with your father?" he asked.

"Yes."

Togbi had noticed how good-looking Vincent was, but in order not to upset Mawusi he said nothing.

"Shall we go into my room?" Mawusi said, "I want to talk to you." He led the way.

"What an occasion!" said Togbi.

"I'm glad you're enjoying yourself. Togbi I am sad because I went into the sitting room and Jiffa was sitting next to Vincent, surrounded by all the important people in the village. How do you think I feel, when I'm just used as a driver for that shrimp?" He bowed his head.

"Don't worry. If Vincent wins the final round he will go to Britain and Jiffa will be yours. I know she loves you."

Mawusi's face lit up. "Do you think so?" he asked.

"Oh yes. I know so"

"What did she say to you when I was away?"

"She was full of praise for you. You see the problem with Jiffa is that she has no confidence. Her parents restricted her so much as a child that she can't make up her own mind."

"Then how can she refuse this arranged marriage?"

"It's just a matter of time, Jiffa will rebel against this arrangement."

"Are you sure?"

"Yes. When you left, she lay on your bed so peacefully, and I know she wished you were around. But I have something to tell you, Mawusi."

"What?"

"I want you to pray that Vincent wins the final round."

"Alright. But will you also pray for me?"

"I will do more than that."

"What do you mean?"

"Whenever I'm with Jiffa, I'll talk about you. That will turn her mind against Vincent."

"Togbi, you will be my friend forever."

They shook hands and went out to join the celebration. After dancing for a while, they went into the sitting room to see what was going on. It was packed with people congratulating Vincent, so they stood at the entrance and watched him answering questions and talking to the elders like a chief, while Jiffa played the role of his queen.

The merriment went on until the early hours of the morning, then before Mawusi went to bed, his father called him.

"I know you're very tired but I want you to do me a great favour."

"What is it, Papa?" Oh lord, not another favour, Mawusi thought.

"I have just been told that Jiffa's mother has been admitted to the general hospital in Adidome, and I want you to take the Agawu family there early tomorrow morning."

"Alright, Papa. What time do they want to leave?"

"Ask Mama Agawu, she will be going with Vincent and Jiffa."

Mawusi went up to Mama who was sitting next to Jiffa. As they spoke, he could sense Jiffa looking tenderly at him.

*C*hapter *T*wenty-five

*N*EXT MORNING, AS MAWUSI DROVE THE Agawus to Adidome, he chatted to Togbi, who was sitting in the front. Mama Agawu talked to Vincent and Jiffa, with a few questions to Mawusi as they went along. When they reached the hospital, Mawusi asked whether he should wait in the car, but Togbi insisted that he came in. They went to the ward, but Jiffa's mother was not on her bed. The nurse told them to see Dr. Appiah

"I sent a message to Mama Agbenyo's family," the doctor said, "I'm glad you have come. I have bad news for you. I'm afraid she is dead."

Jiffa wailed so loudly that Vincent and Mawusi had to help her out of the room. Mama and Togbi remained with the doctor, who gave them the details of Mama Agbenyo's death. He also told them there was no mortuary in the hospital, so Mama Agbenyo's body was being kept in a cold room. The hospital could keep it for one more night if the burial was on the following day. Otherwise he suggested they should move her to a mortuary.

Mama and Togbi followed Dr. Appiah to see the body. Mama Agawu began wailing as soon as she saw it.

Togbi led Mama to the car, where Vincent and Mawusi were comforting Jiffa. Mawusi drove the Agawus back to Kpetwei, but Togbi stayed behind to inform his neighbours.

Papa Agawu was with Chief Kushieto that afternoon, thanking him for the party when the news of Mama Agbenyo's death reached them. They were shocked and offered Jiffa their sympathy. As the Agawu and Kushieto families decided what to do, Jiffa wept her heart out - not just because she was an orphan, but out of fear for the future. Too much had happened in such a short time. Would she live in Adidome, or with the Agawu family? What would she do until Vincent was ready to marry her? Was he the right man for her? Had her parents made a mistake, just as her mother had years ago? At that moment, she wished she had never been born.

The funeral of Mama Agbenyo took place the following day in Adidome. Neighbours and family gathered in the tiny Evangelical church near the tro-tro station. The local priest praised Mama Agbenyo as a devoted mother who worked tirelessly to look after her family.

"Dearly beloved brethren, as she joins today the angels and saints in heaven above, I pray to the Almighty that the soul of our beloved sister Mama Agbenyo may rest in perfect peace and that she may find rest in the bosom of our Almighty Father. May she get the joy and peace which were so sadly denied her in this sinful world."

After the sermon, the congregation sang 'Abide with me' as they accompanied the coffin to the cemetery. Jiffa walked between Mama and Papa Agawu, followed by Vincent and the Kushieto family. Togbi, who had made the coffin as a gift to Mama Agbenyo, followed behind with some of the neighbours. When the coffin was lowered into the ground and covered with soil. Jiffa began to wail and chant.

"Mama, Mama! Why am I alone in this world?"

Mama Agawu led her away.

Vincent returned to school, worried about Jiffa. She was now his responsibility, and he thought about her constantly. One day, as he lay on his bed reading, there was a knock on the door.

"Come in!" he called out. It was Amavi. She handed a box of letters to him. Some were from people he did not know congratulating him. Then there was one from Vera. He read that one immediately.

My dearest Vincent,

Words cannot describe my joy when I heard that you had won the competition. How are you preparing for the final round? I hope and pray that you will make it right to the top. I am sorry I did not see much of you last holidays. But the few times you visited me were enjoyable.

Darling, I hope that after the competition I will see more of you, I am always cheered up by your sweet reassuring words. As I lie here, looking at your photographs and re-reading some of your letters, I feel that you are more than near me. I don't know how I will cope if you go to Britain on the government scholarship. Maybe I shall have to come and join you there later.

As soon as I finish this letter I will write to my friend Henrietta at Tema Secondary School, to tell her about your success. She has been longing to meet you, and I have promised to bring her to your house next holidays. Sweetheart, I hope it will not be long before we are in each other's arms again.

And before I sign off, I say congratulations and good luck for the forthcoming competition.

With all my love
Vera Mensah
PS: I can't wait to be in your arms again.

There were tears in Vincent's eyes as he finished reading because he had lied during the holidays, so that he could go and see Vera. How could he have done that to Jiffa who had nobody except him? Did he genuinely love her? Would he be able to live in peace with her, or would he let her down? These thoughts haunted Vincent and disturbed his concentration. In the end he decided to write to Vera and end their two-year relationship.

My dear Vera,

Sorry I have not written to you since the beginning of term, but I hope you will forgive me. My reason for not writing is that I have had to revise for the competition. I hope you are fine. I received your letter this afternoon, just after I returned from a visit home.

Vincent put the letter aside and lay down. How could he tell Vera he did not love her any more, after she had written such a nice letter to him? They had been together during the holidays, so why had he not told her about his marriage to Jiffa? He had told her he would never leave her. He tore up his unfinished letter and decided to write later.

This time Jiffa was back in Kpetwei for good. She was grateful for the love and kindness Mama and Papa Agawu had shown her. The chief and his family were also supportive and had asked her to come and visit them whenever she wanted.

After she had been back for a few days, Mama Agawu called her in for a chat.

"Your wedding will take place as soon as Vincent has left school. Meanwhile what do you want to do?"

"I don't know, Mama," Jiffa replied.

"There must be something you can do. Listen, why don't you join the local choir? You have a beautiful voice."

Jiffa smiled. "That is a good idea. But who will help you in the house if I go to choir-practice?"

"Don't worry, there isn't much to be done in the evenings. When do you want to start?"

"Whenever you think it's right," Jiffa said humbly.

"I think the earlier the better. Remind me to talk to the choirmaster at church on Sunday."

"I will, Mama." Jiffa looked forward to Sunday. She was excited by the prospect of going out and making new friends.

The time was nine o'clock in the morning. The place, Broadcasting House. The occasion, the final round of the Best Brain competition. Vincent and the other eight contestants had just begun their written paper in a large hall, supervised by two invigilators.

As Vincent started writing, his mind drifted to Vera. How was he going to tell her about Jiffa? Would she come to his house during the Easter holidays? What would he say to his mother if Vera walked in? The harder he tried to concentrate, the worse it became. Before he knew it, one of the invigilators shouted, "Stop work, pens down and fold your arms!" He had barely answered half of the fifty questions.

The contestants were taken to another room to wait for their results. Vincent knew he had not made it and wished he had not been selected at all. When the winners name was announced there were tears of disappointment in his eyes.

News that Vincent had failed to win the competition spread through the Volta Region before he arrived at college. He went to his bedroom sadly to analyze what had gone wrong.

Jiffa heard about it when she got back from choir practice that evening. Secretly, she was delighted. But this did not stop her consoling Mama and Papa Agawu, who were bitterly disappointed.

Jiffa enjoyed the choir immensely and within weeks she had regained her self-confidence. She finished her housework quickly and got to choir practice early. Mama always complimented her beautiful voice any time she sang at home. One day at choir-practice she felt a tap on her shoulder. She turned and saw Mawusi. Her heart sank. What was he doing here? Had he joined the choir because of her? Who had told him she was in the choir?

When choir practice was over, Mawusi offered to walk her home.

"I can go on my own," she said. I've been going alone since I started." Jiffa did not want to be rude to him; but she did not want to encourage him either.

"I'll walk with you because I'm going in that direction," he said.

She could not refuse this and thanked him. As they walked together along the dark path, he told her how sorry he was Vincent had not made it to the top.

"I'm sad for him," Jiffa said, "But delighted for myself."

"Why?" he asked.

"You knew he would have gone to Britain on a scholarship. I don't think you are sad at all."

"I really am sad. I wish to God he had won." Mawusi meant what he said, he wanted Vincent out of the way so that he could marry Jiffa. Not knowing this, Jiffa told him he was the kindest person she had ever known. Mawusi laughed, but said nothing.

"Now tell me why have you joined the choir?"

Mawusi had prepared for this. "I love singing," he said.

"Then why have you waited so long before joining?"

"I hope you don't think I joined because of you?" But the truth was he had overheard his parents discussing Jiffa, and how much she had gained confidence since joining the choir.

"I didn't say that,"

"But you think it," said Mawusi

"How do you know" she asked.

"I know you very well. Now tell me what was on your mind when I tapped you." He took her hand and pulled her closer. At first she resisted, but then she gave in and they kissed. As they neared Mama's house, Mawusi asked her whether she would accompany him to Adidome that Saturday to visit Togbi.

"I would love to," said Jiffa. "But I will have to ask Mama's permission"

"I hope she allows you, because you have not been to thank Togbi for all his help during the burial. You could use that as an excuse."

"That's a good idea. But I can't tell her I shall be going with you."

"You don't need to. Just let me know, and I'll wait for you at the tro-tro station.""

"Alright, I will give you the answer tomorrow at choir-practice."

He could feel that Jiffa was longing to get away before somebody saw them together.

"Goodnight," she said. I'll see you tomorrow."

"Goodnight, and sweet dreams." He stood and watched her enter the house, then he went home.

Jiffa's permission was granted Mama thought it was a good idea, and she talked to her at breakfast.

"Will you stay the night?" Mama asked.

"No: I'll go early in the morning, and come back for supper."

"Papa and I won't be here for supper, we're leaving tomorrow after lunch to spend the weekend with a friend in Togo. I had wanted you to come with us but your idea is important"

"When will you get back?" Jiffa asked.

"Monday morning."

"I hope you have a nice weekend," said Jiffa.

"So do I. I will buy you something nice."

"Thank you Mama. I'm sorry I can't come this time."

"Don't worry about it. Remember to give our greetings to Togbi. He had shown you so much love.

"Yes I was proud to know him."

"Good neighbours are difficult to find."

Jiffa smiled. She was happy to make the trip with Mawusi, and could not wait to tell him that evening at choir-practice.

The news that Jiffa was going to Adidome with him cheered Mawusi up very much. He knew there was no chance of Jiffa changing her mind about Vincent, but he would be on his best behaviour and talk to her in a kind and loving way. In his room that morning, Mawusi rehearsed it. That afternoon he got the car ready for the trip.

Chapter Twenty-six

Early Saturday morning Jiffa left for the station. Mawusi was already waiting and when she got there he got out and opened the door.

"Have you been waiting a long time?" she asked, settling herself in the front seat.

"No." He drove off. "Are you happy to be going back to Adidome?"

"Yes, it will be nice to see Togbi again," she said quietly. As Mawusi drove, he visualized a future with Jiffa. If she agreed to marry him, he would treasure her for the rest of his life.

"Were you pleased I suggested it?" he asked.

"Would I have come otherwise?"

"I don't know, because most of the time I just don't know what you think of me."

"What do you mean?" said Jiffa.

"You know I love you and am prepared to do anything for you, but I don't know how you feel about me.'

"Can I be honest with you?"

"Please do."

"If my marriage had not been arranged years ago, I would seriously consider you. But now there is nothing I can do. I'm an orphan, and I live with Vincent's parents. Do you seriously think I can tell them I'm not going to marry their son?"

"Why not?"

"Even if I was brave enough to tell them, I should have to leave their house. Where can I go?"

"Come to me," said Mawusi.

"How can I repay the bride-price?"

"I'll pay them double what they have paid your parents" As Mawusi said this Jiffa turned and looked at him and their eyes met. He stopped the car.

"Why have you stopped?" she asked.

"I want to talk to you." He put his arm around her. "I love you, Jiffa," he said in a hoarse voice. He drew closer and kissed her again and again, until Jiffa said it was enough. Then they drove off.

When they arrived, Togbi had just returned to his workshop after delivering some of the nursery-school chairs.

"Wezoloo!" he shouted. "I can't believe this!"

Jiffa ran into his arms.

"What a surprise to see you two together!"

"What has brought you here so early?" asked Togbi, looking very happy.

"Do you call twelve o'clock early?' said Jiffa.

"My God! Is it twelve? No wonder my tummy is rumbling."

"You and your big tummy!" Jiffa laughed.

Togbi locked his workshop and made himself comfortable in Mawusi's car.

"I've missed you, Togbi". Jiffa turned round to look at him in the back seat. Togbi winked at her and made signs to indicate that Mawusi had won her love. "Oh, you!" said Jiffa. "Don't start that." She turned away.

"Don't start what?" asked Mawusi, not knowing what was happening behind his back.

"Nothing," said Jiffa.

Togbi laughed loudly, like a big business tycoon.

"What's amusing you, Togbi?" Mawusi was puzzled.

"I'm just happy to see you again, that's all."

They arrived at the house and went straight to Togbi's bedroom.

"Welcome to my residence," Togbi said, laughing he hugged Jiffa again. "I have really missed you." He offered Mawusi the remains of the gin.

"You have reminded me of something, " said Mawusi when he saw the bottle of gin. He left and went to the car.

"I am so happy to see you, have you now forgotten the schoolboy?"

Mawusi was about to come in, but he overheard the word "schoolboy" and stopped.

"Why are you starting this again?" Jiffa asked.

"I just told you I was glad you have come together and you said you were glad too. What did you think I meant?"

"I thought you were glad that we have come to see you together."

"No, no, no: I meant that you have come here together as lovers."

"I didn't understand it like that," said Jiffa. "I'm sorry to have said I was glad."

"Stop being a hypocrite. I'm not a child and I can see what is going on, yet I've been told to keep my mouth shut."

She laughed. "Togbi, when have you ever shut your big mouth about things you see?"

"So can I talk freely about you in front of Mawusi?'

"And what exactly are you going to say. I have come here to thank you for the help you have given me when my mother died, and - "

"There's no need for that," he interrupted. "I'm like a brother or a father to you, and whatever help I can give you in this world, I will not hesitate."

"Oh Togbi!" Jiffa got up and hugged him again.

Mawusi entered with a huge parcel.

"What's this?" asked Togbi. Jiffa let go of him, to see what he was talking about.

"It's for you, said Mawusi.

"Me?" shouted Togbi.

"Yes, you."

"Can I open it now?" he asked.

"If you like." Mawusi smiled nervously and sat down. Togbi put the parcel on his bed and finished serving the drinks. Jiffa sat on the bed beside the parcel.

"This is a big parcel, is this all for Togbi?"

"Why do you want to know?" asked Togbi. "Jiffa, instead of asking questions, go to the kitchen and reheat my okro soup, and then you can prepare some akpene for us."

"You want to get rid of me, don't you?"

"Oh no," said Togbi. "But we have to eat something, and somebody will have to prepare the food. Don't you agree with me Mawusi?"

Jiffa left the room and went into the kitchen.

"She's looking very well," said Togbi.

"She seems happy," said Mawusi.

"Have you persuaded her?"

"Well. It's difficult. She's not a rebel."

"Maybe, but you have managed to persuade her to come all this way with you, what stops you from going ahead? You're too gentle with her."

"I can't use force, it's up to her to choose."

"She has been handed to Vincent on a plate whether she likes it or not. You are the only person who can save her. Oh my God, why did I mention the word plate, my tummy is rumbling again." They both laughed. "I'm going to see how Jiffa is getting on," said Togbi, and left the room.

Mawusi thought about what Togbi had said. He was right. It was up to him to get Jiffa because they loved each other and he would be a good husband for her. The door opened, and in came Jiffa and Togbi with the food. The table was laid, and they ate from the same bowl, chatting and laughing.

Vincent had been depressed since his failure in the regional competition, so he asked permission to come home for the weekend. When he arrived, he found the house empty. He wondered where everybody had gone, but since there was no way of finding out, he went to his bedroom. His thoughts went on to Jiffa. Had she gone to market with his mother? His father would be at the chief's house, but he had no wish to go there. The chief would want to know why he had not won the competition, and Mawusi, whom he despised, would laugh at his failure. Vincent decided to read a book until his mother and Jiffa got back.

After lunch, Togbi, told Jiffa and Mawusi the latest village gossips and Jiffa told Togbi about Mawusi's new role as a chorister.

"I never knew you had a good voice," said Togbi.

Mawusi was about to answer when Jiffa interrupted.

"He hasn't - he only joined because I'm in the choir," she said, laughing.

"That's not true," said Mawusi. "I love singing, so I - "

"Then why didn't you join years ago?" interrupted Jiffa.

Togbi was happy to see them arguing. "Jiffa let Mawusi finish."

"He has nothing more to say. What I said is the truth. Whatever he says is lies."

"Maybe, Jiffa, but please give me the chance to say it," Mawusi was cool.

"I want to hear Mawusi's side of it," said Togbi, laughing.

"So you'd rather hear Mawusi's side than mine?"

"And why not. Men must stick together. I'm sure Mawusi joined the choir because of his love of music."

Mawusi laughed.

"There you go again, Togbi, when Mawusi's name comes up, you are ever ready to give him your support. Is it because he always brings you presents?" Jiffa asked.

"Oh, thanks for reminding me about the present. In fact I planned to open it when you leave, but I have changed my mind. Because I think Jiffa would like to know the contents, wouldn't you?"

"Why not?" said Jiffa. "After all, I introduced you to Mawusi."

"Oh, so you want me to thank you, instead of Mawusi!" said Togbi.

"Of course," she said. Mawusi laughed.

"Alright. Thank you very much, Mrs Mawusi Kushieto," said Togbi. They all laughed.

"Since I am not Mrs Mawusi Kushieto, I don't know whom you are thanking. Just open the parcel."

Togbi opened it. Inside was a beautiful piece of kente cloth, a bottle of whisky and a note.

"My God!" shouted Togbi. He gave the note to Jiffa to read, because he was illiterate.

Dear Togbi,

Thank you very much for the help you gave Jiffa during her mother's illness and death. And thank you for being so kind to her. I cannot think of a nicer friend for Jiffa. I am also grateful for the love you have shown me ever since I met you. I hope our friendship will always remain as solid as it is now.

Thank you once again, Mawusi.

Jiffa was so touched, she got up and embraced Mawusi - he could not believe it. Then she asked Togbi to join her in thanking him. That afternoon Mawusi fixed Togbi's car, while Jiffa slept.

Vincent had been reading David Coppperfield, which he had borrowed from the school library. He fell asleep with the book on his chest, and as he turned on his side, it fell to the floor, and he woke up. He picked the book up and looked at his watch; it was almost six o'clock. He went outside to see whether his mother and Jiffa were back, but there was no sign of anyone. Frustrated and lonely, he sat outside under the mango tree and buried his chin in his hands.

As Mawusi and Jiffa got ready to leave, Togbi thanked them for all the love they had showered on him. He begged them to come back soon, and promised that he would return their visit. Jiffa had had a good sleep and was feeling fresh and ready to go.

"We may come back, if you promise to be nice to me," she said, as Mawusi started the engine.

"Of course I'll be nice to you, please come again, Mrs Mawusi Kushieto." Togbi poked his head through the car window, teasing Jiffa.

"So this is what you mean by being nice to me. Mawusi, let's go. Drive me home!" she shouted.

"You know Togbi loves you, so let him tease you," Mawusi said.

"No! Let's go." Mawusi blew the horn twice as a sign of goodbye.

"I shall miss you very much, come and see me soon!" Togbi shouted as they drove off. He waved to them until the car was out of sight.

"What a wonderful man Togbi is," said Mawusi.

"I know, he has helped me so much. I don't know how to thank him."

"Don't worry, he knows you love him and that is more than that enough."

Mawusi turned to look at Jiffa, "And I really love you."

"I know, please don't rub it in."

"I wouldn't rub it in if you respond to me," his voice was so gentle. "But I find you so negative. Why? Who are you afraid of?"

"You know about my.....

"For heaven's sake don't mention that marriage again," his voice was harsh. "I'm tired of it. You are you and you can make your own decisions if you want to."

It was the first time Jiffa had heard Mawusi raise his voice and she was upset and refused to speak to him. He hated himself for shouting at her, but he had got nowhere by being gentle, even Togbi thought he was too soft.

"Sorry I raised my voice," he said. "It's the last thing I wanted to do. But I become frustrated at times, because - "

"There's nothing to be sorry about," she said.

"I shouted at you and I apologize."

Jiffa was touched by Mawusi's humility. Would Vincent apologize if he were wrong?

"Please talk to me," he begged.

"What can I say?" Jiffa's voice shook and he saw tears in her eyes.

"Tell me why you are crying."

"Nothing, nothing - just take me home!"

"Not unless you tell me the reason for these tears." He stopped the car.

"Why have you stopped again? It's getting late."

"It's tea time and there's no hurry for you to get home, because your aunt and uncle are both away."

"There is a hurry," she said softly.

"You are restricted at home, and because of that you find it difficult to relax. Here we are happily driving home, and suddenly you become all tense. Why?"

"Who told you I am restricted?"

"I can sense it."

"I have no control over my life but..." She broke down and wept.

"I know what you are going through," he whispered. "I hate myself for upsetting you and I'll never do it again."

"It's not your fault I am never relaxed with you. I'm always terrified that somebody may see us together. God knows what trouble that will bring." She looked at Mawusi's face and saw tears in his eyes.

"I love you, Jiffa and I can't bear to see you unhappy." He drew closer and kissed her. She held him very tight, it was something she had never done before. It was like saying "I have a problem, but I don't know how to tell anyone." He responded by tickling her.

"Don't!" she giggled. "Let me go!"

"No." They laughed. "This is the right medicine for you. Whenever I see you in tears, I will tickle you. Now I'll drive you home, because I can see a smile on your face again." Mawusi dried Jiffa's tears, kissed her again, and they drove off.

It was after sunset when he dropped her at the station. He was tempted to drive her home, after all there would be nobody there but he was worried about the gossiping neighbours. He did not care what anyone says, but Jiffa did. She promised to see him at choir practice that evening. After a quick kiss and a hug she got out and walked home.

Vincent was tired of waiting for his parents, and he resigned himself to spending the weekend on his own. What about Jiffa? Did she go with them? Nobody had known he would be coming home that weekend, but he had expected to see them. He got up to go to his bedroom when he heard footsteps and stopped. Jiffa walked quietly into the compound and did not see him. When their eyes met, she jumped.

"Vincent! What are you doing here?"

"Where have you been all day?" he asked, coming over to her.

"I went to Adidome." She thanked her lucky stars that she had not been seen with Mawusi.

"Why?" Vincent looked frustrated and Jiffa knew it was because he had failed to win the competition.

"To thank Togbi for the help he gave me when my mother died."

"Did you go on your own?"

"Yes." She was trembling. Was Vincent suspicious? "Why did you ask?"

"I thought you went with Mama,"

"No," she said, relieved. "Mama and Papa have gone to Togo for the weekend. When did you get here?"

"I've been home since morning." He turned and headed towards his bedroom.

"Do you want supper now?" Jiffa asked.

"Yes, I'm starving. Is there anything to eat?"

"Of course there is. I will reheat some food for you."

Jiffa went to her bedroom, knelt down and thanked God that Vincent had not seen her with Mawusi. She had finished saying her prayers and was changing into casual clothes, when Vincent came into her bedroom without knocking and shut the door behind him. She was amazed.

"Do you want me to do something for you?" she asked.

He moved slowly towards her. "Yes I want you."

Jiffa was terrified, and was about to speak when Vincent grabbed her and pulled her against him.

"Let me go!" She said.

"Let you go where? Are you not my wife?' He pushed her on to the bed and began pulling off her dress.

"Stop! Stop! I'll tell your mother!"

"Oh, Jiffa! I love you!" he groaned, pressing himself against her.

"Stop it!" she shouted again and again. Vincent had undone his clothes and was kissing and fondling her breasts. Jiffa struggled, but he was too strong and in the end she gave in to him.

When it was over, Jiffa sat on her bed and wept bitterly. Vincent sat beside her, looking ashamed.

"Why did you do this to me?" she said. "What am I going to say to your mother? She has barely left the house, and I'm doing the very thing she begged me not to do."

"I'm very sorry. I..."

"Isn't it a bit late to say sorry?"

"Maybe, but why don't you ask me why I did it?" Jiffa knew that she had to obey Vincent, since he was her future husband; so although he had forced her to make love to him she dried her tears and listened.

"I'm frustrated. My world seems to be crumbling. For the first time in my life, I have failed to win a competition and I have let so many people down. I feel rejected, and I need to be loved."

"Who has rejected you? Do you really have to rape me because you have failed in the competition?"

"Please don't use the word rape. I - "

"What do you want me to call it? I didn't ask for sex, you forced me."

"Didn't you enjoy it?" he asked.

"I don't know what you mean. I'm in pain and I shall tell your mother everything when she gets back. I hope you will be here to explain yourself."

"There's nothing to explain," said Vincent, getting up and going to the door. "I've made love to you, and I'm prepared to take the consequences. I shall be in my bedroom if you want me." He got up to leave. "Don't bother to reheat any food, I'm not hungry."

Jiffa sat in her room thinking about the day that had begun so happily and ended so horribly. Was Vincent as good a person as she had thought? Would Mawusi have behaved like this? Vincent had always been a success, and could not face failure, but why should that make him rape her? She dreaded telling Mama. Would she believe her? Suddenly she remembered choir-practice, but it was too late to go now, and anyway she was not in the right frame of mind. She wondered what would happen if she became pregnant. How would she cope? At least, his parents would help her. She got up and saw blood on her bed. She decided to keep the sheet and show it to Mama when she got back.

*C*hapter *T*wenty-seven

*A*T FIRST COCKCROW THE NEXT DAY, Jiffa got up and began her housework. Since she did not know what time Mama and Papa would arrive, she wanted everything to be in order to make them happy. The thought of telling them what had happened the night before frightened her. There was no question of her not telling them, but how would they take it? She could not understand what had come over Vincent for him to rape her. It was time to wake him up so she went over and knocked on his door.

"Come in!" he said.

"Your breakfast is ready," she said, standing in the doorway and avoiding his eyes.

"Why don't you sit down?" he replied, "I want a word with you."

"Speak, I can hear it standing up."

"I shall only talk to you if you sit down."

"No."

"Then you can go," said Vincent, getting out of bed.

Jiffa left his room and went back to her housework. It was Sunday, and normally she would be getting ready for church, but as she had missed choir-practice the day before she would not join the choristers. Moreover she knew she had sinned by making love before marriage and somehow she would feel better praying for forgiveness in her room.

Vincent was very angry with her for walking out on him. He ignored the water Jiffa had taken in to the bathroom, dressed hurriedly and left for school without saying good-bye.

Mama and Papa arrived that afternoon feeling very hungry. After a nice welcome and some hot lunch, Papa left for a meeting at the palace. Jiffa and Mama sat under the mango tree and chatted. Sensing that Mama was tired from sitting, she spread a mat under the tree.

"We had a lovely time and I wish you had come with us," Mama said as Jiffa was plucking up courage to tell Mama what had happened in her absence.

"I hope to go with you one day," Jiffa said quietly.

Mama sensed that Jiffa was uneasy but she could not put her finger on the reason, so she asked about her trip to Adidome.

"It was fine. I was so pleased to see Togbi again. I gave him your greetings."

"I forgot to give you a present for him."

Jiffa remembered the present Mawusi had given Togbi and the joy on his face.

"Was your journey exhausting?" Mama asked, trying to find out why Jiffa seemed so detached.

"Not at all, Mama. But there's something I want to tell you," Jiffa said, suddenly bursting into tears.

"What is it?" asked Mama. "Has something happened while we were away?" Jiffa sobbed loudly, and Mama tried to comfort her. "Please, please Jiffa, tell me what is wrong," she begged her. Eventually, after Jiffa had calmed down and dried her tears, she braved herself and told Mama what had happened between her and Vincent.

"My God! Where is he?" Mama said, sitting up.

"He left this morning without saying goodbye. I suppose he has gone back to school."

"So he came home, raped you, and left?"

"Yes Mama."

"I shall not forgive him for this. Don't worry about it, please leave everything to me. Why don't you bring another mat and lie beside me?"

Jiffa went to fetch the mat, and wanted to tell Mama that she kept the sheet with the blood stain, just in case Vincent denied it, but she was too embarrassed. All the same, she would not wash the blood away, maybe the evidence would be needed one day.

That evening, when her husband got back, Mama told him what had happened. He was very angry, but his wife tried to calm him down.

"Jiffa is not the cause of it," she said. "You're right to be angry with Vincent, but he's back at school, and there's nothing we can do now."

"There's something I can do," he said, looking more and more angry, like a lion, who had failed to catch a goat, that had just crossed its path.

"What?" asked Mama, who felt sorry for both of them. Her son must be crazy to do something like this. Normally he was sympathetic and affectionate to Jiffa, so she was shocked at his behaviour. All the same she would not judge him in his absence. He would face the music when he came home for the Easter holidays.

"I could go to his school and give him a talking to he will never forget," said Papa.

"And what will that achieve?"

"It will shake him because I have never talked to him like that before."

"Papa, don't forget he is taking his final exams in June. It will be wrong to upset him now. You and I know that Jiffa's future depends on Vincent's success. And -"

"What success?" interrupted Papa. "Are you telling me that somebody who behaves like this will succeed in life? Frankly, I have regretted arranging this marriage. I think Jiffa would be better off making her own choice."

"Please don't talk like that," said Mama. "Why don't we asleep on it, and see how we feel tomorrow?"

Vincent got back to school feeling more worried than ever. He had gone against everything his parents had taught him, and put Jiffa in serious trouble. Would she tell them or be too frightened to do so? Would she wait and see if she was pregnant that month, before telling them? And would his parents believe her? Poor Jiffa had enough worries already. She was the last person to deserve this. If she became pregnant he would have to get a job as soon as he left school. It would be difficult, but not impossible. He was prepared to face anything. He decided to write and beg her forgiveness.

My dearest Jiffa,

I am writing this letter in great shame. There is no justification for what I did last weekend. I was frustrated, but that is no excuse. I hate myself for it, and I beg you to forgive me. I hope you don't think that is the kind of person I really am.

Jiffa, I love you dearly, and doing what I did has somehow made me realize how much I love you. You may think I don't respect you but that is not true. I did what I did because of how I was feeling. Please, please , forgive me. Only if you forgive me will I be able to look you in the eyes again.

I don't know whether you have told my parents or not. I hope you have, but if not I will tell them when I come home. I have decided not to come home for the Easter holidays, but stay here and prepare for my final exams. I will miss you very much, but never mind, because after the exams we will be together forever.

I have nothing to add to what I have said. It sounds stupid, but I hope you will think of me as the person writing this letter and not of what I have done, I love you, and I will cherish you forever. Before I sign off, I want to tell you how much I think of you, and please take care of yourself.

With endless love and kisses from your future husband.

Bye-bye, Vincent.

Jiffa received Vincent's letter a week later. She read it carefully and showed it to Mama. It was then that Jiffa told her she had kept the sheet on which they had made love since there had been nobody at home, and she thought Vincent might deny it. She brought the sheet and showed it to Mama.

"I don't want you to wash the blood. Keep it, and I will show it to him when he gets back."

During the weeks that followed, Mama noticed changes in Jiffa. She looked tired and could not wake up as early as before to perform her morning duties. Since Mama always ate from the same bowl with her she also noticed a change in her appetite, but said nothing. She would talk to her when Vincent came home.

Papa Agawu was going with Chief Kushieto to the Volta Regional Council of Chiefs the weekend Vincent came home. He arrived looking tired. Mama was in the sitting room reading her bible when he entered.

"Wezoloo," said his mother but there was no smile on her face. Vincent realised that he was in trouble, but he was ready for anything.

"Hello, Mama." They shook hands and he sat down. She closed the bible and put it on the table beside her. "Is Papa in?" he asked.

"No. Your father is away for the weekend." Vincent was secretly pleased about this, he could deal with his mother because she understood him better.

"Why are you looking so tired?" His mother asked.

"I had difficulty getting transport."

Mama knew that was not the reason. "I thought the transportation problem was getting better these days?"

"It depends, sometimes it's easy, but I was unlucky today." He asked after Jiffa.

"I think she is in her room," Mama replied. "Why don't you go and greet her?"

Vincent knocked on Jiffa's door, but there was no response, so he entered. Jiffa was asleep. He stood and looked at her for a while; then he kissed her. She opened her eyes.

"What are you doing in my room?" Her voice was unfriendly.

"Please! I haven't come to harm you. Mama asked me to call you. I'm sorry if you think that whenever you see me I'm coming to rape you. I've apologized for what I have done, and I beg you to forgive me."

Jiffa got up and followed him to the sitting room.

"Why did you wake her up?" Mama asked.

Vincent sat beside Jiffa on the sofa. "I'm sorry. I don't seem to do anything right these days." He shook his head, while Jiffa and Mama looked at him.

"Vincent," said his mother. "Do you know how tired you look? I'm sure you are having nightmares and sleepless nights, because of what you did to Jiffa. If you don't take my advice, you will suffer one day. I have not brought you up to behave in this disgusting way. What respect do you have for women if you can go into Jiffa's room and rape her? I -"

"Mama please - "

"Let me finish!" shouted his mother, banging her hand on the table. She had never shouted at him before, and it frightened him.

"Sorry I interrupted," he said, shaking his head. Jiffa watched quietly.

"I'm disgusted by your behaviour towards Jiffa. If you think you can take the law into your own hands and treat people any way you want, I tell you again that you will suffer in life. Your father and I regret arranging this marriage."

Tears ran down Jiffa's face when she heard this. Had Togbi been right to say she would regret not marrying Mawusi, who respected her so much and would never treat her like that. Was she going to suffer, as her mother did, for marrying the wrong man? She dried her tears and listened to Mama.

"Vincent, you alone know why you did what you did. But I expect you realize that Jiffa is pregnant."

Jiffa put her fingers in her ears - she knew she did not feel right in herself, but had not told Mama.

"Oh my God!" said Vincent. He ran his hand through his hair. "Mama, I don't know what to say. I - "

"There's nothing to say. You have done exactly what your father and I begged you not to do. If you don't obey us, we will leave your life for you. I am sure you know better than any of us here, maybe because we are illiterates. My son, book knowledge is not the only thing in life. There are people who have never entered a classroom before, but they have more knowledge of life than many intellectuals."

"Mama, what I did to Jiffa was wrong. It's got nothing to do with being clever. I regret - " Vincent started weeping. He knelt at Jiffa's feet and begged her forgiveness.

Jiffa was also in tears but she had nothing to say. What was there to forgive? She was pregnant and Vincent was asking for forgiveness - for what?

"Jiffa, please dry your tears," said Mama. "You must not cry, it is not good for the baby. I am going to look after you until you give birth. And as soon as Vincent completes his exams your wedding will be celebrated. It is unfortunate that this has happened, but the love I have for you is even stronger than before, so dry your tears."

Vincent rose from his knees and sat down, his head bowed in shame.

" I don't want to drive a wedge between you two. You are carrying his child and I beg you to forgive him, I will leave you to talk thing calmly with him while I dash over to see Mama Kushieto." Jiffa's heart sank, Mawusi was bound to find out what had happened.

As weeks turned into months, Jiffa's early morning sickness became obvious. She vomited everything she ate, and was too tired to do anything so she gave up the choir and stayed at home. She had visits from some of the choristers and covered up by telling them she had malaria.

Mawusi had come to see her, and he mentioned it to his mother, who was a close friend of Mama Agawu and shared secrets with her.

"I wish Jiffa's malaria would go, so that she can come back to the choir," he said, while he was helping his mother in the kitchen.

"What malaria?" she asked.

"Did Mama Agawu not tell you that Jiffa is ill?"

"Oh yes, she told me".

"Then why are you behaving as if you don't know?"

That girl is not suffering from malaria: she is pregnant."

"What?" shouted Mawusi, stopping what he was doing. "Who caused it?"

"For heavens sake, don't shout. It's the biggest secret Mama Agawu has ever told me, and I promised not to repeat it. I don't know why I am telling you."

"Sorry I shouted; but who caused it?"

"You know she is to marry Vincent," said his mother.

"Is he the father?"

"Yes."

"I thought he was in school," said Mawusi.

"He is, but he came home one weekend when his parents were in Togo, and raped her."

Mawusi shook his head in disgust. Now he knew why Jiffa had not turned up for the choir practice that day.

"Please don't tell anyone about this, otherwise Mama Agawu will never trust me again."

"I won't." Mawusi kept shaking his head in disbelief.

"At the moment Mama and I are busy putting things together for the wedding."

If his mother knew how he felt, she would not talk about weddings. Mawusi felt as if someone had pieced his heart with a sharp instrument. He left his mother, went to his bedroom and wept. Although he loved Togbi, he ruled out going to Adidome to tell him, because he could not keep secrets. And how could Togbi help? The girl he loved was pregnant. There was nothing anyone could do to change that.

That evening, Mawusi made up his mind to leave Kpetwei and spend more time in Segakope. He would stop thinking about Jiffa, but his dream of marrying her was dead.

Chapter Twenty-eight

*E*IGHTEEN YEARS LATER, AS JIFFA SAT on the coach to Kpetwei, her mind went back to Mawusi. He was now the chief of Kpetwei. Should she have married him, rather than Vincent? He had tried so hard to persuade her. Should she have listened to Togbi, and rebelled against the marriage her parents had arranged for her? With hindsight, it looked as if she could have made her own choice, but she had been too young to understand what was happening.

Jiffa arrived at Kpetwei looking very tired. As she came through the wooden gate she could see Mama sitting under the mango-tree, reading her bible. Since Papa's death, she had lived alone, but she was never lonely, because neighbours visited her frequently. Not wanting to give her a fright, Jiffa shut the gate hard.

Mama raised her head. "Jiffa, Wezoloo!" She put the bible down, got up, and ran gently to embrace her.

"What's wrong?" she asked, looking at her face. "Talk to me. Is something wrong with the children?"

Jiffa shook her head.

"Come and sit down." Mama was worried to see Jiffa like that. "What is it, my daughter?"

"Mama, I don't think Vincent wants me any more."

"Oh God! Jiffa, what are you talking about?" Mama looked carefully at her and saw the bruises on her face. "Have you been fighting?" She could also see that Jiffa had lost weight and was tired.

"Vincent beat me, Mama, my marriage is falling apart."

"I'm shocked to hear this," Mama replied. "Why did Vincent raise his hand to you? When did it happen?"

"Last night. Vincent's character has changed so much. He has stopped eating my food, and I'm lucky to see him before midnight."

"What! Doesn't he see the children?"

"Not as much as he used to." Jiffa dried her tears.

"Where was he when you left?"

"At home but I'm sure he will be going out."

"Did he know you were coming to see me?"

"No he doesn't speak to me."

"God save my son, he is in danger of losing the one good thing in his life," said Mama sadly. "I fear for him."

"Mama, I'm tired of Vincent's behaviour. I wish God would show me what is behind it."

"Don't worry, Jiffa, rest your mind. Did you tell the children you were coming here?"

"I told Emefa, but I asked her to keep it to herself."

"How are Essenam and Kobla?"

"They are both well. Emefa says hello. She wanted to come with me."

"I wish you had brought her, but it doesn't matter because I will go back with you tomorrow".

"Thank you, Mama"

After supper, Jiffa went to bed in Vincent's room. Nothing had changed. The single chair was in the same place, so was the book shelf with a few books on it, including the dictionary which Vincent had given her years ago to look up the word jeopardise. Jiffa sat on the bed and wept, wondering why her marriage was now in jeopardy.

The night was long for her. She thought about Vincent and the first time she had laid beside him in that bed. As she thought of the good things that he had done for her, she fell asleep and dreamt that she was making love to him and that they were happy. When she woke up, she thought about the dream, and realized why she had been dreaming about sex, because Vincent had not made love to her for a long time.

At home the following evening, Vincent was getting dressed to go out when Jiffa and his mother arrived. Jiffa offered Mama a chair and went into Vincent's bedroom to call him.

"Where have you been?" he asked when he saw Jiffa.

"Your mother is waiting for you in the sitting room."

"Oh! So you went to tell tales." He came up to Jiffa and pointed his finger at her. "I hope you have told her the truth. If not, I will make your life miserable."

"Don't threaten me," Jiffa said before leaving the room. Vincent sat on his bed, wondering how to escape. If his mother wanted to talk to him, how could he brush her aside and drive off. But how could he disappoint Vera this evening?

He came into the sitting room to welcome his mother, looking very smart in a white suit.

"Are you going out?" asked Mama in a hard voice.

"Yes, Mama." He sat down.

"Where are the children?" asked Jiffa.

"Next door. Its Zara's birthday, and they have been invited," he answered Jiffa without looking at her.

"I hope you realize why I am here," said Mama.

"No," he replied, looking at his watch.

"I have come all this way to talk to you. So you must cancel whatever you are doing this evening and listen to me."

"Mama. I have a very important meeting."

"Vincent, I was not born yesterday. Even businessmen rest on Sundays. Ring your office and tell them that you cannot attend this important meeting."

"But Mama..."

"If you don't ring them, I will ask Jiffa to ring on your behalf."

"I don't want her to do anything for me."

"Why?" asked Mama quietly.

"She can answer that herself," said Vincent rudely.

"Vincent, I am talking to you," shouted his mother. "I am your mother, and without me you would not be in this world, let alone be a pompous man because you have a good job. If you don't listen to me now, I will leave your mansion and I shall not want to see you in my mud hut ever again."

Vincent realised the seriousness in his mother's voice and asked her to wait while he went to his bedroom and rang the office.

"Why can't you use the telephone here?" Mama asked, but Vincent went out without answering. Jiffa was tempted to listen to the call from down stairs but could not do so in front of her mother- in -law.

He came back looking angry, and sat down heavily.

"Did your office accept your apology?" asked Mama

"Yes," said Vincent, taking a deep breath.

"I'm glad you have time to listen to me," Mama said, "What has happened between you and Jiffa? I'm not here to side with either of you, but to hear both sides. And since I have already heard Jiffa's side of the story. I would like you to answer three things. Firstly, why are you not talking to her? Secondly, why don't you eat her food? And finally, why did you beat her?"

"Mama, you said you weren't going to take sides, but it looks as if you are already siding with her," Vincent responded.

"I am asking you a few questions. If you want me to ask Jiffa questions, I will do so willingly. But I'm not going to ignore the fact that there are bruises on her face."

Vincent took a deep breath, sat quietly for a few minutes and then spoke to his mother in a quiet voice. "Mama, since we got married, I have never raised a finger against Jiffa. But recently she has become a nagging wife. Whatever I do, she complains. If I come back from work a little bit late, she asks me all sorts of questions. No man wants to live with a nagging woman. Jiffa is in danger of losing me."

Mama Agawu turned to Jiffa. Is it true that you nag him?" she asked quietly.

"Maybe I do, Mama, but there's a good reason for it. Do you know that he has moved from his matrimonial bedroom into a spare room?"

"What?" shouted Mama, almost jumping out of her chair? "Since when did you move out?"

"Last week." Vincent was surprised at Mama's anger.

"Why?" Mama stood in front of him.

"I couldn't stand her nagging any more. As I said, if she doesn't stop she will drive me away."

"Do you have another woman?" asked Mama waving her arm. Vincent did not answer. "I'm asking you a question and I want a reply."

"No, Mama."

Mama looked at him and knew he was lying.

"Listen to me carefully. Today may be the last day you see me. I am old and my days on earth are numbered. If you don't take my advice now, you will live to regret it. Your late father and I chose Jiffa as your wife. She suffered during her childhood, and we prayed that she may find happiness in marriage. You have three beautiful children, a house and a very good job. What else could a man wish for? But what I have seen today alarms me. Why have you moved out of the bedroom? Why are you not speaking to her? Jiffa is not your housekeeper, she is your wife, and so long as I have breath in my body I shall not approve of any other woman in your life."

Jiffa started weeping, and Vincent bowed his head in shame.

"Vincent, take me to the spare bedroom," Mama said. They left the sitting room and went upstairs. Jiffa went to the kitchen to tell Ajovi to prepare supper. Then she left for Zara's house.

As mother and son entered the spare bedroom, with its fitted wardrobes and mirrors, Vincent shut the door and sat next to his mother on the sofa.

"I want you to move out of this room because I want to sleep here tonight."

"There is another room for you."

"No, I prefer this one." She smiled, and Vincent smiled back. "I'm sorry to be hard on you, but Jiffa is my choice, and I will not approve of any other woman. You don't have to tell me who the woman is, but I'm going to see that you move back into your matrimonial bedroom now,"

Vincent got up and began collecting his things. He put all his dirty shirts on the floor, and his suits on the bed. As he made the pile, Mama spotted a white shirt with red lipstick on it. She picked it up quickly, and called Vincent.

"Who put this on your shirt?" She showed the lipstick mark to him.

"Where did you find it?"

"On the floor."

Vincent looked ashamed.

"Tell me. Who is this woman?"

"Mama! I'm forty-one and you are questioning me like a child," he replied angrily.

"It's exactly because you are not a child that I am questioning you. I would not have bothered if you were a child."

"I'm sorry to raise my voice at you. Forgive me," he said and took the shirt from her.

"I forgive you, but I want you to do something for me"

"What?"

"After you have collected your things, I want you to call Jiffa and apologise"

"We are both in the wrong so why should I apologise?"

"How is she in the wrong?"

"But Mama..."

"Listen to me, Jiffa is not in the wrong. Put yourself in her position and think of how you would feel if your wife moved out of the matrimonial bedroom."

"But I'm moving back..."

"And what about the lipstick on your shirt?"

"Alright, I will apologise."

Vincent hugged his mother and thanked her, then he continued with his packing. Without knocking Emefa came in.

"Grandma!" she shouted. She hugged Mama and sat on her lap.

"Mama," said Vincent, "Seeing Emefa sitting on your lap reminds me of the day I found Jiffa crying in the gari-shed, and brought her into the sitting room to chat with us."

"Oh yes..." Mama Agawu thought back to that day, eighteen years ago. It was a mirror of today, she told herself. After all was Vincent not going to see a girlfriend today? Thank God she had stopped him on both occasions. Mama was thinking of sending Emefa to call her mother when suddenly Essenam and Kobla run into the room followed by Jiffa. They climbed onto their grandmother's lap and hugged her. Emefa got off Mama's lap, and Essenam took her place. Jiffa sat beside Mama, while Vincent sat on a chair thinking of what to say.

After talking and laughing with the children, Mama told them to wait for her in the sitting room, because she was going to discuss something with their parents. Essenam did not want to leave, but Emefa ordered her out. They all left and shut the door behind them. Then Mama turned to Jiffa.

"Vincent and I have had a good talk and he has agreed to move back into your room immediately."

Jiffa was pleased, but did not show it.

"I have listened to you both," continued Mama, "and as I said before I'm not going to give judgment. All I ask is both of you should set good examples for your children to follow. If you can't deal with a problem, come and tell me. Nagging Vincent will not solve anything."

Then she tuned to Vincent. "And if Jiffa annoys you, I am sure you know where to find me. You have no right to beat her. This is the last time I want to see such a thing. Before I go downstairs to see my grandchildren, I want you to come and sit next to Jiffa and ask her to forgive you."

Vincent looked at Jiffa and saw tears in her eyes.

"Please forgive me. I'm sorry for what I did."

Jiffa accepted his apology. Mama saw that they needed to be alone so she made her way to the door.

"I'm also sorry to have become a nagging wife," said Jiffa sadly. "But it's only because I love you so much."

"I know, and I'm very lucky to have you. Mama is right, I'm in danger of losing you," said Vincent. He drew Jiffa gently towards him and kissed her. Jiffa was pleased to see Vincent being kind and loving again. She wanted to spend every moment with him, to love and cherish him forever. But as he made love to her that evening his mind was on Vera.

Chapter Twenty-nine

BEFORE EMEFA AND KOBLA WENT BACK to school, they were relieved to see that their parents had patched up their differences. Vincent came home in the evenings, told Essenam stories and shared jokes with Jiffa, as they had done in the past. But deep down he was disturbed because he had become a servant with two masters. He wanted to serve both Jiffa and Vera, but it was impossible. Since he started paying more attention to his family, Vera was seeing less of him. He had had lunch with her a couple of days ago and he made it clear that he could not continue seeing her in the evenings because of his family, so they should agree to see each other in the afternoon. But yesterday when he went to her flat at lunch time she confronted him.

"We've been together only three months and I'm already seeing changes in you."

"What changes?" asked Vincent softly.

"You used to take me out in the evenings, so now that we have agreed to see each other only in the afternoon, what will I do with my evenings?"

"Listen I love you dearly, but you must understand that I have a family. Please don't put too much pressure on me."

"I don't want to put any pressure on you, but you have promised me many things, and I have seen nothing."

"Have patience, sweetheart - "

"Patience! For how long? Are you changing your mind about me again?"

"You know that I only ended our friendship because of my mother."

"Is your mother telling you what to do again? I'm tired of mother's boys. Either you take your own decisions, or you're still a boy taking orders from your mother. I want to know what my position is."

Vincent felt himself being torn apart. He could see that Vera had cause to complain. But how would Jiffa react if he told her he was marrying Vera? She had suffered enough, and he did not want to hurt her any more.

"Don't ever doubt my love for you," he said. "I just need time to think things over, but I shall keep my promise."

"Are you saying we shall get married?"

"Yes," said Vincent firmly, but his mind was confused.

"I don't want to wait another eighteen years, so please put a date on it."

"Give me time, Vera. I'm a married man, and I have difficult hurdles to cross. As I said, earlier, I shall keep my promise."

But Vera had no intention of being patient.

One cloudy Friday morning, Vincent was at work when his intercom rang.

It was Vera. Vincent wondered why she had come to see him instead of ringing and why she should come in the morning when he was seeing her at lunchtime. There was a knock on his door, and Vera entered, looking as smart as ever.

"What a cheerful sight on a dull morning!" he said.

She looked round. "You've got a very nice office," she commented. There were three armchairs, a sofa and a small centre table with fresh flowers on it. Behind the door was a glass-fronted bookcase. Vincent's mahogany desk was beautifully polished, and the blue carpet was brand new.

"I'm glad you like it," he said. "When I took over as Assistant Director, I had it redecorated."

"Are you pleased with the result?" asked Vera, admiring the quality of the finished work.

"Yes. But if you like it, then I am more pleased." They laughed.

"Would you like some tea or coffee?"

"No, thank you."

"I thought I was seeing you at lunch time,"

"I'm afraid not," Vera said,

"Why?"

"I'm seeing my doctor."

"You don't look ill to me."

"I'm not ill, I'm pregnant"

"What? How long have you known this?" Vincent's face was tense with shock.

"About two months."

"Why didn't you tell me?" he asked hoarsely.

"I'm telling you now." Her voice was hard.

"But isn't it a bit late?"

"Late for what?" she asked

"To terminate it."

"You must be joking. I'm going to have a baby, your baby! If you don't want any trouble, I suggest you come and see me this evening to discuss our marriage plans. Otherwise I'll come to your house."

"But Vera - "

"But nothing. I thought you would be pleased to hear about my pregnancy, but you're not. Your idea of having me back in your life was to have your fun and abandon me, wasn't it? No, Vincent. This time I have been smart."

"Are you telling me that you became pregnant deliberately?"

"If you have unprotected sex then you take the consequences," she said. "What time should I expect you this evening?"

"Straight after work," he said tensely.

"I want you to take me out to supper."

"I can't. I have to be with my family and you know that."

"I don't know that. I'm also your wife. You'll have to share your evenings equally between us."

"I can't take this pressure, Vera, you are pushing me too far."

Vera got up to leave. I'll see you for supper this evening, otherwise.."

She left the office in a huff. Vincent sat with his head buried in his hands. What was he to do? The only way to prevent Vera making trouble was to give in to her. But what effect would that have upon his family? It was Emefa's birthday that weekend and with this problem around his neck, would he be able to enjoy it? Jiffa had been so loving to him lately, he must avoid hurting her. Could he persuade Vera to terminate the pregnancy? Would Jiffa put up with him taking a second wife? From the way Vera was behaving now, she might even want to move into his house. What an impossible situation!

He could no longer concentrate on his work, so he called in his secretary and told her he was not feeling very well so he was going home.

His secretary, Mary was suspicious because she had seen Vera leaving angrily. "What about your meeting with Mr. Quaye this afternoon?" she asked.

"Give him my apologies. I'll ring and fix another date on Monday."

"Alright."

Vincent picked up his briefcase and went to his car. He drove home feeling worried and wondering what would happen if he did not give in to Vera. Should he tell Jiffa the truth and set himself free? No, it would be too much for her to accept. If she got to know later, would she leave him? Would his children hate him for letting the family down? What would his own mother think of him? The only answer was to do whatever Vera wanted.

Jiffa was having a late breakfast when the telephone rang.

"Hello," she said, answering the phone. It was Emefa. "Darling, how are you? What can I do for you? Right. Not at all. It's your birthday, so invite whoever you want. We're both looking forward to seeing you tomorrow. He is very well. Come on - tell me now. Alright, alright. I look forward to hearing all about it when I see you tomorrow. No, you can ask a few more friends if you wish. I love you, too. She's fine, but she was very grumpy this morning when she left for school. Because I refused to give her something she asked for. I knew you would say that." They both laughed. "Everything's fine at home. Oh, I've asked Mama to come to your party. That's why I invited her. Bye."

Jiffa went back to finish her breakfast. Then she rang the confectioners and booked a birthday cake for Emefa. She was in the middle of booking the chairs and table when Vincent arrived.

"Are you home for lunch?" she asked, following him to the bedroom.

"No."

"You look worried, what's wrong?"

"I have a bad headache." He took off his coat and sat down heavily on the bed; Jiffa sat beside him.

"Have you taken anything?"

"No, I'll do it now." Vincent took some pain killers and went to bed.

Jiffa sat beside him and rubbed his back affectionately. "Get some sleep, that will make you feel better."

"Could you stay for a while?"

Jiffa sat and looked at his unhappy face. "If there's anything I can do to help, tell me." Vincent was restless, struggling to decide whether to tell her the truth or not.

"You do everything for me. I will rest now, but I have to go to a meeting this evening."

"How could you if you are not feeling well?" she asked, raising her voice.

"I hope to feel better by then."

"Can't you cancel the meeting?"

"I'd love to, but it's too important..." Vincent put his arm around Jiffa. "I shan't be having supper at home tonight.'

"Why?"

He took a deep breath. "The meeting is at a hotel, so we will eat there."

"Oh ... Essenam will miss you. She has got used to seeing you in the evenings and listening to your stories."

"I can't help it, but I'll buy Essenam a nice present to make up for it."

"Talking of presents, I thought I'd buy Emefa's birthday present this afternoon."

"Me, too, but I can't."

"Don't worry about presents now Just relax and get better."

"Thank you, Jiffa."

"By the way, I just had a call from Emefa telling me the number of friends she has invited - fifty, but I told her to ask a few more if she wants to."

"She's lucky to have a loving mother."

"And a loving father." said Jiffa.

"Yes, loving parents," Vincent smiled nervously. "What time is my mother arriving on Sunday?"

"Early in the morning, I think."

"Did she tell you how long she was staying?"

"A week."

Vincent looked even more worried when he learnt that his mother was staying on after the party. How could he go and see Vera in the evenings if his mother was here? He shut his eyes in fear of the inevitable.

"I'll leave you to rest," said Jiffa, seeing his eyes shut.

"Thanks, Jiffa. I love you,"

"I love you, too," whispered Jiffa.

He was unable to sleep for a long time. His father had told him years ago that a bad woman can destroy a man's life. Vera was not bad, but she was demanding, and would not compromise. He had met her only a few months ago, but she had already exhausted him physically and mentally. After lunch she always insisted on having sex. If this went on much longer, his work was bound to suffer.

Vincent left home just after tea time and drove to Vera's flat. She opened the door to let him in, wearing a dressing gown. She went into the kitchen and came back with two bottles of beer.

"How did you get on with the doctor?" he asked, sipping his drink.

"It was fine." Vera sat down and crossed her legs. "I'm sorry I left your office in a huff."

Vincent gave her a false smile. "Don't worry about that. We have more important things to think of."

"Well, since you are here. I'd like to put a few things to you. First of all, I want you to meet my parents and fix a day for our engagement. Secondly we have to make a date for the wedding."

"But - "

"Do let me finish!" she raised her voice.

"Alright," Vincent said, looking miserable.

"I don't want to have the wedding after the baby . It must be done before. And finally I want you to think very carefully about what I'm going to say next."

"And what are you going to say?"

"I would like your wife to know that I am expecting your baby. Otherwise I'll tell her myself."

"Listen, it's up to me to decide whether or not to tell my wife." Vincent replied angrily.

"It's up to both of us. I want her to know that she's not the only woman in your life. Her three children are not the only ones who will inherit what you have. My baby will also have a share."

"Vera. How could you talk like this when - "

"Now, lastly - "

"What else have you got to say?" he shouted.

"If you listen, you'll hear."

"You'll get your way, so go ahead," he said.

"I haven't had my way yet, have I?"

"That doesn't surprise me, because if this is your true character I now see why at your age you are still single!"

"What's wrong with my character?" shouted Vera.

"Stop screaming, I'm not deaf." Vincent was so angry he couldn't even drink his beer.

"You stupid man!" Vera shouted, "When we first met, you gave me sugar-coated words, now is the time to put them into practice."

Vincent could not believe his ears, but he did not want to enflame her anger, so he sat and watched her waving her arms in the air.

"If you don't do what I have said I'll come to your house and talk to you there." Vera sat quietly for a moment, trying to get her breath back.

"Have you finished?" Vincent asked, sarcastically.

"No," she said sharply.

"Well why don't you finish quickly because I'd like to go home and think."

"I'm glad, because I don't feel like going to supper with someone like you."

Vincent felt relieved.

"Before our engagement, I want to meet your mother," said Vera just as Vincent got up to leave.

"I can't introduce you to my mother. She will never approve of you."

"Oh I see! Did you know that when you made me pregnant?"

Vincent said nothing.

"It's about time your family realized that you have a second wife," Vera continued. "I am not prepared to be a mistress whom you visit only when it suits you. What do you think I am - a fool? I'll meet your family, whether you like it or not."

Vincent was furious, but said nothing.

"When am I going to see you again?" Vera demanded.

"When do you want to see me?"

"Tomorrow evening," she said deliberately, waiting to make a scene if he said no.

But Vincent agreed, "All right, I'll see you then."

Chapter Thirty

$\mathscr{I}$T WAS EARLY IN THE MORNING, Jiffa was getting dressed when the telephone rang. She received it.

"Hello?" she said into the receiver. "I'm leaving now to pick you up. Oh, that's wonderful - I'll wait for you here then. You promised to tell me something yesterday - what was it? Okay, see you then. Bye-bye."

"Who rang?" Vincent asked. He was still in bed, struggling with his conscience. Vera had asked to see him that evening, but he could not leave his children and was also worried about how to handle her while his mother was staying.

"It was Emefa," Jiffa replied. "She's getting a lift back from school."

"That saves you the trouble of going."

"Absolutely. So why don't we have breakfast together?"

Jiffa drove Ajovi and Essenam to the market, leaving Vincent at home to welcome the children. Unsure of what to do, he decided to call Vera.

"Hello, I hope I have not woken you, I want to apologise for yesterday." That was not why he had rung, but her voice was so unfriendly he thought saying sorry might lighten things up. "I don't think I can make it this evening. Please be reasonable. I'm not feeling well, so let's forget tonight. Listen, it will be unwise for you to come here - I shall tell my wife about you when the time comes. Don't push me - that will only make the situation worse. No, I am not terrified of my wife. Do let me finish. I just don't want to upset her. Hello, hello ...."

Vincent shook his head in disbelief.

Jiffa returned to find Vincent looking worried and miserable. She asked him what was wrong.

"My headache is back again."

"Have you taken any medicine?'

"No." Vincent picked up Essenam and placed her on his lap.

"Shall I bring you some aspirin?"

"No. I will lie down." He carried Essenam to the bedroom.

"Do you want me to ring the doctor?"

"No. It's not too bad at the moment. I'll ring him if it becomes worse."

"Alright. Have some rest," Jiffa said, "I will be back shortly."

Jiffa was in the middle of preparing some pastry when the door opened and Emefa and Kobla ran in and embraced her.

"Where's daddy?" asked Kobla.

"In bed."

Emefa looked at her watch. "But it's almost midday, why is he still in bed?"

"Can we go and say hello to him?" asked Kobla.

"Yes, let's go and see him," Jiffa said, leading the way.

"Hello!" shouted Vincent. Essenam woke up. Emefa and Kobla ran into their father's arms and lay beside him.

"Hello," said Essenam softly.

"How are you?" Kobla asked her.

"I'm sleepy," They all laughed.

"Please don't disturb your father," Jiffa said, "he's not feeling well."

"I'm fine, now that I have seen my children." He gave Emefa a peck. "Happy Birthday in advance."

Jiffa opened the drawer, got out her Polaroid camera, and took pictures of them. Emefa took her turn, and so did Kobla. Essenam wanted to try, but she was not allowed. The children shouted with joy as they saw their pictures. Meanwhile the table was being laid in the garden, and when it was announced that food was ready they rushed out.

Vincent took the children shopping and bought Emefa her birthday present. When they left, Jiffa called all the workers into the garden to tell them what she wanted them to do.

"We will be having about sixty teenagers and twenty couples for the party tomorrow," said Jiffa.

"Madame," said Ibrahim the gardener," You told us about the fifty teenagers, but not the twenty couples."

"I'm becoming forgetful lately. It must be old age." The workers laughed and so did Jiffa.

"You don't look old at all, Madame," said Salifu, the day watchman.

"You wait until I show you my gray hair," Jiffa replied.

Salifu laughed.

"Now, one hundred chairs and sixty tables will be delivered this afternoon. I want Ibrahim and Salifu to arrange them in the garden."

"Yes, Madame."

"Victor, I want you to go into all the spare rooms and clean then thoroughly, and polish the furniture in the sitting room. When the drinks arrive this afternoon, put them in the fridge. I have ordered a hundred glasses, plates, and cutlery. They will be delivered tomorrow, and you will be in charge of them as well."

"Yes, Madame," said Victor.

"Madame, is Frank coming to work today?" asked Salifu.

"Oh yes - I'd forgotten. He doesn't work on weekends."

"He told me Master had asked him to come to work today," said Salifu.

"Wonderful, if Frank comes, I'll tell him to go to Kpetwei and collect Mama Agawu."

"Madame ," said Ajovi. You said that you would meet grandma at the station tomorrow morning."

"I've changed my mind - she will be too tired if she comes by public transport."

"It will be nice to see grandma again," said Ajovi

"She will be staying on for a week after the party," Jiffa informed her.

"That will be wonderful," said Ajovi, rubbing her palms together. "I like her very much."

"I know and she likes you too. Now, let's all go and begin our tasks."

"What should I do?" asked Ajovi.

"We are in charge of the food," said Jiffa. "Are there any questions?"

Victor was just about to speak, when Frank appeared.

"Hello Mr Driver," said Jiffa.

Frank smiled and shook hands with her and the other workers.

"Are you going out with your master?"

"No. He told me I would be needed to run a few errands."

"I want to give your master a surprise."

Frank smiled.

"Go to Kpetwei and pick Mama. She will not be expecting you, so just in case she is not in, go to the chief's palace, she will be there."

"Yes, Madame."

"Frank have you had lunch?"

"Yes, Madame, I just had some very hot akpene and okro stew." They all laughed.

"I hope you don't fall asleep behind the steering wheel," said Jiffa.

"No Madame."

Ajovi gave the keys to Frank, he said goodbye and drove off.

"Victor, you were about to ask me a question, weren't you?"

"I've forgotten."

"You're only twenty-one. If you're forgetful now, God knows what will happen when you're my age," said Jiffa.

"When he's your age, Madame, I'm sure he will forget his name," said Ibrahim.

They all laughed at Victor and left to go and begin with their tasks.

Vera was lying in bed, feeling sick and wishing Vincent was with her. What should she do if he failed to come that evening? She had threatened to go to his house, but would she have the courage? How would his wife take it? Would his children be there? What if Vincent was so angry that he refused to see her again? Her pregnancy was her only hold over him, once the secret came out, what next? Suddenly she felt very sick, rushed to the bathroom and vomited. Thinking of what to do afterwards, she decided to phone her friend for advice.

"Hello, Henrietta! It's Vera. I'm not very well - I'd rather tell you face-face. Can I come and see you? Alright. What time? See you soon"

Henrietta could not understand why Vera's voice sounded very low. It was only a few days ago that she had called and told her of the wonderful time she was having with Vincent. What could have happened for her to sound so low? She left immediately to see her.

Henrietta arrived and knocked several times before Vera came to open the door.

"I thought you weren't in," said Henrietta, following her into the sitting room.

"Sorry you have been knocking for a long time. I was feeling sick," Vera explained.

"What is wrong with you?"

"Henrietta, I should have listened to you!"

"What's the matter?"

"I'm pregnant.'

"Oh, lord" Henrietta shook her head. "Have you told Vincent?"

"Yes."

"What did he say?"

Vera began to weep.

"Don't cry,"

"He wanted me to terminate it."

"What! I thought he wanted to marry you."

"He has changed his mind."

"Good heavens! What are you going to do now?'

"I don't know." Vera began to weep again. Suddenly she choked and rushed out. Henrietta waited for her, shaking her head in disbelief. How could Vera allow herself to be used by Vincent like this? Vera came back, sat down heavily, and sighed.

"Listen, I'm confused," Henrietta said. "I want to know whether Vincent will stand by his promise."

"He doesn't want to, but I'm going to make him."

"Sorry, but you cannot force a man to marry you if he doesn't want to."

"But he promised me."

"Promises can be broken."

"I'm not going to let him. I'll make his life miserable."

"How?"

"I'll go to his house and disgrace him in front of his wife."

"I don't think that is such a good idea."

"Then what can I do?"

"There's no easy answer. If I were you I would wait and hope he changes his mind. Putting pressure on him will only make matters worse."

"I can't just hope," Vera cried, "I feel used - can't you see?"

"Yes, but it was up to you to avoid becoming pregnant."

"So you're saying it's my fault?"

"No, but you have to take some responsibility for it."

"I agree - but I loved him. He told me he wanted me as his second wife, and I thought he meant it."

"That's the way of men; sweet words today and a bitter pill tomorrow. You're not sixteen. At your age you should have known better."

"How could I have been so stupid? I should have seen the danger signals when he stopped seeing me in the evenings."

"When do you see him then?"

"In the afternoons. Yesterday I went to his office and told him I wanted to see him in the evening."

"Did he come?"

"Yes, but we had a huge row and he left."

"When are you seeing him again?'

"He was supposed to come here tonight, but he rang me this morning to say he can't. I put the telephone down on him."

"What were his reasons?"

"He said he wasn't feeling well."

"What will you do if he doesn't come?"

"I don't know, that's why I rang you." Vera was desperate.

"I think Vincent loves you but he can't make up his mind. If I were you, I would give him a chance to think. Don't go to his house and create more trouble for yourself. If he can not come tonight, don't worry, I'm sure he will come tomorrow."

"Alright - but supposing he doesn't come tomorrow?'

"Vera, Vincent must be just as worried about your pregnancy as you. He can't refuse to see you. Have patience: you will be alright." Henrietta patted her shoulder gently.

"Thanks," Vera replied. "I'll ring you tomorrow."

"Promise me that you will not have a row with him when he comes to see you. It will only drive him away."

"I promise."

Then Henrietta said goodbye and left.

Chapter Thirty-one

$\mathscr{M}$AMA HAD ARRIVED BACK FROM THE chief's palace when she heard a knock.

"Wezoloo! She called out. Frank came in and shook hands with her, and Mama offered him some water. "Have you come alone, or with my son?"

"I have come to take you to Accra," said Frank.

"Oh, but l am supposed to come tomorrow."

"Madame changed her mind"

"Oh, what a surprise!'

Mama went to her to collect her suitcase, and asked Frank to carry it into the car while she locked up.

"I need to talk to the chief's mother about the change of plan, so drive me to the palace."

Frank did as he was told, and waited at the gate. Just after Mama had gone into the house, the chief sent a messenger to call him. Chief Mawusi Kushieto was having a conversation with an elderly man when Frank came in and bowed.

"I hear you have come to take Mama Agawu to Accra,"

"Yes, chief."

"I would like you to give a message to your Madame"

"Yes, chief." Frank was standing in front of the chief, with his hands behind his back.

"Could you tell Madame Jiffa Agawu that Chief Mawusi of Kpetwei is sending her a special invitation to attend the forthcoming village yam festival in a week's time."

"Yes chief."

"And tell your Madame that you met someone called Togbi, who will also be very happy to see her".

"Yes chief," said Frank.

Mama Agawu and chief Mawusi's mother came into the sitting room.

"Frank! I thought you were waiting in the car," said Mama.

"I sent for him," said Chief Mawusi. "I wanted to send a message to Jiffa."

"Can't I deliver the message for you? Or do you think I am too old and forgetful?" asked Mama. They all laughed. Mama shook hands with Togbi, and said goodbye to the chief and his mother.

Vincent and the children arrived from town with huge presents. He had bought dresses and shoes for them and some African cloths for Jiffa. He was happily watching the children as they shouted with excitement and held up their presents.

"Say a big thank you to your father," said Jiffa.

"Now take your things to your bedrooms, have your baths, and then come down for supper. I have a big surprise for you."

"What is it?" they asked.

"A surprise is a surprise. I will only tell you after you have done what I said." The children rushed to their bathrooms. Ajovi helped Essenam with her presents, and then bathed her.

Vincent followed Jiffa quietly into the bedroom.

"How's your headache?" She asked.

"Well..."

"What do you mean, well...?"

Vincent lay on the bed, and watched Jiffa putting her presents into the wardrobe.

"My headache's better, but I'm exhausted." Vincent did not know whether to go and see Vera or stay at home. He had been worrying about it all day.

"Why don't you have a rest before supper?"

I would prefer to have a bath. Why don't we bath together?"

"Why not?"

Vincent and Jiffa went into the sitting room to have a drink before supper. They were in deep conversation when the door opened and in came

186

Mama with Frank following behind, carrying her luggage. Vincent had no idea that Jiffa had sent Frank to fetch his mother. He welcomed her with a warm embrace.

"Wezoloo!" cried Jiffa. She seated Mama and offered her a glass of water.

"I wasn't expecting you tonight," said Vincent.

"It was a surprise to me, too. I was to come tomorrow, but I was in the house when your driver arrived to pick me up. So here I am."

"I'm so glad you were able to come," said Jiffa. Vincent sat next to his mother and chatted with her. There was no question of him going out now that Mama had arrived. So he called Frank and told him to go home and come in early the next day.

Frank turned to Jiffa. Madame, I have a message from the Chief of Kpetwei."

"What did he say?"

"He said he is inviting you specially to the forthcoming yam festival, and Togbi will be there too."

"That is wonderful. I can't wait to see them," Jiffa could not hide her joy.

"Do you really want to go?" said Vincent with a sharp voice.

"Of course she will want to attend the yam festival, and I hope you're not going to stop her," said Mama.

"I would not dream of stopping her," Vincent replied.

Emefa heard Mama's voice and rushed downstairs, calling Kobla and Essenam to come too. The children spent the evening chatting happily with their grandmother. After supper they showed her their presents. Mama was pleased to see Jiffa and the children relaxed and happy. She was tired after the journey, but before she went to bed, she told her grandchildren a story.

"One day a man called Kwasi went hunting in the forest, and after he had searched in vain for many hours he sat under a tree to rest. Soon afterwards he heard someone singing. He looked round to see where the song was coming from, and saw a tortoise dancing slowly towards him, singing as it came. These were the words of his song:

'You love trouble, trouble doesn't love you.
It's man who hunts for trouble but trouble doesn't hunt for man.'

Kwasi was astonished, and immediately saw that the tortoise could make him rich and famous; so he snatched it up and set off home. The tortoise asked him to promise not to tell anyone that it could sing and dance, so he promised. When he got home he locked the tortoise up in his bedroom and went to the palm-wine bar to tell his friends about the tortoise. They laughed, and said they didn't believe him, but he said he was prepared to display its amazing powers to the entire village.

The news that Kwasi had caught a dancing tortoise spread through the village. The chief summoned him and asked him whether the rumour was true. Kwasi confirmed it, and even boasted that the tortoise sang and danced for him every evening. The chief did not believe him, but Kwasi said the chief could have his head cut off if he was proved to be liar. The chief called his elders and fixed a day on which everyone should come to the village square and the tortoise would sing and dance. If Kwasi was speaking the truth the chief was prepared to give him half his wealth and a chieftaincy title. But if he was deceiving the entire village then he would have his head chopped off.

On that day, none of the villagers went farming or hunting, they all gathered in the village square. Shortly after everyone had assembled, Kwasi appeared with the tortoise. Everyone was waiting to see the wonders that the tortoise was going to perform, and after the spokesman had announced why they had assembled, the chief commanded the hunter to go ahead with the show.

The hunter told the tortoise to dance, but nothing happened. He tried again; still nothing happened. He shouted and pleaded with it; but the tortoise remained still and silent, its head withdrawn inside its shell. Gradually the crowd began to boo and laugh at Kwasi, and in the end the chief ordered Kwasi to be taken away. After the executioner had announced that his job was done the tortoise raised its head slowly out of its shell, got up on its hind legs and danced slowly back into the forest, singing as it went:

'*You love trouble: trouble doesn't love you.*
It's man who hunts for trouble: trouble doesn't hunt for man.'

When villagers heard the words of the song, they realized that if Kwasi had left the tortoise in the forest, he would be alive today."

Essenam was fast asleep before Mama finished her story. Emefa and Kobla thanked their grandmother and went to bed.

Jiffa and Vincent were already in bed, finalizing their plans for the party. Terrified and worried about what Vera might do, Vincent thought of going to her flat first thing in the morning. He could tell her he was going away for a week and that would cover the time his mother would be spending with them. If he told Vera the truth she would call him a mother's boy.

Finally he fell asleep. And dreamt that Vera came to the house and disgraced him in front of his family. He woke up from the nightmare sweating with horror. He was so relieved when he saw Jiffa asleep beside him he kissed her and drew her closer.

Vincent was still asleep when Jiffa got up to prepare Emefa a special birthday breakfast. She put a bottle of champagne on the table, to celebrate her eighteen years with Vincent. Eighteen difficult years together, thanks to her mother-in-law, who had always been the rock of the family. No words could thank Mama for the motherly love and kindness she had given her family.

Jiffa had just sent Ajovi to wake the children, when a car pulled up in front of the house. She went out to see who it was.

"Good morning, Madame." It was the driver from the confectioners, delivering Emefa's birthday cake.

"Come in." Jiffa opened the door, and the driver came in with a box. He opened it and showed her the cake.

"Wonderful!" Jiffa exclaimed. "It's exactly what I asked for." She thanked the driver, and he left.

Then she went into the bedroom to wake Vincent and tell him about the cake.

"What's the time?" he asked.

"Almost eight," said Jiffa.

Vincent was still stretching. "Oh my God! I've got to go out this morning."

"But Vincent, we're all going to church to thank God on Emefa's birthday. You must come."

"Here we go again," said Vincent. "I can't go out in the morning or the evenings. Whatever I do there's something to stop me. I'm fed up!"

"What have I done to make you angry this morning?"

"You haven't done anything. I'm just frustrated."

"What about?" I'm your wife, please tell me."

"Nothing. Leave me alone."

"I can't leave you alone if you are frustrated. We're married, and you must tell me what is worrying you."

"I'll tell you later. Now please leave me alone."

Mama and the children were admiring the cake when Jiffa went down stairs. Essenam wanted a piece of it but Emefa opened her eyes wide at her, and she shrank like a mouse.

Vincent joined them later. He was surprised at the trouble Jiffa had taken to make a lovely spread and was ashamed for shouting at her. After breakfast the children dressed in their new outfits and joined Mama in the sitting room. Jiffa came down in a long pink silk gown, with matching accessories, and Vincent followed in his dark suit. Mama admired the beauty of her family, and asked Vincent to take some photographs before leaving.

Vera had waited in vain for Vincent the previous evening. As she lay in bed that morning, she decided to ignore Henrietta's advice and go to Vincent's house that evening if he failed to come and see her, regardless of what might happen. It was all very well for Henrietta to advise her not to go, but she had a husband, and did not know what it was like to be pregnant and unmarried. The thought of going to see Vincent that evening gave her strength.

Lunch was ready when the Agawu family returned from church. Victor served drinks in the sitting room, while Jiffa took pictures. Meanwhile Ajovi was busy laying the table, while the children chatted with their grandmother.

Vincent was very quiet during lunch, Jiffa noticed, but she ignored it and concentrated on the family. After lunch he called Jiffa into the garage.

"I'm going out to buy a few things for Emefa's party."

"Today is Sunday, all the shops are shut."

"I'm not going to a shop."

"Then where are you going?"

"I've ordered something for her, and I'm going to collect it."

Jiffa knew it was not true, but she did not want an argument at that moment. She nodded, and Vincent drove off.

Vera had just finished lunch, and was watching a movie, when she heard a knock. It was Vincent.

"I thought I would never see you again," she said.

"Can I come in?" he asked

"Of course." Vera smiled and offered him a chair on the balcony.

"I wasn't expecting this friendly reception," said Vincent.

Vera brought out two bottles of beer and glasses, and they served themselves.

"Why didn't you come last night?" she asked.

"I told you, I wasn't feeling well."

"I don't believe you."

"That's your problem."

"Look, I'm expecting your child, and I want to see more of you."

"I know, and I'll do my best to support you. But I can't come here every evening."

"Now I realize you just needed a woman to go to bed with and throw away."

"That's not true."

"Then what is the truth?"

"I love you dearly," said Vincent. "I want you to give me time to sort things out."

"Sort what out? All you have to do is to come with me to see my parents. Then we can think of the engagement."

"That sounds simple, but I need time to think."

"I'm fed up with that old tune - Give me time, give me time. If that's all you have to say, I'd prefer you had not come here."

"Are you telling me to go away?'

"Yes, unless you have something definite to tell me."

Vincent got up to leave; Vera grabbed his tie and pulled him back into his chair.

"Stop it!" Vincent shouted, "If you had not been pregnant, I would have slapped you."

"Try it.'

"I will not because you're pregnant. But don't you dare do that again, or..."

"Or what?"

"Nothing," said Vincent.

"You've shown me your true character," said Vera angrily. "I regret everything."

"What about you?" Vincent retorted, "I thought you were a sweet, loving woman I could marry, now I have my doubts."

"So you don't want to marry me?"

"I do, but it doesn't help when you behave like this.'

"Like what?"

"You know perfectly well what I mean."

"Why have you come here? I was having a nice time sitting quietly, now you have upset me."

"I'm sorry Vera, but I wish you would be more patient with me," he said gently.

"If I am, will you treat me better?"

What a sad voice, thought Vincent. "I'll do my best." He said, now feeling sorry for her.

"What can I do to make you happy?" He asked.

"I want to have you here with me." She fought back her tears.

"You mustn't cry because it's not good for the baby." They went into the sitting room and he held her in his arms. "I love you," he whispered.

Vera looked at him tearfully. "I love you, too".

He kissed her tenderly then she begged him to stay with her. He kissed her again, took her to bed and made love repeatedly. As they lay chatting, Vera could imagine the marriage she had always longed for. He was still playing with her smooth body, when suddenly he remembered Emefa's party. He looked at his watch, and realised that he was in trouble. He leapt out of bed, and dressed hurriedly.

"I must go," he said, taking his car keys.

"Don't rush out like this."

"I have to be at home by eight, we have guests coming."

"When shall I see you again?"

Vincent opened the door. "I'll ring you tomorrow." He ran out and drove off.

Vincent had come in, had sex with her, and run away. Now Vera was alone in her room with nobody to talk to. Enough was enough. She would tell Vincent next week that he would have to divide his evenings between her and his wife. Either he came to live with her, or she would go and live with him.

Chapter Thirty-two

$\mathscr{S}$OON AFTER VINCENT LEFT THE HOUSE, his mother noticed his absence. She called Jiffa into the garden and asked of her son's whereabouts.

"He's gone out to buy something for Emefa," Jiffa replied.

"Why didn't he tell me where he was going?"

"I don't know, Mama maybe he will not be long."

"I hope he won't, because I have something to discuss with him before the party."

The guests were expected shortly, so Jiffa asked the children to get dressed. Mama was ready and waiting in the sitting room when the children and their mother came in. She looked unhappy and Jiffa asked why.

"How can I be happy? Today is a special day for the family, and where is Vincent?" Jiffa said nothing.

"Please let me know when he comes back," Mama continued. "I hope he isn't going to start that stupidity again."

Jiffa left Mama and went to the kitchen to dish out the food.

Iddrusi and Salifu were fixing lights in the garden, and Victor looked after the drinks. Vincent was supposed to be in charge of the music, but since he was not there Jiffa took over. She put on a Stevie Wonder record, and Emefa came out of her bedroom and began dancing. She looked so beautiful, her hair was combed back in a half-bow and her white lace dress made her look stunning.

Emefa went into the garden to welcome her friends, and there were shouts of "Happy Birthday!" Just then the sitting room door opened, and in came Vincent. His mother was quick to spot him.

"What do you think you're doing?" she asked angrily.

"What's the matter, Mama?" Vincent replied.

Jiffa saw them talking and passed by without a comment. She was also angry, but the time was wrong to start a fight.

"You have been out since lunch time, and only now you arrive home," Mama said.

"I had things to do in town." Vincent walked away from his mother to have a quick shower and change.

"It's entirely up to you," Mama called out after him. "In this world we reap what we sow."

Vincent said nothing, his mother was right: he would reap what he had sown in Vera. Life was difficult enough without remarks like that.

By the time Vincent came out again, wearing a white T-shirt and trousers, the party was gaining momentum. Teenagers packed the dance floor. A few couples had also arrived, and were enjoying themselves. Essenam was by her grandmother's side until her friend Phoebe arrived with her mother, then they started playing together. Vincent took over the music when the party was in full swing.

Jiffa decided to take a break from dishing out food and join Mama in the sitting room for a chat. Shortly after that Emefa came in with a tall looking gentleman dressed in black trousers and white jacket with a black bow tie. He wore spectacles with small round lenses. Emefa introduced him as Prosper, her boyfriend.

"Pleased to meet you," he said as he shook hands with Mama and Jiffa and took a seat. Vincent over heard them, and came over to introduce himself.

"I'm Vincent Agawu, Emefa's father," he said, shaking his hand.

"Prosper Tamakloe," the young man replied quietly.

"What is your father's name?"

"E.J. Tamakloe."

"Is he a High Court judge?"

"Yes sir," said Prosper shyly.

"I'm very pleased to meet you," said Vincent, shaking hands with him again.

"And what does your mother do?"

"She is also a lawyer by profession, but she doesn't practice."

"What does she do?" asked Jiffa.

"She looks after my father."

"Do you have any brothers and sisters?" Jiffa wanted to know everything. Vincent got up to put on another record.

"Yes, three brothers and a sister." Prosper felt more relaxed talking to Jiffa.

"What number are you?"

"The last born."

"So you're the baby of the house?"

Prosper laughed. Emefa looked at him with loving eyes. Vincent joined them again.

"Are you also at Achimota?" he asked.

"Yes sir."

Emefa was pleased by the way her parents had received Prosper. She had been terrified at the thought of introducing him as her boyfriend. After a short pause, Emefa whispered something in her mother's ear.

"Of course you can," Jiffa said aloud.

Emefa turned to Prosper, "Will you help me cut my birthday cake?" she asked.

"Yes I will," he said, smiling.

"I want you to make a short speech," said Emefa.

"Why didn't you tell me earlier?" Prosper asked.

"Oh I don't want anything elaborate. A couple of sentences is all."

"Alright," he replied, "I can do that."

They all laughed. Prosper and Emefa got up and went into the garden.

When Prosper left, the Agawus praised his manners. Mama was happy to see her grand daughter with such a nice young man.

"What a polite boy," said Jiffa.

"Yes," said Vincent, trying hard to make things up with his mother and wife.

Jiffa said nothing and went to join her friends in the garden. She was happy to see the teenagers dancing and enjoying themselves. It was good that Emefa had brought her boy friend to greet them. She could not have done that at Emefa's age. Even if her marriage had not been arranged, her parents would not allow her to bring her boyfriend home, it was considered wrong to have a boyfriend. Emefa was lucky, she was free to choose any boy she loved, provided he was sensible and gentle.

Jiffa wished her parents were alive today to see how the world had moved on. The days of arranged marriages were over. Nowadays, you could choose for yourself. She called Victor to bring the birthday cake outside so that Emefa could cut it.

Vincent stopped the music, and took the microphone, "Attention please, ladies and gentlemen. I call on Emefa Agawu and Prosper Tamakloe to come forward and cut this cake." The teenagers clapped and cheered as Emefa and Prosper walked arm-in-arm to the cake, smiling shyly.

Vincent then called for silence. "Before the cake is cut, Prosper Tamakloe will say a few words." There was more cheering and clapping, Vincent called for silence again, and Prosper took the microphone.

"The Agawu family, ladies and gentlemen, I'm greatly honoured to be invited by Emefa to help her cut this enormous cake on her eighteenth birthday. May she enjoy this day to the fullest and we all hope it will be the beginning of many such occasions. Happy birthday, Emefa!" He gave her a peck and they cut the cake. There were more cheers. All the teenagers knew Prosper was Emefa's boyfriend and after the cake cutting there were shouts of "Mrs Emefa Tamakloe!" Vincent went into the sitting room to put on some soft music and the dancing began again.

The party went on until the early hours of the morning. Just before midnight, Prosper was chatting when he felt a tap. He turned round and saw Mr. Asare, his mother's driver, who had come to take him home.

"How did you find me?" he asked.

"A lady pointed you out," Mr Asare took a seat.

"You have met before, haven't you?"

"I remember giving her a lift yesterday, but I don't know her name."

"I'm sure she can introduce herself." Emefa said as she introduced herself to Mr Asare.

"What can I offer you?" Emefa asked.

"Well a glass of beer would do no harm."

Emefa excused herself.

"What a beautiful girl," said Mr Asare.

"Do you only give lifts to beautiful girls?" Prosper asked.

"Of course I do. Wouldn't you?" he asked Prosper.

"Well I don't mind giving lifts to ugly girls too."

"If that is the case, why have you chosen this beauty queen as your girlfriend?"

Emefa returned with a drink and a piece of her birthday cake for Mr Asare. He thanked her and wished her a happy birthday. He soon finished his drink and stood up.

"Shall we go now?" he said to Prosper.

"I'm going into the sitting room to say goodbye to Emefa's parents, Could you wait for me in the car?" Prosper replied.

Mr Asare shook hands with Emefa and left.

"Mummy, Prosper has come to say goodbye," said Emefa.

"Thank you for coming." Jiffa said and she and Vincent shook hands with him. Emefa walked with him to his car. Prosper took a letter from his pocket and gave it to her.

"What is it?" she asked.

"It's your birthday present."

"Thank you very much." She gave him a peck and Mr Asare opened the back door for Prosper. She waved as they drove off. Emefa went in to read the letter.

My Dearest Emefa,

My parents and I will be going to Britain for the summer holidays after my exams in June. I want you to come with us. If your answer is yes, please ring me tomorrow so that I can ask my father to book your ticket. We will be away for three months; I hope your parents will not mind you going away for that length of time.

I should have told you this before, but I thought it would be better to do it on this special day. I look forward to seeing you tonight.

All my love.

Prosper

PS Don't forget to ring me tomorrow.

Emefa could not believe what she was reading. She wished she could ring Prosper that minute and say, "Yes, yes, yes!" She rushed out of her bedroom to show the letter to her mother in the sitting room, but she heard some of her friends calling her to say goodbye, so she thanked them for coming. Almost everyone had left, and the house helps were clearing up. Emefa went into the sitting room and found her mother sitting with her feet up.

"Mummy, I want to show something to you and daddy, Where is he?"

"Some where in the garden."

"And where is grandma?"

"She went to bed ages ago."

"Mummy, aren't you exhausted?"

"Yes, but I am pleased that the party has gone so well. Have you seen your presents?"

"Where?"

Jiffa pointed at a table in the corner of the room, which was overflowing with Emefa's presents.

"Oh, I'm very lucky."

"What was the news you wanted to tell me yesterday?'

"I wanted to introduce Prosper"

"He's a real gentleman," Jiffa said, "I like him very much,"

"He's extremely kind. Look at the birthday present he has given me." Emefa gave the letter to her mother.

"My God! Emefa, you're very lucky." Jiffa gave the letter back to her, and they hugged each other.

"I feel like ringing him now," she said.

Vincent entered the sitting room laughing.

"Daddy, who were you laughing with?" asked Emefa.

Vincent sat beside Jiffa. "Phoebe's parents. They were looking for her and I told them she was fast asleep in Essenam's bedroom."

"I suppose Essenam is also asleep?" Emefa asked.

"Yes," said Jiffa. "So too is Kobla. Show the letter to your father."

"What letter?" asked Vincent. Emefa handed it to him.

"What is it about?" he asked.

"You read it," said Jiffa, irritated.

"Emefa, you are lucky to be mixing with a family like that" said Vincent.

"I've just told her that," said Jiffa.

"Maybe, but you don't know how rich these people are."

"I know "

"Have you been to Prospers house before?" he asked

"Yes," Emefa replied shyly.

"Where do they live?" asked Jiffa, trying to relax her daughter.

"McCarthy Hill."

"Well, that's not a place for the poor, is it?" said Jiffa. Emefa laughed. Vincent was listening, but his mind was on Vera and the mess he had got himself into.

"Their house is more than twice the size of ours. It makes this house look small."

"Our ten bedroom house small?"

"Mummy, you must see theirs. It's enormous!"

"I'm sure," said Vincent. "And I'm sure they have a house in Britain, too. They would not take you to a hotel."

"Will you allow me to go?" Emefa asked her parents.

"No, I don't think you should," said Vincent. Jiffa looked at him sharply.

"Daddy!" said Emefa.

"I'm only joking. I'm jealous of the wonderful time you will have. I hope to meet Prosper's family soon."

"I'm sure you will. I'll ring Prosper tomorrow and tell him."

"What do you mean, tomorrow," asked Vincent. It's almost three in the morning."

"Daddy, will you be going to work?"

"Why?"

"You're still sitting here at three a.m, what time will you sleep and wake up?"

"I'm glad you care so much about my health. I'll take tomorrow off," Vincent replied.

Jiffa listened carefully, but said nothing.

"Today's my birthday, so I hope I'll be given whatever I ask for," said Emefa.

"Don't behave like Essenam," said Jifffa.

"I'm not. But I want daddy to give me something."

"Look here, young lady, I have already bought you two big presents, which you haven't even opened. What else do you want?"

"I haven't had time to open any of my presents."

"What about Prosper's present?" Vincent asked.

"Dad, its only a letter."

"Well, it's the most expensive letter I have ever seen."

"Daddy, please listen. I want to put something to you." Emefa was so excited.

"Go ahead."

Jiffa yawned and stretched.

"Since grandma is here and we are all home, why don't you take a few days off work?"

Vincent paused and scratched his head. "I suppose I could," he replied. "I haven't had any holidays this year."

Emefa hugged her mother and father.

"Thank you both for the trouble you have taken to organize this party for me."

"It was a pleasure to do it, you're a caring daughter, and you deserve even more than this." Jiffa was thinking of the way Emefa had stood by her when she had had trouble with Vincent.

"I'm flattered, Mummy. All I can say is I love you both dearly and I want us to live together happily." She hugged her father again, then her mother, said goodnight, and went to her bedroom.

Vincent and Jiffa were very pleased that Emefa had brought Prosper home to meet them. It showed what respect she had for them, even though it had not been easy for her to do it. They remembered vividly what it had been like when they were her age.

Chapter Thirty-three

*E*MEFA LAY AWAKE ALL NIGHT, THINKING about Prosper. How lucky she was to have met him. She had known him only a year and he had been so kind to her. What a birthday present. She would ring and thank him first thing in the morning. Looking at the calendar she counted the weeks to the end of June. She looked in her wardrobe to see which of her clothes would be suitable for the trip. In the morning she would start choosing what to take with her. There was no question of her sleeping now, all of her thoughts were on Prosper. There were so many pretty girls in his class, yet he chose her as his girlfriend. She got up and looked in the mirror to see how pretty she was, then went back to bed again - not to sleep, but to look at his photograph.

It was late morning when Emefa woke up. She got ready and came into the sitting room. Victor and Ajovi were busy tidying up and she called them.

"Thank you both for everything you did yesterday." They smiled happily and Emefa asked, "Did you enjoy the party?"

"Very much," Victor replied. "I ate and drank as if there were no tomorrow." He laughed.

"Maybe there will be no tomorrow," said Emefa.

"Victor is just greedy," said Ajovi.

"What about you?" Emefa asked her.

"I ate sensibly and drank very little."

"Ajovi, you are a liar," said Victor. "I saw you eating and drinking and dancing." They all laughed.

"Well, a birthday comes only once a year, so it's good you all enjoyed it" Emefa then went into the garden to thank Iddrisu and Salifu. The party would not have been successful without their help.

Everyone was busily having breakfast when Emefa came in.

"I'm sorry to be late." Taking her seat, she really looked happy and ready to help herself when the telephone rang. She received it.

"Hello? Emefa speaking. No - I was about to ring and thank you for the most wonderful present I have ever had in my life. Yes, they're thrilled. It was lovely to see you yesterday," Emefa said into the receiver, "No, tell me. I couldn't sleep either. I was thinking about you. I'd love to, but I'll have to ask my mum. No, I'll ring you back later."

Emefa went back to the dinning room to have her breakfast.

"Who were you talking to?" asked Vincent

"Prosper."

"Did you thank him for the present?' asked Jiffa

"Yes."

"What present?" asked Mama. Emefa told her grandmother. She was very happy for her grand-daughter, but still very unhappy with her son since yesterday afternoon when he had come back from town. She had seen his crumpled tie and tangled hair. And had not been satisfied with the answers he gave her. Mama hoped her family's happiness was not built on sand. "That's wonderful!" said Mama. She hugged Emefa.

"Did you say you are going to Britain?" Kobla asked his sister.

"Yes, didn't you hear the first time?" asked Vincent.

"Daddy why don't you pay for me to go too?" asked Kobla.

"Who told you I was paying for Emefa?"

"I think you're still asleep, Kobla," said Jiffa. "Why don't you go back to bed?"

"I'm not asleep," said Kobla angrily.

"Daddy is not paying for my ticket," said Emefa. "It's Prospers parents who are paying."

"You are lucky, Emefa, I wish I were you," said Kobla.

"Never wish you are anybody," said Mama. Be content with what you have."

"Thank you, Mama" said Kobla. Everyone except Emefa had finished eating, and Kobla was quick to comment.

"It's only because I spent a long time on the telephone," said Emefa.

"How can you say Emefa eats slowly?" asked Jiffa. "What about Essenam?"

"Mummy, Essenam is a child, so it's understandable."

"Where is she?" asked Emefa.

"Can't you guess?" said Jiffa

"Still in bed, probably."

"Yes, she's in my bedroom,'" said Mama.

Vincent went into the sitting room to read the newspapers. Mama Agawu went into the garden for fresh air. Kobla left to see his friend, leaving Jiffa and Emefa alone.

"Can I ask you a favour, Mum?"

"It depends." Jiffa stood looking at Emefa.

"You know I was talking to Prosper on the telephone?"

"Yes, what did he say?"

"He thanked you all for receiving him so well."

"It was our pleasure to have him. Considering what he has just given you I think we ought to thank him."

"He asked me to come to the beach with him this morning, if you permit?"

Jiffa paused for a moment. "It's alright by me, but I don't know your father's plans."

"Shall I ask him?" Emefa asked.

"No, I'll go. You finish your breakfast."

As Jiffa was going into the sitting room, she over heard Vincent on the telephone and stopped to listen.

"If she rings again," he was saying, "tell her I'll be away for a few days and I will ring her when I get back. Thank you. Goodbye."

Vincent looked startled when Jiffa entered.

"Aren't you going to work today?" she asked.

"No, I'm taking four days off."

After overhearing Vincent's telephone conversation, Jiffa was suspicious. Vincent was worried, since he did not know whether Jiffa had overheard his conversation or not.

"Prosper has asked Emefa to go to the beach this morning, and I wanted to know whether you were taking them anywhere before I agree to it."

"No, I'm not," said Vincent. "She can go."

Jiffa went out, shaking her head - how many lies had Vincent told her and how many more was he prepared to tell? She hoped the truth would come to light one day.

Emefa was delighted that she could go to the beach. She rushed to the telephone and rang Prosper.

"Hello - its Emefa - I'm so glad he enjoyed himself. Yes he rang me this morning, and I'm returning his call - alright I will hold – why? I had to finish my breakfast - my brother said the same thing to me. Any way, what time do you want us to go? Yes they said I could go. Wouldn't it be better if I came in a taxi? Alright I will wait. See you soon."

Emefa put down the receiver and went to her bedroom to get her swimming things ready. Jiffa went into the garden to talk to Mama. Kobla had already gone to see Paul, while Essenam and her friend Phoebe had just woken up, and were having their bath.

Emefa went out to the garden to join her mother and grandmother.

"What did Prosper say?" Jiffa asked

"He's sending their driver to pick me up."

"I could have taken you myself."

"I did not want to bother you after yesterday."

"You are a sensible girl," said Mama. Emefa thanked her.

"Aren't you going to pack your swimming things?" asked Jiffa.

"I have already done that." Emefa could sense that her mother and grandmother wanted to be alone but they were too polite to tell her to go away, so she excused herself.

Mama had a long talk with Jiffa about Vincent, saying she did not like what she had seen. Jiffa told her what she had overheard.

"Is that why he can't come and talk to us?'

"I don't know, but I think he is ashamed of something," said Jiffa.

"From the way you say he reacted when you went into the sitting room, I think he has a problem," Mama said.

"I wish I knew what it was."

They were still locked in deep conversation when Ajovi came into the garden, followed by a middle-aged man in a light blue shirt and dark trousers, to greet Mama and Jiffa.

"I have come to collect Emefa," said the man.

"What is your name?" Jiffa asked.

"Mr Asare."

Jiffa offered Mr Asare a chair and asked Ajovi to call Emefa. She emerged in her flowery flared skirt and red blouse, with a chain belt around her slim waist. A pair of smart slippers displayed her dainty feet and she topped it all off with her black sunglasses. She moved beautifully towards them with her swimming things in a white leather bag. Emefa really looked grown up.

"Hello, Mr Asare,"

"Do you know each other?" asked Jiffa.

"Yes. He gave us lift home from school and we met again yesterday," said Emefa.

"Thank you very much for bringing them home for me," Jiffa said. "But were you at the party, because I did not see you."

"Yes and no," he replied. "I came to collect Prosper, and I had a glass of beer."

"Well I hope you will come to Emefa's nineteenth birthday party and have something more than just a glass of beer."

"I will definitely come, if I am invited." They all laughed, and Mr. Asare stood up and took Emefa's bag.

"Have you said good bye to your father?" asked Jiffa.

"Yes." Emefa hugged her mother and grandmother, said goodbye and left.

Vera was in bed that morning when her mother phoned and said she had had a fall and was not well. Vera agreed to go and spend a few days with her before leaving on a business trip. She rang Vincent's office, and was told by the secretary to ring later, because Vincent was not yet in. When she rang again, his secretary said he was away for four days.

She did not believe it. Why had Vincent not told her about this yesterday? Was he trying to avoid her? She needed money and would go to his house to collect it when she got back. She was digesting what the secretary had told her and wondering what the truth was when she heard a knock on her door. She rushed to open it, hoping it was Vincent. But it was her friend Henrietta.

"Hi! Come in." Vera was disappointed, but did not show it. They sat on the balcony.

"How are you?" said Henrietta. "I have not seen you for some time, and I decided to pass by and see how you are."

"I'm fine, but confused."

"Has he been to see you?"

"Yes, he came here yesterday."

"Well, you can't complain, can you?"

"Of course I can. I saw him briefly yesterday and today I rang his office and was told he's gone away for four days."

"Did he tell you he was going away?'

"No."

"Maybe he forgot."

"No, Henrietta, there is something behind this."

"What do you mean?"

"I'm sure he hasn't gone anywhere."

"You mean you think he's at home?"

"I'm sure he is."

"What are you going to do?"

"I shall ring him at home, to find out the truth."

"And if his wife takes the call, what will you say?"

"I'll say I want to speak to Vincent."

"I wouldn't dare ring a married man at home."

"Henrietta, I'm desperate. I need to see him; I want to talk to him. I'm carrying his child, and he's playing games with me."

"You must take part of the blame. You knew Vincent was married before you gave yourself to him."

"That kind of talk doesn't help. You seem to be siding with him," said Vera angrily.

"No, I'm not. But if my husband found another woman in town I would be upset, wouldn't I?" said Henrietta quietly.

"So you see me as a dangerous person, do you?'

"No. But you could destroy Vincent's life if you're not careful. If you take a wrong step now, your future and that of your unborn baby will be damaged and Vincent will hate you, do you want that?"

"I should hate him. He has used me and I'm bitter."

"But you mustn't do anything to hurt his wife."

"Stop talking about Vincent's wife! I don't even know her and you keep telling me not to hurt her."

"You can be angry with me if you want, Vera I don't care. I know what it's like to be with a man for a long time, how long did you say they've been together?"

"Eighteen years," Vera said quietly. She could see an element of truth in what Henrietta was saying, but could not bring herself to agree with her.

"Eighteen hard years," said Henrietta. "And it will only take one day to destroy everything."

"I know what you mean. But at thirty-four I'm not going to let Vincent use me as a dustbin to dump the waste he doesn't need. I'm sorry, but he's going to pay for it."

"You shouldn't have allowed him to dump the waste in you in the first place. Now it has got stuck, what are you going to do?"

"That's up to me." She looked at her watch. "Heavens! I must be going."

"Where to?"

"My mum had a fall and she rang to tell me."

"How bad was the fall?" Henrietta had known Vera's mother for years. "Please give her my love. I will visit her some other time. How long will you be away for?"

"A few days"

"Have you told Vincent?"

"That was why I tried calling him."

"Just supposing he comes here when you have left, what will you do?"

"That's why I want to ring him, but you said I shouldn't. I am so confused, I don't know what to do!"

"Let's sit down again, I've got an idea," said Henrietta. "Why don't you ring him at home, and if his wife receives it, put the receiver down."

"What will I gain from that?"

"You're right, that's no good". She thought for a moment." I've got it. Ring his house, and if his wife answers ask to speak to him. If he isn't in don't leave your name."

"Alright, I'll try that." They went into the sitting room and Vera nervously dialled Vincent's number.

"May I speak to Vincent please? No, I'll ring back later." She hung up and took in a deep breath.

"Wasn't he there?" asked Henrietta. Vera shook her head in despair and said nothing. "Answer me - wasn't he there?'

"He was there."

"Why didn't you speak to him?"

"He was in the swimming pool. Vincent is a liar! I'm going to teach him a lesson."

"Be careful, Vera. Why don't you ring him again when you get to your mother's?"

Vera went into her bedroom and brought out a small travelling bag. "I'll do that," she said, locking up.

"Do you want a lift?" Henrietta asked her.

"Yes , but where were you going?" Vera asked.

"The centre of town, to do some shopping."

"Lucky you. Just dump me at the station and I'll take a taxi."

They left the flat, got into car, and drove off.

Chapter Thirty-four

AFTER JIFFA PUT DOWN THE RECEIVER she stood for a while, wondering who the caller might have been. The woman had not left her name. And only that morning she had overheard Vincent telling his secretary to tell someone that he would call her when he got back. Was it the same person? Should she tell Vincent that a woman had rung him and had refused to leave her name? Or should she wait for more clues? She decided to wait and went to the kitchen to get lunch ready.

Vincent was in the swimming pool with Essenam and her friend Phoebe. As he played with them, he was thinking about Vera. Should he go and see her after lunch and tell her he was going away? Or should he leave it to his secretary? He longed to go to Vera, but his mother was there and yesterday she had been very angry when he came home. He did not want to worsen the situation. Jiffa had not asked him where he had been; that was also haunting him. He was in a trap, how could he escape? Just then Jiffa came out and called him to lunch.

Prosper was waiting impatiently when Emefa arrived. She thanked Mr Asare as he opened the door for her.

"Hi! You really look beautiful. Happy birthday!" Prosper embraced Emefa.

"I hope you are not going back in time?" She was really happy in Prosper's arms

"I want to."

"Then wait until I am nineteen."

Mr Asare packed the car and came over to Prosper and Emefa.

"Where can I find your mother?" Mr Asare watched them and thought how sweet young love can be. Just wait until it's old, he thought, then it will be a different story all together.

"She's on the rooftop," said Prosper.

"I'd like to say hello to her," said Mr Asare.

"I also want to see her," said Emefa.

"Then let's go up." Prosper led the way up the spiral staircase, which led to the roof. Mrs Tamakloe was having her nails manicured when they appeared.

"Hello," she said when Emefa walked in. She told the manicurist to wait while she hugged her. Then she turned to Mr Asare. "Could you take the Range Rover? I want you to go and collect some drinks from my agent. I have already rung and ordered them, so they will be ready when you arrive. Take John with you, he is in the pantry."

"Thank you, Madame." Mr Asare said goodbye and left. Mrs Tamakloe turned to Emefa.

"I want to wish you a belated, happy birthday and I am happy that you can come to Britain with us," she said, quietly and slowly. Prosper stood watching.

"Thank you so much for asking me," Emefa replied.

"It will be a pleasure. Have you been there before?"

"No."

"Well, next month you will. Meanwhile I shall get in touch with your parents next week and fix a date to meet them."

"We're leaving for Bortianor beach now," Prosper said to his mother.

"Alright," said Mrs Tamakloe. "What time shall I expect you home?"

"Tea-time"

"Alright. Have you got everything you need?"

"Yes, thank you."

"Alright. I'll be here when you get back."

They left and as they drove off along the Winneba road towards Bortianor beach, Prosper played some cool music. Then he turned and looked at Emefa and smiled.

"Why didn't you drive yourself to my party yesterday?" she asked.

"I never drive after dark, because of my eyes."

"Have you seen an optician?"

"Yes. My father wants me to have a check up when I'm in Britain."

"Does it affect your reading?"

"No, but I have frequent headaches."

"Poor you. Why haven't you told me this before?"

"Sweet heart I am sorry for not telling you."

"I forgive you" They laughed.

"Look at you, when we first met you were very shy, now you are so grown up," Prosper said.

"Yes, now I am eighteen."

"Do you remember when we first met?"

"I remember it vividly," said Emefa. "That Christmas dance."

"Yes..." said Prosper slowly."I must say you have grown up a lot since then," he added.

"Why do you say that?"

"I remember you didn't want me to come to your house, because you were terrified of your parents. And made excuses for not coming to see me."

"I know."

"Yesterday must have been frightening for you?"

"I rehearsed your introduction several times at school." They laughed. Prosper turned left off the main road on to the untarred road, which led to Bortainor.

"Your parents don't look very strict to me."

"They are not. But something made me shrink from taking you home to meet them. Do you know what my father asked me after you left?"

"No, I meant to ask you."

"They were all saying how nice you were, then my father asked me whether I have been to your house before. I nearly said no and then I hesitated and said yes. He asked how often, and I said a couple of times."

"You liar! How many times have you been to my house? Count them."

"Prosper, you can't live in this world of ours without telling a few lies," said Emefa. Prosper parked the car under some coconut trees, and they got out.

The Tamakloes owned a chalet on the beach. Prosper opened it up so that they could change. He had already put on his swimming trunks at home, so he took off his shirt and trousers. Then he stood and watched Emefa, who was putting on her bikini.

"You have the most beautiful body I've ever seen." said Prosper, putting his arm around her.

"You always say that. How many have you seen?"

"Quite a few. When you come to the beach every day you see all shapes and sizes."

"Do you come here everyday?"

"Not when I'm in school."

"Stop playing the fool with me, Prosper."

"Do you think I'm playing the fool?" They lay down on the beach.

"Yes. When you saw my parents yesterday you behaved like a real gentleman. I wish they could see you now."

"What about you? Didn't you do the same when you first met my parents? You're still nervous when you see them. Weren't you pleased that I put on my best behaviour yesterday?"

"Yes. But I wish you'd put it on now."

"I looked at you and your mother carefully. You resemble her very much. She looks so young, I thought she was your sister."

"I know, everyone says that."

"Your father's very lucky to have a wife like that. If I were in his shoes, I'd never look at another woman."

"Stop exaggerating, my mother's not a beauty queen. And I don't believe you when you talk of not looking at other women."

"Why?"

"Because it's a man's disease to chase women, whether he has a beauty queen at home or not. Am I telling lies?"

"Come on," said Prosper. "Let's have a swim." They got up, arm in arm and ran into the sea.

After lunch, Mama went to her room to read her bible, while Jiffa and Essenam took Phoebe home. Jiffa returned later without Essenam, who wanted to stay on and play. When she got home she noticed that Vincent was not there and asked Ajovi of his whereabouts.

"Master has just gone out," she replied.

"Did he say where he was going?"

"No, Madame."

Jiffa went to Mama's bedroom.

"Oh, you're back," Mama said, "I thought you'd be out for a while." She closed the bible and put it under her pillow. Jiffa sat beside her.

"I did not want to leave you alone in the house."

"Where's Vincent?"

"I don't know. I came to ask you."

212

"Didn't he go into the garden after lunch?"

"Yes, but Ajovi says he has gone out."

"Why didn't he tell me where he was going?" asked Mama.

"Maybe he thought you would stop him."

"Why should I?"

"Well, that's what he thinks, and that's why he was moody at lunch."

"I'm glad I have seen this for myself, Jiffa, now I know why you nag him. Fancy going out without telling your wife!" she said waving her arms. "Where is his respect for you?"

"I'm glad you have seen it, too," Jiffa said, "I shall not ask him anything when he gets back, I will just watch him."

"I will do the same," said Mama, "I was a fool to question him when he came back yesterday. All he did was tell me lies. Vincent has changed, Jiffa, and I'm worried."

"I did not bother to ask him anything," said Jiffa. "I saw his crumpled shirt and tangled hair, but I said nothing. I don't want any more rows in the house, especially when the children are here. It's bad for them to see us arguing. They had enough of that last holidays. It's their half term, and I don't want to upset them anymore."

"I agree. Do you want me to speak to him?"

"No. He will not tell you the truth. He has a serious problem on his mind."

"How do you know?" asked Mama

"Since last week he has been having headaches, he looks moody and he has started going out in the evenings without telling me. I can only assume he has a problem."

"You may be right. And where is he now?"

"God knows," said Jiffa. She was about to say something when the telephone rang. She went into the sitting room to answer it.

"Hello? He's not in at the moment. If you give me your name and number, he'll ring you back. Did you ring earlier?"

Vera now knew Vincent was in and was trying to avoid her. She would not ring him again, but rather go to his house when she got back.

Jiffa was about to ask the caller whether anything was wrong and why she did not want to leave her name, but the person had hung up. She was now certain that Vincent was in trouble. She went into Mama's room and told her what had happened.

213

"Don't worry too much, Jiffa. I will be here until Friday morning. If these mysterious telephone calls continue, I'll talk to him."

"I hope he tells you the truth."

Mama was dozing off and her last words were almost inaudible.

Jiffa was sitting in the garden pasting photographs into her album when Vincent arrived. He came into the garden and sat beside her. He had been to Vera's flat, but she was not in and after waiting for a while he decided to come home. Jiffa had not addressed a word to him since he returned the previous evening. Now he was desperate and longed for her to talk to him, but when Jiffa saw him she merely glanced at him and went on with what she was doing. Vincent put his feet up on the garden table and called Ajovi to bring him a bottle of beer with two glasses.

"Will you share a bottle with me?" he asked Jiffa.

"No. Thank you. I don't feel like drinking."

"Please! Just a glass won't do you any harm."

"Is it a must that I should drink?" she said coldly. Ajovi brought the drink and went back to the house.

"It's not a must, but I'm trying to make things up with you."

"Make what up?" asked Jiffa, she stopped what she was doing and looked at him.

"You know what I mean, since yesterday you have been very cold towards me and I don't know what I have done."

"Do you think you have done something?"

"I don't know. But you and my mother seem to. By the way where is she?"

"She's asleep."

"The two of you make me feel uneasy. It's like I'm being watched and it's horrible."

"I'm sorry you feel that way." She went on with what she was doing, happy that he was carrying his guilty conscience around. He was longing for her to release him, but she would not. Wasn't he the same person who called her a nagging wife?

Vincent sipped his drink in silence. "What time is Emefa coming back?" he asked. Jiffa did not raise her head.

"Before supper."

"Where's Kobla?"

"He's gone to see Paul." Vincent was trying hard to ease the atmosphere, but Jiffa would not budge. She began humming a hymn. When she finished the first hymn, she was thinking of the second when she heard Mama asking for her.

"I'm here!" she called. Mama came into the garden.

"You've been asleep for ages, Mama," said Vincent. Mama took a seat and was about to question Vincent, but Jiffa signalled her not to.

"Yes. I was tired after my journey."

"I'm sure you were," said Jiffa.

"Jiffa, thank you so much for sending the driver to pick me up. I would have been far more tired if I had come by public transport."

Vincent jumped in to answer his mother. "From today, Mama, I will always see to it that one of my drivers will come to collect you."

"That's very kind of you."

"Do you want a drink?" he asked his mother.

"Yes, please." Vincent went into the house to get more drinks. Jiffa turned to Mama and thanked her for not asking him any questions.

"Don't worry, I'm not going to. Did he tell you where he has been?"

"No. He hoped I would ask, but I didn't."

"Excellent."

Vincent returned with the drinks. Mama stopped talking and began admiring the photographs. Vincent served his mother and helped himself.

"Jiffa, are you really not having a drink with us?" he asked.

"I have already told you, I don't feel like drinking." Ajovi came into the garden to tell Jiffa that Emefa was on the telephone, she left at once.

"Hello? Why? Alright. How is Prosper? And how was the beach? I'm glad. Tell me all about it when you get back. Thanks for calling me. Bye"

Emefa was a daughter worth having, thought Jiffa. During her last holidays she had stayed home to keep her company because Vincent was behaving stupidly. She was delighted that her daughter had found happiness with Prosper. She thanked God for this beautiful friendship. Instead of going back to the garden, Jiffa went to the kitchen to see whether Ajovi had finished making supper and to tell her to fetch Essenam from Phoebe's house.

When she left, Vincent asked his mother why Jiffa was moody.

"Is she?" asked Mama.

"Yes. I find it hard to be with her when she's like this."

"I don't think she's moody. Maybe she's tired."

"I know when she's trying to avoid me."

"What have you done?"

"I want you to ask her," said Vincent.

"Can't you ask her yourself?"

"Mama. She's refusing to talk to me. I'm desperate. I came home this afternoon longing to be with her, but as soon as I saw her face I felt like running away." Vincent wanted his mother to ask him where he had gone that afternoon but she did not.

"I think you're imagining it. Jiffa and I have had a wonderful time this afternoon. She was full of fun. And I haven't noticed any moodiness."

"I'm glad she had fun with you. Maybe I am imagining it." They heard footsteps coming from the gate and looked up, thinking it was Emefa. Instead Kobla appeared.

"Hi, Mama. You were sitting here when I left this morning. Haven't you moved?"

"No, I have been waiting for you to come and move me," Mama replied. They laughed and went into the house.

Chapter Thirty-five

MAMA AND JIFFA WERE CHATTING IN the sitting room after supper when Emefa walked in with Mr Asare.

"Hello," said Jifffa. She shook hands with Mr Asare, and Emefa hugged her grandmother. Then they thanked him and said goodbye.

Emefa told them all about her trip to Bortianor beach and gave them Prosper's greetings.

"He is a very good looking boy," said Mama.

"Oh yes," said Jiffa.

"Mummy, Prosper liked you very much," Emefa said.

"I liked him, too."

"Do you know what he said about you?"

"No, tell me," Jiffa said eagerly.

"He couldn't believe you were my mother, he thought you were my big sister. They all laughed.

"What else did he say?" asked Mama.

"He said you're a beautiful woman, and if he married someone as pretty as you he would never look at another woman."

Jiffa was flattered, and her mind went back to the days when she was nicknamed Beauty.

"I wish your father could hear this," said Mama.

"Where is he?" asked Emefa.

"He and Kobla are in Essenam's bedroom telling her a story."

"I must go and say hello to him. Mummy, could you please tell Ajovi to put all the presents in my bedroom? I will open them before I going to bed." Emefa went to see her father.

"I'm glad to see Emefa looking very happy," said Jiffa.

"Me too," said Mama. "She's a lovely girl and I hope she grows up into a wonderful woman like her mother."

Jiffa laughed. "What an evening of compliments!" she said.

"You deserve them. You've gone through many difficulties in life, but you have emerged a winner. When your mother and father died, I wondered what would become of you. I prayed daily for God to help you through the difficult times in your life."

Jiffa looked at Mama quietly, thinking about her past. "Yes, those were the days when I wished I have never been born. Without the help of you and Papa, I don't know what I would have done." When Jiffa mentioned Papa Agawu's name, Mama's face became sad.

"When Papa died, part of my life went with him. Sometimes I wonder how I have lived without him. It's only thanks to you and Vincent, who have helped me in my time of need."

"Mama, we have to thank you. Without you, where would we be?"

"Thank you, Jiffa. Talking to you always makes me feel good."

"I feel the same; that's why I enjoy your visits."

"I wish I could stay longer, but I hate to leave my house empty for too long, it looks unloved."

"Anyway, I will be coming to the Kpetwei yam festival in a fortnight, so I'll stay a few days with you."

"That will be lovely. Did you notice that Vincent was trying to stop you going?'

"Oh yes. I hope he won't stop me, because I want to see Togbi."

"Togbi has a big contract in Kpetwei, so he spends quite a lot of time there."

"What is he doing?" asked Jiffa.

"Chief Mawusi has asked him to do all the carpentry for the extension of the palace."

"That's good news." Jiffa remembered the days when Togbi made nursery school chairs, and laughed to herself.

"He has done a marvellous job for the chief and he's doing other jobs in the village."

"I can't wait to see him. I love to hear news about Adidome."

"Have you been there since your mother died?'

"No. I would like to go and stay with Togbi for a day or two after the festival."

"It would be good for you to see what has become of Adidome since you left."

"Mama, the problem is because I grew up in Kpetwei, I have never felt part of Adidome and since my parents' death whatever roots I had got withered."

Mama started dozing off and Jiffa told her she should go to bed.

"Was I falling asleep?"

"Yes, you're tired." Jiffa followed her into her bedroom and said goodnight. As she passed Essenam's bedroom she could hear Vincent laughing with Emefa and Kobla; presumably Essenam was asleep. She thought of going in to join them, but changed her mind and went to her own bedroom.

After their happy half term, Emefa and Kobla were sad to go back to school. As Jiffa and Mama waited to drive them back, the children hugged their father and thanked him for the presents he had given them. Vincent waved as Jiffa drove off, and went back into the house to wait for Essenam to come back from school.

He went into the sitting room, feeling confused. He had been trying to ring Vera since Monday, but there was never a reply. He had been to her flat but she had not been there. Had something happened, or had she gone on one of her business trips? He doubted whether she would go abroad without telling him. As he lay on the sofa, wondering what to do, the telephone rang. He rushed to it, hoping it was Vera.

"Hello - Mr Agawu speaking. Oh, hello! Yes, we very much want to meet you too. Thank you for the wonderful present you have given Emefa. When shall we meet? Yes, that will be fine. Can I have your address please? Alright, that will be fine - that's very kind of you. Thanks - bye."

Vincent sat thinking about the Tamakloe family. What were they like? How big was their house which Emefa said made his own house look so small? He couldn't wait to meet them. Then his mind returned to Vera. He was about to dial her number when the door opened and Essenam came in with Ajovi.

Vincent put down the telephone and picked up Essenam.

"Daddy, where's mum?" she asked.

Vincent sat down on the sofa and put her on his lap. "She has taken Emefa and Kobla back to school."

"But I wanted to go with them..."

"Don't be sad, I'll take you there next weekend."

"Thank you daddy." Ajovi called Essenam to come and change and have her bath. She ran upstairs.

Jiffa returned later, with a huge load of shopping. She and Mama had gone to the market on their way home. Most of what she had bought were provisions for her mother-in-law to take back to Kpetwei. Vincent told his mother and Jiffa about Mrs Tamakloe's invitation and they were pleased.

Vera was exhausted when she returned to her flat on Thursday evening. She had already made up her mind to go to Vincent's house the following day, unless he came to see her. As she lay on her bed, wondering how Vincent would react when he saw her, she fell fast asleep.

On the last evening of Mama's stay, Jiffa and Vincent decided to have champagne in the garden. Vincent was delighted that his mother's stay had come to a happy end. He asked them to sit in the garden and relax, while he waited on them.

"That's kind of you," said Mama. Vincent made a joke and went into the house to get the drinks.

"He's doing his best to please us," said Jiffa.

"Yes, I can see that. I think he's ashamed of his moody behaviour."

Essenam came to her mother covered in dirt, so Jiffa called Ajovi and asked her to run a bath and put Essenam in it.

"Do you know I still have not asked him where he went on Sunday afternoon"? said Jiffa.

"If I were you, I would put it out of my mind."

"Alright, Mama."

"Who knows, he may even tell you himself."

Jiffa was about to answer when she saw a woman coming into the house. She told Mama to look up. The woman was dressed glamorously in a green and white-striped skirt, white blouse and green neck scarf. Jiffa and Mama sat silently as she approached.

"Good evening," said the woman.

"Can I help you?" asked Jiffa politely.

"Yes, I would like to know whether this is Vincent Agawu's residence."

"Yes, it is," Mama said, examining the woman from head to toe. Her carefully styled, straightened hair, heavy make up, and low heeled slippers displaying her bright red toenails.

"Is he in?"

"Yes," said Jiffa." Please take a seat, he will be with you soon."

Vincent came out of the house carrying a tray with a bottle of champagne and three glasses. Jiffa called to him to hurry up, because there was a visitor waiting for him. When Vincent saw Vera he stopped dead, his eyes wide open. His heart was beating very fast and his hands were shaking so much that he nearly dropped the tray. His mother and Jiffa watched him carefully.

"Is anything wrong?" Jiffa asked. Vincent said nothing, but came over and put the tray on the garden table. Then he faced the woman.

"Vera! What are you doing here?" He had no idea what to do. Jiffa and his mother watched them in amazement.

"Do you really want to know?"

"What is the matter, Vincent?" asked Mama. He did not answer. "Young lady, I am Vincent's mother, what is the matter?'

Vera was about to answer, but Vincent grabbed her hands and dragged her out of the chair.

"Leave me alone!" Vera shouted.

Mama and Jiffa got to their feet to stop Vincent.

"I will not!" he shouted.

"Then I'll tell them everything!" shouted Vera, breaking away from him.

"What have you got to tell?" asked Mama. She took Vera's hand and asked her to sit down. Jiffa could not believe what she was seeing. Vincent rushed at Vera again, but was stopped by his mother.

"Now tell me why you have come here," Mama said, still holding Vera's hand.

Vera took a deep breath. "I have come to see Vincent."

"Why?"

"I am expecting his child."

"You liar! shouted Vincent. "Get out of this house immediately!"

"She is not going to get out." said Mama

"I'm not a liar, you are a liar," screamed Vera. "You told your secretary to tell me you were going away for four days. I rang this house twice, and you were in. You liar!"

Jiffa was in a daze. She had never thought such a thing could ever happen to her. Mama was listening carefully.

"Didn't you say you would marry me?" Vera shouted, "Now that I'm pregnant you won't even see me."

"Shut up and get out of here!" shouted Vincent.

"Is that all you have to say?" said Vera.

221

Vincent did not know what to do. He leaned against a pawpaw tree and said nothing.

"Vera," said Mama. "Where did you meet my son?'

"I met him when I was at Ola Secondary school." Mama nodded. Vincent had mentioned the name Vera to her years before, in Kpetwei, as a girlfriend whom he was going to see. It was the day after Papa had told him he was to marry Jiffa. So this was the girl she stopped Vincent from going to see.

"That was a long time ago. Have you been seeing him ever since then?"

"Mama, stop asking questions!" shouted Vincent.

"Why should I? I want to know what's going on, why it's going on, and when it started."

Jiffa was dumbfounded. She just listened. But what she was hearing was too much to bear, and she started crying.

"Vera, please answer my question," Mama repeated.

"No. We met recently on a flight and we started seeing each other again."

"Vincent!" shouted Mama. "Today your true character has come out. Now I know why you have been beating Jiffa and treating her badly."

"That is not true. I didn't treat Jiffa badly because of this woman."

"Don't call me this woman!" shouted Vera. She got up and thanked Mama Agawu for listening to her. As she walked past Vincent, he shouted at her.

"You ought to be ashamed of yourself for coming here! I don't want to see you ever again!"

Vera stopped and faced him. "May be you don't, but I want to see you. Coming here is just the beginning. You will be seeing me in your office next time." She left angrily.

Vincent stood helplessly, watching as Vera left. Jiffa sat weeping, while his mother stared at him as if he were a stranger. Then Mama spoke.

"My son, this evening we have seen a drama which none of us have expected. I'm so pleased to have been here when it was performed. It would have been terrible for Jiffa to experience it alone. And if she came all the way to Kpetwei and told me about it, I don't think I would have enjoyed it. Since the drama is over, it's time I went home."

As Mama got up to leave the garden, Jiffa spoke for the first time. "Mama, I have nobody in this world except you. If you're going home, I'll come with you." Mama hugged Jiffa and helped her dry her tears.

They left Vincent in the garden and went into the house. A few minutes later, Vincent came into the sitting room and sat down beside his mother. Neither of them spoke.

Ajovi was in the kitchen getting supper ready when Jiffa called her. "Go to Mama's bedroom and collect her suitcase," she ordered. Then Jiffa went to her bedroom and began emptying everything from her wardrobe into suitcases. Ajovi came down with Mama's suitcase and went into Jiffa's bedroom to ask her what to do next. She gave her two empty suitcases one for Essenam and one for herself. Jiffa was about to take a suitcase out of the room when Vincent came in and shut the door.

"I want to talk to you," he said

"Talk to me?"

"Yes."

Jiffa put the suitcase down and sat on the bed. "What have you got to say?"

"I beg you to forgive me."

"Oh no, Vincent, it's too late. I have very little time. Please open the door for me."

"Jiffa we are married?"

"Oh! Are we? If we are married you would not have created this mess." She went back to packing her things.

"Please, I am begging you to stay."

"I'm going away to make room for your second wife. I have had enough." Jiffa began to cry.

"We have three children to think about, Jiffa."

"If I stay with you my children's lives will be in jeopardy." As she said the word jeopardy, she remembered the first time Vincent had used it. He stood in front of the door with tears in his eyes.

"Jiffa, please change your mind."

"Oh no. This time I am going. I have no home to go to, I am aware of that, but I can assure you that I shall never sleep in the street. And even if I do, will I be the first?"

There was a knock on the door.

"Who is it?" asked Vincent

"Ajovi."

"Let her in!" shouted Jiffa. He opened the door.

"I've finished packing Essenam's things, Madame," she said.

"Have you taken them down?'

"Yes."

"Take these suitcases, and put everything in the car." As Ajovi took the suitcases out of the room, Vincent went up to Jiffa and was about to touch her.

"Don't touch me! I'm not good enough for you." She shouted.

Vincent could not believe it. Suddenly he was just like a piece of dirt who nobody wanted to see or touch. .

"Please forgive me," he said. Mama called Jiffa to hurry up so that they could leave.

"Alright, Mama - I'm coming," she replied.

AsVincent heard his mother's hard voice calling Jifffa he knew there was nothing he could do to stop her going. He followed her into the sitting room. Ajovi finished loading the car and came into the sitting room.

"Where is Essenam?" asked Jiffa.

"In the bath."

"Get her out and dress her quickly. We're going to Kpetwei." Ajovi ran upstairs.

Jiffa helped Mama into the car. Vincent followed them outside and stood helplessly. A few minutes later, Ajovi and Essenam came out and got into the car.

As Jiffa reversed her white Peugeot out of the garage, Vincent wept. He could not wave to them, neither could he stop them, in a twinkling of an eye they were all gone and the whole drama was over. The only person left in his big house, apart from himself, was the night watchman. Vincent went sadly into the garden and collected the drinks tray, then he went into his bedroom and changed.

Chapter Thirty-six

---

*V*ERA ARRIVED HOME FEELING PROUD AND happy. Then, before she packed for her trip, she made a quick call.

"Hello, its Vera - last night. Fine. Alright. Not on the telephone. Alright. Bye."

Vera was rushing from room to room collecting all the things she would need. Then she heard a knock. Thinking it was Henrietta she opened the door and Vincent walked in.

"How dare you come to my house and disgrace me!" he said

"If you don't get out of here I'll call the police," said Vera. She ran to the telephone, but Vincent took it from her and threw it on the floor.

"You stupid woman!"

"I am not a stupid woman, and I came to your house to - "

"Shut up!"

Vera was terrified. She wanted to run out, but he locked the door and put the key in his pocket.

"When you met me on that flight and saw my position in life, you thought you could trap me into marriage. Do you think I would marry a woman like you?"

There was a knock on the door. Vincent opened it, thinking it might be another man coming to see Vera. Instead Henrietta came in.

"Answer my question!" he shouted.

"What question?" asked Vera.

"I asked whether you deliberately became pregnant so that I would marry you."

Henrietta asked Vincent what was going on.

"Ask your friend, she will tell you," he said

"What's wrong, Vera?" asked Henrietta. Vincent sat down.

"Don't ask me," said Vera. "Why can't he tell you - liar! Vincent the liar!"

Henrietta turned to Vincent and asked him to tell her what was happening.

"Is Vera your friend?" he asked.

"Yes, she is, my name is Henrietta," she said, shaking hands with him.

"If she's your friend, then you must be very careful."

"Why?" asked Vera.

"Shut up - I'm not talking to you."

"You may not be talking to me, but you are talking about me so I have every reason to interrupt."

"Vera," said Henrietta. "Please calm down and let me listen to him."

"You should be ashamed of what you have done this evening," Vincent said.

"What has she done?" Henrietta was getting irritated by what was going on.

"You look like a sensible lady, so I'll tell you the whole story."

Henrietta crossed her legs and folded her arms.

"I met Vera more than eighteen years ago," said Vincent. She was my first girlfriend, but just before I left the sixth form my parents arranged that I should marry my cousin. It was heartbreaking." Henrietta already knew all that, but she did not interrupt. "Vera wrote and told me how sad she was, but I had no alternative but to accept the marriage my parents had arranged. I never saw or heard from her again until three months ago, on a flight from Italy. I sat next to her and we recognized each other. I had always wondered what life would have been like if I had married Vera, so when I saw her again I renewed my old love for her."

"When did you say you met her?" asked Henrietta.

"I started seeing her three months ago. Last week she came to my office to tell me she was pregnant. It was a shock. I love her, and was thinking of marrying her; but I'm a married man, and I have to talk to my wife about it before I take any steps. Vera deliberately became pregnant for me to - "

"You liar!" said Vera.

"Please keep quiet," said Henrietta

"To cut a long story short, I came to Vera's flat last Sunday and she threatened to come to my house if I didn't visit her every evening. How can I do that? She started threatening to come to my house if I don't do exactly what she said. I had permanent headaches from the fear that she might suddenly appear in my house. Last week was my eldest daughter's birthday, and she asked me to take four days off work."

"Where is your daughter at school?" asked Henrietta.

"Achimota" said Vincent.

"Oh, my husband's nephew is in the same school."

"What does your husband do?"

"He's an architect".

"I must meet him. We are always looking for architects."

"What do you do?" asked Henrietta. Vera had already told her, but she had forgotten.

"I work for the Standard Housing Corporation. Your husband and I could do business together." They laughed.

"Can I hear the rest of the story?" said Henrietta.

"Yes. Because it was a big family occasion, I invited my mother from Kpetwei and she stayed for a week. I took four days off work to be with the family. I intended to tell Vera when I came here on Sunday, but the first thing she asked me was when I was going to marry her. It is so off -putting. You don't push any man into marriage, let alone a married man! I left a message with my secretary to tell anyone who rang me that I was away. When my secretary told her, she rang my house and learned the truth. Anyway, today was my mother's last evening with us, I was giving her and my wife champagne in the garden when Vera arrived."

Henrietta shook her head. She had warned Vera not to go.

"I can't tell how I felt."

"I can imagine," said Henrietta.

Vincent bowed his head. "This girl has ruined my life."

"Don't call me this girl," shouted Vera. "It's all very well for you, but what about me, carrying your baby?"

"Stop shouting!" said Henrietta

"Stop shouting yourself. I'm the one in the fire, and only I know how hot it is. If you are going to side with Vincent, go away!"

"If you had told me on the telephone that you had been to Vincent's house, I would not have wasted any time coming here. Now that I see you can solve your own problems, I'll leave you." Henrietta got up to go, but Vincent held her back.

"Wait, we will leave together."

"Yes I want you both out! said Vera angrily.

"You don't need to tell me again," said Vincent. "Today is the last time I will come here." Vincent and Henrietta stood up to leave.

"I know where to find you," said Vera.

"You can try if you want, but next time you won't have it so easy."

Vincent and Henrietta left. Henrietta advised Vincent to go the following day and see Jiffa. "You must beg her to forgive you," she said. Vincent thanked her, and left.

Jiffa was in tears as she drove off to Kpetwei. She could not discuss anything in the car because of Ajovi. As she wept, Mama tried to cheer her up. Jiffa thanked God that Vera had not appeared on Emefa's birthday and destroyed her party. Emefa's friends would have gossiped about it at school and her relationship with Prosper would have been ruined. Would all this have happened if she had been allowed to choose her own husband?

Vincent arrived home and went straight to bed. He thought about what he would say to Jiffa when he saw her. Would she accept his apology? How should he approach the subject? What reception would he get? Should he buy her a present? What present could make up for this? He blamed himself for going back to Vera: for eighteen years he had lived happily with Jiffa, and Vera had destroyed it overnight. After the baby is born, he would have nothing more to do with her. He lay wake for a long time and thought about what had happened.

Jiffa arrived at Kpetwei just before midnight. She had left everything behind and was now going to starting life again in the village. While Ajovi unpacked the car, Mama Agawu called Jiffa into the sitting room.

"Before you go to bed, I'd like to thank you for the way you controlled your temper when you heard what had been going on between Vera and Vincent. If my love for you was great before this evening; it's now even greater. You're only human, and I'm sure you are thinking that if you had been allowed to choose your own husband this would not have happened. I can't help thinking that myself; but I'm not going to allow your eighteen years with Vincent to come to naught. I shall sleep on it, and think of a solution. Meanwhile, have a good rest, and lets talk tomorrow."

That night, Mama shared her bed with Essenam. Ajovi slept on the veranda and Jiffa slept in her old bedroom. As she lay on the grass mattress, Jiffa thought of the memories that the room brought back. It was in this room, eighteen years ago, that Vincent had broken her virginity, which had forced Mama to arrange a wedding before the birth. Today she was lying miserably in the same room. Everything she and Vincent had worked for all these years would be taken by Vera. Had she been right to leave the house? What if Vera came there and Vincent did not bother with her any more? Should she have swallowed her pride and stayed? If Vincent came to apologize for what had happened, should she accept him? If she did not would it be the end their marriage? What would Mawusi think if he heard of it? Would he laugh and say, I told you so? She fell asleep, and woke up at the first cockcrow.

Chapter Thirty-seven

HAVING DECIDED THE NIGHT BEFORE TO go to Kpetwei, Vincent woke up at dawn. It was unlikely that he would return that day, so he packed a few things and set off. Worried and ashamed, he tried to think of ways to convince Jiffa to come back to him. What would he do if she refused? Should he come back alone? If Jiffa really loved him, she would not allow this to destroy their marriage. He was prepared to do anything to make up for what had happened.

Jiffa lay awake pondering over what had happened when she heard a knock on her door. "Come in."

Ajovi entered.

"Mama wants you to come and have breakfast."

"Where is Essenam?"

"She's asleep."

"Could you take some water into the bathroom for me?"

"I have already done it."

"Tell Mama I will be with her shortly." Jiffa joined Mama under the mango tree for some porridge.

"You look beautiful!" said Mama. Jiffa smiled and sat down. Ajovi brought her a bowl of porridge. "Are you going somewhere?" Mama asked.

"Yes, to see the chief." Jiffa was not eating.

"You must eat," said Mama quietly.

"I'm not hungry."

"I know, but if you don't eat you will get ill."

Jiffa looked at Mama, shook her head, and tears filled her eyes.

"Please don't cry again," Mama said. "I want us to talk about what you should do, all this weeping is bad for you. I beg you, dry your tears."

Jiffa went back into her bedroom and lay down. Mama finished her breakfast and was about to go over and see her when Vincent drove up. As he approached his mother he knew he was in for an unpleasant scene. Mama would have said "Wezoloo" as a sign of welcome. If she was denying him that, then he realised how badly he had offended her.

"How are you, Mama?"

"I'm fine."

Vincent offered a hand shake, but it was refused. He sat and bowed his head.

"Mama. I have come to apologize."

"I'm not the one you should apologize to."

He looked at her, but she turned away.

"Can you please tell me where Jiffa is?"

"In her bedroom."

Deep down Mama was delighted that Vincent had come, it showed he cared about Jiffa. But she was not going to be friendly to him.

Jiffa was lying face down when she heard a knock on the door.

"Come in," she said. Thinking it was Ajovi; she did not raise her head. There was silence, so she looked up. "What do you want here?" she asked.

Vincent locked the door and went over to her. "Jiffa, I beg you to forgive me," he said quietly. She did not answer, so he sat beside her. "Please stop crying. Believe me, what happened yesterday will never happen again. I love you dearly and I'll do anything you want to put this right."

Jiffa dried her tears and looked at him. "I don't want anything, just go away and leave me in peace."

"Please, please for give me." He knelt down in front of her.

"Go to your second wife."

"She's not my wife."

"Then what is she?"

Vincent could not answer. He got up and sat beside her.

"Now I realize why you have been behaving so badly towards me and the children. Beating me and shouting at me, just because of a woman." Fresh tears came into Jiffa's eyes as she thought of Vincent's behavior in the past few months. "Why should I come back for you to hurt me again?"

"Listen - please listen. I have realised my mistake and I'm here to make it up, so don't push me away."

"I'm not pushing you away, you have pushed your family away!"

"Are you saying you want to leave me?'

"Because of the respect I have for your mother, I want her to be present to hear my answer." Jiffa got up and went to the door, then realized that Vincent had locked it.

"Open the door: I want to see your mother." Jiffa stood by the door, and Vincent came towards her.

"Please don't leave me," he moved closer to her.

Jiffa was worried that Vincent might force a kiss upon her.

"Don't touch me!" shouted Jiffa.

"I love you, please don't leave me! If you do, I will be finished. I need you and the children need us both." Vincent was in tears. But Jiffa did not give in.

"Do you know how near you came to destroying the children? If that girl friend of yours had come during the party, what do you think would have happened?"

"Don't make me suffer more than I'm suffering already. I want us to start life afresh."

"I can't start life afresh when your girlfriend is expecting your child. Open this door at once."

Vincent tried to take her hand, but she pushed him away.

"Open the door!" she shouted.

Mama was reading her bible when Jiffa and Vincent came in.

"Can I please have a word with you" said Jiffa softly. Mama closed the bible. Jiffa sat beside her on the sofa and Vincent sat opposite in an armchair.

"What have you got to say?"

Jiffa could not speak instead she started crying.

"Vincent, what have you done to her?" Mama said.

"Nothing, Mama, I went to her room to apologize and she suggested we should come and talk to you."

"I'm wondering whether we were right to arrange a marriage for Jiffa..."

"But Mama - "

"Shut up! I am talking."

Vincent shook his head and looked at his mother.

"You have sinned against the God you worship. When you married Jiffa and took the vows, did you mean what you said?"

"Yes Mama." Vincent was prepared for the worst: he knew his mother would talk and talk, but this was extreme.

"So why have you broken your matrimonial vows?"

"Mama, I've made a mistake, and I'm begging for forgiveness."

"You think you can go and make love to another woman and when she is pregnant then come and beg your wife for forgiveness? Vincent, the world is not like that. If Jiffa is not good enough for you, go and live with Vera."

"Jiffa is good for me. I love and need her. She is the mother of my children. I deeply regret what has happened, and I'll never do it again.'

"That's cheap to say. Are you telling me you won't make love to your girlfriend until the baby is born? Or are you saying that woman won't want another child from you? If it's children you need, Jiffa has given you three and she could have had more if it were not for her hysterectomy."

"I know all that, Mama."

"Then how could you be so wicked? I have always loved and respected you, but since last night a big question mark hangs over it."

There was a knock on the door.

"Come in," said Mama. Ajovi entered and went to Jiffa.

"Essenam wants to see you. Shall I bring her in after breakfast?"

"Please do," Jiffa replied, Ajovi went out.

For the first time since they came in to the sitting room, Jiffa spoke.

"Vincent, I have heard your apologies; but even if I forgive you, how am I to forget what has happened? We have always lived as one family, but that will change when the baby is born. And what are you going to do about that woman after she has her baby? Are you going to abandon her, or will she move in and live with us?"

"She is not going to move in with us, because she has her own flat." Vincent replied. Mama looked at him in disgust.

"And how will you spend your time?" asked Jiffa.

"What do you mean?"

"I mean your evenings and weekends. Will you divide your time between us?"

"No, you are my wife and that's all I care about."

"If that were true, why is your girlfriend pregnant?" Mama asked, shaking her head.

"I'm trying to undo the damage I have caused, Mama, please don't make it harder." Essenam ran into the sitting-room and when she saw her father she ran into his arms. Vincent lifted her up and kissed her.

"Daddy, why didn't you come with us last night?"

Vincent looked at Jiffa and his mother. "I wanted to come this morning."

"I missed you."

"And I missed you, too." He kissed her again.

"Will you take me home to see Phoebe?"

"If you want." Vincent knew that if he kept Essenam, Jiffa would have to follow him back.

"When can we go and see Phoebe?"

"Tomorrow," said Vincent.

Jiffa realized that Vincent had come for the night. Mama called Ajovi to take Essenam to the village shop and buy her a bar of chocolate.

When they left Mama turned to Vincent. "For the sake of my grand-children, I will do everything in my power to see you together again," Jiffa looked at her. "I'm not going to have my grand-children suffer because their father has been stupid. I have seen enough broken homes, and I don't want one in my own family." Vincent was inwardly much happier with his mother's change of tone.

"When Essenam asked you why you did not come with us last night, you were embarrassed, and told her a lie. Will you tell lies to Kobla and Emefa when they ask why their mother now lives in Kpetwei and you in Accra? Vincent, if you start telling lies, you will never stop. Have you seen how you have been struggling with yourself since that woman came into your life?"

"Mama, I beg you to forgive me" He knelt in front of his mother. You're right. But I promise, I'm going to turn over a new leaf."

"Stand up. Yes maybe you will change. But I don't think I shall be alive to see it."

Jiffa started crying . She had seen so much death since her childhood, and the idea of Mama dying made her very sad. Vincent tried to comfort her. "I thank God that I am alive to see what Vincent has made of the marriage I arranged."

Ajovi came in with Essenam to ask them where she should serve lunch.

"Under the mango tree," said Mama. Essenam followed Ajovi to the kitchen.

"Mama, have you got any painkillers?" asked Jiffa.

"What's wrong with you?" asked Vincent.

"I have a headache."

Mama went to her bedroom and brought back a small box containing all sorts of tablets. Some wrapped in pieces of paper, others in bottles. Vincent went to the kitchen to get some water.

"Why don't you have some lunch and take a rest?" he asked.

"I have no appetite: I'll go and lie down." Jiffa took the tablets and went to bed.

Chapter Thirty-eight

VINCENT FOLLOWED JIFFA AND SAT BESIDE her on the bed. "Can I do anything for you?" he asked. She shook her head. "Shall I massage the back of your neck?" She still did not answer. Vincent drew closer and took her hand. She did not resist, but just looked at him." I'll do anything for you," he whispered.

"I don't want anything, I want you and our family to stay intact."

"But you have me," said Vincent. He moved closer to her.

"No, I haven't. You have gone."

"No, I'm here with you and I need you more than ever."

Jiffa looked at him and knew that he meant it. His face was pinched with the fear that she might leave him.

"I love you," he whispered. He came closer to kiss her, but Jiffa turned away. Vincent forced her and she gave in. He was about to lie down beside her when the door opened and Essenam ran in. Vincent lifted her on to the bed.

"I have been looking for you, Mum."

Jiffa drew Essenam towards her. "What for?"

"To tell me a story."

On her flight to Italy, Vera's thoughts were on Vincent. She planned to go to his office when she got back and ask him what the future held for her and the baby. It might be a blessing in disguise that his wife had left him. After he had cooled down he would probably ask her to come and live with him. As for Henrietta, she was history. Now she had learnt to pick her friends more carefully. She thought of all the promises Vincent had given her. Poor Vincent, his wife had stood in the way. Vera was now prepared to be extra nice to win back his love. What had happened was just a hiccup.

Mama lay under the mango tree after lunch and thought of her family. Vincent and Jiffa could not live without each other. It was time Vincent realized that. Poor Jiffa was vulnerable, she needed security and reassurance from Vincent. If Mama had not been alive, what would Jiffa do? Where would she go? And worse of all who would help her? Mama decided talk to Vincent that evening. She would not disturb them now, because they might be talking things over. Jiffa needed to get it out of her system so that she could stop crying.

After Vincent had told her a few stories. Essenam fell asleep.
"I hope you've for given me, he whispered to Jiffa.
"What do you want me to say?" she replied.
"I want a positive answer. Please help me, I'm confused." He drew closer.
"I can see you are confused, but before I give you an answer, I'd like to ask you some questions. Am I not a good wife?"
"Oh you are wonderful!"
"Haven't I been a good mother to the children?"
"You have been fantastic."
"So why..." She choked and could not speak any more.
"Please don't cry," Vincent implored, "I love you and I am prepared to do anything for you. I'm here to take you home where you belong. What else do you want? I know how you feel, but I promise you'll see a changed Vincent. I haven't slept all night, because I've been thinking of you. And - "
"Will you ever leave me?" she interrupted.
"Never. I wish you knew how I feel about you. Believe me - I know it's a hard thing for you to accept..."
"It's very hard for me to accept you."
"Please try." They looked into each other eyes. "I beg you to forgive me."
Jiffa was about to speak, but Vincent moved closer and kissed her. He wanted to make love to her, but she stopped him. They held each other. She was deeply hurt, but she did not push Vincent away because who else had she got. It was exactly what she needed to make her feel loved. If she left him, who would protect her children? How would Emefa and Kobla feel

if they heard that their parents had divorced? Suddenly she remembered the Tamakloes.

"Vincent," she said softly. "When are we going to see Prospers parents?"

"Tomorrow evening. Why?"

"I had forgotten all about it."

"I hope you will come?"

Jiffa paused. "I don't think so."

"Why not"

"I don't feel like going anywhere."

"Jiffa, going to see the Tamakloes is important for Emefa. Let's put our own problems aside and think of our daughter. Do you want her to travel without knowing the people she is going with?"

"I still have a headache, so let's see how I feel tomorrow."

"Let's stop talking. I'm sure you'll feel better after a good sleep."

"You're probably right. I couldn't sleep last night." She took a deep breath.

"But what about your second wife?"

"Please Jiffa, let's leave her out of it. I want you to get some sleep."

Vincent decided to give Jiffa a gentle massage on the neck to relieve the tension. In the process, he thought of how much he had hurt her. Fighting back tears, he realized that she had given him all her love and he had abused it. All she needed was someone to love and care for her; she had trusted him and now look at the end result. Surely there was something he could do to repair this damage. Jiffa fell asleep with her head resting on him.

In the middle of preparing supper, Ajovi wondered why her madam had been weeping so much and refusing to eat. She had not been in the garden when Vera arrived, so she did not know what had gone on. She had been puzzled by the sudden rush to Kpetwei. And why did her master stay behind only to appear this morning? From the look of things he was here to beg his wife's forgiveness, but why couldn't they solve the problem at home? Oh well, she was only a servant, and it was none of her business...

Mama had finished having supper and tiding her wardrobe when she heard Essenam asking for her.

"I'm in my bedroom."

Essenam came in with father. Mama ignored Vincent and took Essenam in her arms. They sat on her bed. Vincent stood and looked at them.

"Have you had a good sleep?" Mama asked Essenam.

"Yes."

"Me too," said Mama.

"Mum is still sleeping, shall I go and wake her up?"

"No, your mother needs to rest. She has a headache, so don't disturb her, now why don't you go and ask Ajovi to bath you, and give you supper?"

"Alright, grand-mama." Essenam left the room. Mama sat on the bed and looked at her son.

"May I have a word with you?" said Vincent in a sad voice.

"Yes, sit down," she replied. He sat beside her.

"I have had a long talk to Jiffa, and I've begged her to forgive me." Vincent bowed his head.

"What did she say?" Mama asked calmly.

"I think she is prepared to forgive me."

"How is her headache?"

"I massaged her neck and I'm sure that helped."

"I hope you realize how much you've hurt her?"

"Yes, Mama, but I'll do anything to make it up to her."

Mama Agawu felt sorry for her son. He had obviously not thought of the consequences when he allowed Vera back into his life. "Have you told her that?" she asked.

"Yes I have. I want her back. I need her, Mama. Please help me."

"So that you can hurt her again?"

"No, Mama, no. Never, never again." He fought back tears. "I love Jiffa, but of late I've taken her for granted. I've realized my mistake and I want you to forgive me. Don't make me suffer any more, because my nerves are on edge and I'll have a breakdown from torturing myself. I beg you to forgive me!" He bowed his head and wept. His mother had never seen him like that before, and she took pity on him.

"Stop crying, I know how much you love Jiffa. I don't think you could live without each other. Jiffa does not deserve to be treated like this. Vincent, there's something I have not told you before, but I will now."

He raised his head. "What, Mama?"

"You remember that shortly after her father's death, Jiffa gave up her education?"

"Yes." He dried his tears.

"Did we tell you why?" asked Mama

"Yes I remember you said there was no money to pay her fees."

"That was not the real reason."

"So what was it?"

"Jiffa's father was very strict, and he never allowed her to go out. After his death, Jiffa's mother became worried that she would not be able to keep an eye on her and if she started going out secretly with men and became pregnant, it would bring great shame to the Agbenyo family. To avoid that, her mother decided that Jiffa should give up schooling and come and live with us, so that we could keep an eye on her."

"So Jiffa sacrificed her education in order to marry me!" said Vincent gently.

"Yes."

He shook his head in disbelief. "And now look at how I've repaid her." Fresh tears came into his eyes. His mother watched as he failed to fight them back.

"I want you to promise me something," said Mama.

"I'll do anything."

"I am in my seventies and my days on earth are numbered. I want you to promise me that you will never ever leave Jiffa, that you will never hurt her like this again and that you will live with her in peace. She has done a lot for you and the children and you must not think she is a fool. I warn you, if after my death you treat her like dirt because she has nobody to turn to, my ghost will haunt you and you will suffer. If Papa had been alive today, he would be ashamed of you." Tears came into Mama's eyes when she thought of her late husband. Vincent watched his mother weeping and realized how much he had hurt her. He moved closer to her and took her hands.

"I'm deeply sorry to have brought such misery into the family. I promise you that from this moment I'll take very special care of Jiffa." His mother looked at him. "I love you very much, Mama, thank you for all that you've done for me." Mama smiled. Vincent left her room and went to see his wife.

Jiffa was awake when Vincent entered the room.

"Where have you been?" she asked.

He sat down beside her. "I was talking to Mama."

"What's she doing?"

"Arranging her wardrobe"

"What's the time?"

"It's supper time. Did you have a good sleep?"

"Yes." Jiffa stretched and yawned.

"I think you need to rest a bit more," said Vincent.

"No, I'm all right now."

"How's your headache?" Vincent held her hand and rubbed it gently.

"I don't know until I get up."

"Try and get rid of it by tomorrow because I want to take you home."

Jiffa looked at him and did not answer.

"Will you come" he asked in a low voice. She nodded.

"What do you want me to do for you? Buy you a house? A car? Anything, anything. Just say it, Jiffa please say something!"

"No," she whispered. "Nothing. I only want you." Vincent looked at her, and realized that she was the most precious treasure in his life. He drew her closer and held her tight.

"I'll do anything I can to make you happy," he said, and kissed her.

Chapter Thirty-nine

JIFFA DECIDED TO HAVE SUPPER IN bed, so Vincent called Ajovi to come and serve them both. Ajovi brought the food and told Vincent that his mother would like to see him.

"Vincent, please tell Jiffa that I'd like to come and see her after she has finished eating," Mama said.

"Yes Mama," Vincent replied.

"How is her headache?"

"Much better."

"Please encourage her to eat: she has not had any food since last night."

"Alright, Mama."

Vincent went through to Jiffa, who was helping herself to okro soup.

"I'm glad you are eating," he said, sitting down beside her.

"Why?"

"Mama tells me you haven't eaten since last night."

"Yes, I had no appetite"

"Whether you have appetite or not, you must try and eat."

"May be, but I couldn't."

"Have you got your appetite back now?"

"A bit."

"Do you know why?"

"No tell me."

"Will you believe me?"

"It depends on what you say."

She stopped eating and looked at him.

"It's because you've seen me."

Jiffa did not answer. She knew it was true. "Why did your mother call you?" she asked.

"Oh, she wants to come in and see you."

"Why didn't you tell me?"

"There's no hurry. She will come when you finish eating"

"All the same, you should have told me when you came in."

"Yes, darling."

"When have you ever called me darling?" she asked.

"I'm starting today."

"Is that what you call Vera?"

Jiffa, please let's keep off that subject."

"How can we keep off it?"

"I don't want to be reminded of what happened last night."

"Maybe you don't. But since she is going to be part of your life I'll have to get used to her name, and - " Jiffa stopped talking and eating.

"Aren't you going to eat any more?" Vincent asked.

"No. I've had enough."

"Please have a bit more. Mama said I should make sure that you eat."

"Why?"

"She's worried about you."

"I hope you know she is very unhappy"

"Yes, I do. Please forgive me," Vincent whispered. "I will never do it again." He went to the door and called Ajovi to come and collect the plates. As she was about to leave the room, Jiffa asked her to bring Essenam to see her before she went to bed.

"Did my massage help your headache?" Vincent asked.

"Yes. Who taught you?"

"I learnt it when I was at college."

Jiffa remembered how she had given up her education because of Vincent and now he had let her down. Vincent thought of what his mother had told him. He braced himself to tell her.

"Jiffa, Mama has just told me …. " There was a knock at the door.

"Come in," said Vincent. Mama entered.

"I hope I'm not intruding," she said, sitting down.

"Not at all," said Jiffa.

"How is your headache?" asked Mama.

"Much better."

"Jiffa, I've had a long talk to Vincent, and I beg you to put everything behind you and go back home. For the sake of the children, I don't want you two to separate. I know it is a difficult thing to accept, but it's the only solution. Neither of you will benefit from a divorce, what's the point? Would it not be eighteen wasted years?"

"Yes, Mama" said Jiffa.

"But I warn you again, Vincent, if you treat Jiffa badly you will never find peace on earth. I shall not approve of any woman except the one I've given you, so I hope you'll find yourself another mother to introduce Vera to. I don't want to hear that Vera has moved into the house - if that happens - "

"Mama, that will never happen, so don't worry," Vincent interrupted. "At the moment Vera is in Italy. When she gets back I'm going to - "

"How do you know she's gone to Italy?"

"I went to her flat last night after you left."

"What did she say?"

"We had a row."

"Did you?" said Mama. Jiffa was listening carefully.

"Yes. She was proud of what she did. I would not tolerate it."

"Vincent, what happens between you and Vera has nothing to do with me," Mama replied, "I only care about Jiffa and the children."

There was a knock on the door.

"Come in," said Vincent.

Ajovi entered with Essenam, who went straight to her mother.

"Mum, Ajovi had told me a story."

"Did you thank her?" asked Jiffa.

"Yes."

"Good girl," said Vincent. He lifted Essenam up and kissed her.

"Good night, Dad," Essenam said, then she went and hugged her grandmother.

"Goodnight, grand-mama. May I sleep in your bed tonight?'

"Yes, my love," said Mama. Ajovi took Essenam out. "I will leave you two in peace, because I'm very tired. Vincent, what are your plans for tomorrow?" asked Mama.

"We'll go home after breakfast, because Jiffa and I have to go and see Prosper's parents."

"Will you go separately?"

"Yes, Mama - I have to take my car back," said Jiffa.

"No, darling," said Vincent "I'm not going to let you do that.

Mama could sense they wanted to be alone. "I'll leave you to sort that out," she said, "Sleep well, Jiffa. I hope you feel better tomorrow."

"Thank you, Mama," Jiffa replied. Mama got up and left.

"Do you want me to leave my car here?" Jiffa asked Vincent after Mama Agawu left the room.

"Yes. I'll send Frank to collect it."

Jiffa said nothing. She got up, changed into her nightdress, and went back to bed. Vincent lay down beside her. "You were about to tell me something before your mother came in - what was it?"

"I can't remember." He moved closer to her. "I'm so glad you're feeling better. I'm happy we're together again." He bent over and kissed her. Jiffa responded hungrily and Vincent realized how much he had starved her sexually since Vera came into his life. That night they made love repeatedly.

Ajovi was up at dawn, to finish with all her housework. After preparing breakfast, she woke Mama. Essenam followed her into the bathroom. As Mama had her breakfast, she asked Ajovi to go and wake her master and madam. Ajovi knocked on the door several times but there was no reply. She went to tell Mama. The old woman was not surprised, she had known from the look in her son's eyes the previous night that he would not give Jiffa a chance to sleep.

Mama spent the morning with Essenam in her bedroom while Ajovi packed the suitcases. Late that morning Jiffa and Vincent woke up, exhausted. They had a quick wash and came into Mama's room.

"Did you sleep well?" Mama asked Jiffa.

"Yes." Vincent smiled and asked Essenam to help Ajovi to pack the car.

"Jiffa, have you had any breakfast?" Mama asked.

"No, Mama, we ought to go now." said Vincent.

"I think Jiffa can answer the question herself," Mama replied.

Jiffa smiled. "I agree with Vincent," she said. "I think we ought to leave immediately. It's our fault that we have overslept."

Mama was pleased to hear Jiffa supporting Vincent.

"I'm glad you overslept," she said, "You needed it. I hope Vincent will let you rest when you get home.

"I'll do anything she wants. It's up to her to say it, and it shall be done," he replied

"I want you to keep me informed," Mama said to Jiffa. "Don't argue with him, just come to me. I'll do the talking for you."

"I wish someone would do the talking for me," said Vincent. They all laughed.

There was a knock on the door and Ajovi came in to say that everything was ready for them to leave. Vincent and Jiffa thanked Mama. Mama could see tears in Jiffa's eyes as they waved goodbye and drove off.

They had driven a short distance when Jiffa turned to Vincent.

"I'm sad to leave your mother behind," she said.

"I know. I'm sad, too."

"Maybe we should have taken her with us," said Jiffa.

"I don't think she wants to leave Kpetwei."

"Vincent, if she doesn't want to come, it's because she can't stand another scene like last Friday."

"I know what you mean, but I don't think that is the reason. I beg you not to talk about last Friday. Let's think of the future, not the past." Jiffa looked at him and thought of Vera.

A few miles out of the village, Jiffa remembered something. "Could you do me a favour?" she asked.

"Yes darling, anything you say." Vincent was only too pleased to do her a favour.

"I'd like to go back to the village to see Chief Mawusi."

Vincent turned the car round and headed back to the village. "Why do you want to see him?"

"He has been very kind to me in the past and it would be wrong for me to leave the village without saying hello."

"I suppose you're right." Vincent agreed. He did not like the idea, but he had to put up with it.

When they arrived at the palace, Vincent waited in the car and thought about Mawusi. Why should Jiffa want to see someone who hated him? He did not hate Mawusi, but ever since he had known him there had been an uneasiness between them. It was difficult to understand why, because they had nothing in common. As he sat wondering why Jiffa was visiting the Chief, she reappeared.

"That was quick," he said as they drove off.

"Mawusi and Togbi were both out," Jiffa replied.

"Where?"

"Segakope."

"What for?"

"Didn't you know his father had a poultry farm there?"

"No. How did you know?" he asked. Jiffa said nothing so Vincent repeated, "How did you know Mawusi's father had a poultry farm at Segakope?"

"I'm going to tell you something I've kept from you all this time," Jiffa said.

"What?"

"I'll tell you when we get home."

"No, tell me now."

"I want us to be alone."

"Don't bother about Ajovi," Vincent said, "She's playing with Essenam."

"I don't know how to begin."

"Please tell me. Darling, there's nothing you need be afraid of, so please don't hide anything from me."

"Would you also promise not to hide anything from me?'

"Yes, I do."

"Then will you tell me what your mother said last night?"

Vincent remembered. "Yes, but ladies first."

"I know you hate Mawusi..." Jiffa began.

"I don't hate him, he hates me."

"Listen, I can understand if Mawusi hates you."

"Why?"

"Because he was in love with me."

"What? said Vincent. "And did you love him?"

Jiffa could see that Vincent was jealous and she was pleased. "I'll give you the answer when we get home."

*C*hapter *F*orty

*I*T WAS JUST BEFORE TEA-TIME WHEN they arrived home. Essenam was fast asleep, so Ajovi took her to bed and Victor unpacked the car. Vincent followed Jiffa into the bedroom.

"Darling, I want you to tell me about Mawusi," he said angrily.

"There's nothing to be angry about." Jiffa stretched herself on the bed. She was right. What right did he have to be angry?

"I'm sorry if I sounded angry," he replied.

Jiffa called Ajovi and told her to bring some cold beer and prepare some hot snacks. Ajovi brought the drinks at once and they drank in silence for a while.

"Vincent," Jiffa said softly. "If I had been allowed to choose my own husband, I would have chosen Mawusi."

"What are you saying?" he shouted.

"There's no need to shout," her voice was very soft. "What I wanted to tell you is that Mawusi did all he could to get me as his wife."

"And what exactly did he do?" Vincent was so angry, but it made her happy.

"Before my mother died, Mawusi came to Adidome to visit me. It was he who drove Togbi and I to visit her in hospital. He - "

"Jiffa I am surprised you've hidden all this from me," Vincent interrupted.

"I'm not hiding anything. My parents had already decided that I should marry you and I was not going to go against their wishes."

"So you would not have married me if you had your wish?" He shook his head.

"And would you have married me if you had your choice? she asked with a false smile.

"Yes I would."

"Don't be a liar. If you would have chosen me then why is your long time lover pregnant?"

"Darling, let's not talk about Vera any more." Vincent lay beside Jiffa. "I'm glad to have you back. It was terrible when you left me here. I was unable to sleep, I thought of you all night. Jiffa, please don't ever leave me. I will not survive if you do."

"We human beings never appreciate what we have until it's out of our hands," said Jiffa.

"Well I hope you will never be out of my hands, not now and not ever. Jiffa I will cherish you forever." Vincent kissed her.

"Now I want you to tell me what your mother said."

"It will upset you."

"Me, upset! Listen, just tell me because nothing will ever upset me again."

So Vincent told her.

"I thought you knew already," she said.

"No, I did not. If I had, I would not have allowed it," he replied.

"I'm sure you wouldn't. But Vincent, the best thing you ever did was to encourage me to go back to school after I had Kobla."

"Well I'm glad to have done that. Can you imagine how I would have felt, if I had not kept my promise?"

"How would you have felt?"

Vincent was thinking of what to say when Ajovi came in with the hot snacks. Jiffa took a nap afterwards, while Vincent read a novel.

Mr Justice Tamakloe and his wife had decided to give the Agawus a warm welcome. Mrs Tamakloe invited her brother- in- law and his wife to join them. She asked the cook to prepare her favourite dish of chicken with almonds and the butler to choose the best wine from the cellar. The sitting room had been thoroughly cleaned and the furniture carefully polished.

The Tamakloes were in the garden when Henrietta arrived. She told Mrs Tamakloe that Bright would not be able to come, because his business partner had arrived from abroad and they had to catch up with some work. He sent his apologies for letting her down.

"Don't worry," Mrs Tamakloe said, "Bright just called me and explained."

"I know, but he wanted me to tell you all the same," said Henrietta, following Mrs. Tamakloe into sitting room. "Have your guests arrived?"

"No, you're the first."

"For once, I have arrived early," Henrietta said, laughing.

Jiffa woke up feeling fresh and after dressing beautifully, her husband praised her.

"I want you to know that you are the prettiest woman I have ever seen."

Jiffa was flattered. "Thank you, but please let's hurry because we have a long way to go."

"Today is Sunday, there will be no traffic," said Vincent.

"I'll wait for you in the sitting room." Jiffa got up and walked out majestically. Victor was tiding up when she came into the room.

"Madam you look beautiful," Victor said, his eyes fixed on her.

"Thank you very much." Then she heard Vincent's footsteps.

"Darling shall we go," Vincent said. Victor watched them as they got into the black Mercedes and drove away.

The Tamakloes were talking and laughing in the sitting room when the house help came in and announced the arrival of their guests.

"Show them in," Mrs Tamakloe said. As Jiffa and Vincent entered there was a round of introductions. When Vincent set eyes on Henrietta his heart missed a beat.

"Hi!" said Henrietta.

"Hello," said Vincent. The others looked at them. Jiffa was standing beside Mr Tamakloe who was admiring Jiffa.

"Have you two met before?" asked Mrs Tamakloe.

"Yes, we have a friend in common," said Henrietta. Vincent was relieved that the friend's name was not mentioned. The butler brought drinks, and they all sat down. Henrietta examined Jiffa from head to toe as she sat and chatted with Mr Tamakloe. What a beautiful lady, she thought. What is Vincent doing with Vera if he has a woman like this at home? Vincent realised that Henrietta was looking at him, so they left the sitting room to talk outside.

"I can't tell you how I felt when I saw you," said Vincent.

"Come on - tell me," she laughed.

"I thought you would mention Vera's name and how we had met."

Henrietta laughed even louder. "Maybe I should have done that."

"Thank you for saving me from the embarrassment," Vincent said.

"But why should I embarrass you in front of people you have never met?"

"You're a sensible lady," said Vincent. "Vera would have done just that."

"Oh, her!" said Henrietta. "I don't think she ever wants to see me again."

"Why?" asked Vincent.

"She thought I was on your side. When she left for Italy she did not even let me know. Normally she would ring and tell me."

"It sounds as if I have ruined your relationship."

"If she can't take criticism that's her problem. She expected me to approve of her coming to your house and creating a scene. In fact, I feel like exposing her real character to you."

"Please do," Vincent replied.

"From the moment she knew your position in life, she set out to get you. I wasn't at all surprised when she told me she was pregnant."

"So she trapped me on purpose?"

"I would not rule it out. But why on earth did you go after Vera when you have such a beautiful wife at home?"

"Henrietta, I'm a man and it's our illness. I think every man is infected with it. I know Jiffa is beautiful, but..." he shook his head.

"I gather your marriage was an arranged one," said Henrietta.

"Who told you?"

"Who else would tell me?"

"I despise Vera for what she did and I curse her every day for it."

"I'm so glad you've been able to persuade your wife to come back."

"Thank you very much for your advice. It was a good thing I went to Kpetwei. She was in very low spirits when I got here. I had to beg for forgiveness until my mouth was dried up before she accepted my apology. Now we are together, but our life will never be the same again."

"I'm not surprised. I don't know what would happen if my husband did that to me."

"Listen, I've asked her to forgive me, and even asked to buy her anything she wants."

"What did she say to that?"

"She doesn't want anything."

"What did you have in mind?"

"I thought of buying her a house, but the house we have is in her name, so what is the point in having another?"

"Why don't you buy her a car?"

"She has one already."

"So what are you going to do?"

"I don't know. Can you help?"

Mrs Tamakloe came out to tell them supper was ready. They went into the dining room. Jiffa and Mr Tamakloe were already seated and busily chatting and laughing. There were two servants to wait on them - one to serve the men, the other the ladies. The butler had already put out several decanters of wine.

As food was served and they started eating, Mr Tamakloe told a funny story and Jiffa choked, Mr Tamakloe patted her tenderly on the back. All evening he had been admiring Jiffa's beauty and saying flattering things to her. When supper was over, they went into the sitting room to talk about Emefa and Prosper's forthcoming trip. Jiffa was delighted for her daughter. She could see Emefa sharing a wonderful life with Prosper. She really liked the Tamakloes and that made her very happy.

Chapter Four-one

Vincent and Jiffa left McCarthy Hill more cheerful then when they had arrived. They thanked the Tamakloes and promised to return their invitation. There was silence in the car as they drove along the empty roads. Jiffa broke it with a slight cough.

"Shall I pat your back?" Vincent asked.

"No, I'm fine." Her voice was soft.

"You needed it when Mr Tamakloe did it," he said.

Jiffa had sensed Vincent's jealousy during supper, and she was pleased. "Yes, he patted me on the back because I needed it, but now I don't."

Vincent wondered how to start a conversation with a woman he had hurt so badly.

"I have asked you to tell me what you want, so that I can give it to you, but you have not given me an answer."

"I have no answer, because I don't want anything," she said.

"Come off it, Jiffa, you must want something."

She knew he was desperate to buy her love, but she was not prepared to sell. Gone were the days when he behaved badly and then gave her a present to keep her quiet.

"Come off what, Vincent? You asked me a question, and I have given you an answer. Forgive me, but I'm rather tired and I would be grateful if we could keep off this subject."

It was after midnight when they arrived home. Jiffa went straight to the bedroom, with Vincent following closely behind. Shortly after they had changed into their nightclothes, there was a knock on the door.

Ajovi entered, holding a piece of paper.

"What is it?" Vincent asked.

"There was a telephone call for you from Korle Bu Hospital. And you must ring this number as soon as you get back." Ajovi handed him the piece of paper and left.

"Why should I ring the hospital?" he said to himself. Jiffa lay on the bed and said nothing. Vincent thought of going into the sitting room to make the call, but did not want Jiffa to be suspicious. Moreover, he knew Vera was abroad, so he was not worried. He sat on the bed and dialled the number.

"Hello," he said into the receiver, "May I speak to Dr. Agyekumhene. Alright, I will be there shortly. I have to go to the hospital," he said to Jiffa.

"Why?"

"Vera has had an accident, and she has asked to see me."

"Alright." Jiffa watched him leave.

Vincent arrived at the hospital and was directed to Dr. Agyekumhene, who told him that Vera was not seriously injured, but had lost her baby. He took Vincent to see her. She was in tears when she saw him.

"I am sorry to hear what has happened," Vincent said and he kissed her forehead and sat down beside her.

"I'll leave you and come back later," said the doctor. Vera had cuts on her face and both arms.

"Please tell me what happened." Vincent felt really sorry for her.

"There's nothing to say," she sobbed. "I had an accident and I've lost the baby. So that's that."

"I thought you were in Italy," he said. "What happened?"

Vera told him that the taxi she took from the airport had swerved off the road and hit a tree.

"Then what happened?" he asked.

"I don't know. When I regained consciousness the doctor told me I had lost my baby." She wept bitterly and Vincent helped her dry her tears.

"There's nothing to say, except that I'm sorry. I'll go now and come back in the morning. Try to get some sleep." He kissed her and left.

Jiffa was reading a novel when Vincent got back. She had found it difficult to go to sleep. Here she was alone in bed, while her husband was in hospital visiting a pregnant girlfriend. She wished she knew what was wrong with Vera, and why Vincent was needed so urgently. Shortly after three o'clock, Vincent arrived.

When he found Jiffa was still awake, he asked her why she had not gone to sleep.

"Why do you want to know?" she replied. Jiffa had made up her mind not to ask Vincent any questions when he came back. His life was up to him, and he could do whatever he liked with it.

"I was expecting to find you asleep."

"Don't expect anything from me. I'm in this house only because of my children. As far as you are concerned..." She stopped. She had been determined not to say anything to him, but she was doing just the opposite.

"Listen, Jiffa." Vincent sat beside her. "I have treated you badly, but I have begged for forgiveness. Are you not prepared to forgive me?" She did not answer. "I know you won't ask me what happened when I went to the hospital."

"Why should I ask?"

"Because it's to do with both of us. Vera has lost the baby in an accident and you should know about it."

"Vera losing her baby has nothing to do with me," Jiffa relpied, "I'm not going to be happy about it. It's your affair, and you have to deal with it."

"Jiffa, I want you to listen carefully." His voice was very gentle and he drew her closer to him. Then he closed her book and put it on her bedside table. He was expecting her to resist, but she did not. It was a good sign. "I love you, Jiffa," he whispered.

"Oh, do you?" she said sarcastically. Vincent got off the bed and undressed. Jiffa was right to doubt his love. Vera had been a problem between them, and even when he was making love to Jiffa, it had become a duty rather than a pleasure. But now that it was all over, he was ready to embrace his wife.

During the months after Vera's accident, life between Jiffa and Vincent gradually returned to normal. Vincent came home as soon as he finished work and was very loving to Jiffa. They joked and played together as if they were teenagers and their love making went from strength to strength. Jiffa appreciated every moment.

Vincent saw Vera once after she was discharged from hospital. He promised her a lump sum of money to help her business and made it clear that he would not marry her.

One Friday evening, Jiffa was in the sitting room listening to the news when Vincent came in.

"Darling," he said, "why don't we go and see Mama this weekend?"

"That's a good idea," Jiffa said. "I have been thinking of her lately and since you became a good boy I have not told her."

"That's why I want us to go,"

"I can't wait to see Mama, she is the soul of my life," said Jiffa.

"Why don't we go and pack a few things to take with us?" Vincent said.

Jiffa had even noticed a change in the words Vincent used. These days everything was 'we' instead of 'I' - she only hoped it would last.

Chapter Forty-two

MAMA AGAWU WAS HAVING BREAKFAST UNDER her mango tree when Vincent drove in.

"Wezoloo!" she called, her voice was quivery.

Essenam opened the door and ran into Mama's arms. Ajovi unpacked the car, while Jiffa and Vincent walked arm in arm towards her and sat down.

"Oh, I'm so happy to see you all!"

Vincent was delighted to see his mother happy and Mama could see the change in her son. But she would still later warn Jiffa to be on the look out, because a leopard never changes its spots, and if a thief promises to give up stealing, everyone should remember that stealing is in his fingertips, and he can always go back to it.

"How have you been since we last saw you, Mama?" Vincent asked, concenred that his mother was looking frail and thin.

"Not very well. I have had to go twice to the doctor," she said.

"Why didn't you send us a telegram?" Jiffa asked, looking worried.

"I did not want to bother you. The chief has been wonderful to me."

Jiffa sensed that perhaps Mawusi was doing this for Mama because he still loved her.

"Vincent, I would like you and Jiffa to go and see the chief and thank him for the love he has given me." Mama said.

It was the last thing Vincent wanted to do, but if it was what his mother wanted, then he would do it.

"Very well!" Vincent said. Then he told his mother about Vera losing the baby. Like Jiffa, Mama took no joy from it.

"I hope you have learnt a big lesson from what happened. I am not going to give you a lecture. But look at me: I am getting old and I will not be here forever. If you take my advice, it will be good for you. If you don't, it will be entirely up to you."

Jiffa was sad to hear Mama talking like that, and tried to cheer her up. "Mama, Vincent has changed a great deal towards me. These, days he gets home very early, so Essenam and I have time to be with him. He has done all sorts of nice things for us. And..."

Vincent jumped in. "Also, Mama, what Jiffa does not know is that next month I'm taking her on holidays to America."

"What?" Jiffa cried. She hugged Vincent. "Why haven't you told me earlier?"

Mama looked at them with joy. They were behaving like teenagers who had just found love.

"It's a surprise," Vincent replied.

Jiffa now realized why he had wanted them to visit his mother. "I wish you would come with us, Mama," said Jiffa.

"I wish I could too. But my health has not been kind to me lately. In fact, I have to go and see my doctor tomorrow morning."

"Vincent and I will take you there and bring you back. But why don't you come and live with us?" said Jiffa, "I don't want you to be here alone." She had tried many times to persuade her, but the old lady had always resisted.

"I will reconsider your offer this time and since you two are happy, I think I too will be happy living with you. This is the kind of happiness I have been waiting to see."

Mama became very tired and went into her bedroom. Jiffa and Vincent also decided have a rest.

"I am always cheerful when I see Mama," said Jiffa.

"You don't need to tell me. But I'm a bit worried about her," said Vincent.

"Yes, she looks frail. I'm pleased we've persuaded her to come and live with us. I'll look after her very well. Now listen, we mustn't forget to go over and thank the chief on Mama's behalf."

"We won't forget, but don't think for a moment that I'll allow you to come with me," said Vincent.

"What do you mean?" Jiffa asked sharply.

"You know why, don't you?" he said with a false smile.

"Vincent stop being childish. You don't want me to see Chief Mawusi because he used to love me. How could you be so jealous? If - "

"Listen, Jiffa, if a man has once loved you, you are forever in his memory. It doesn't matter how long you have been apart, as soon as you meet again, his love will be rekindled." Vincent immediately regretted saying this.

"Was that what happened to you and Vera?" Jiffa asked.

"Yes."

Jiffa shook her head.

Vincent saw that he would be a fool to hide anything from her, because she had only just begun believing and trusting him again. "Don't be disgusted by what I have said." He took her hand. "I hope whatever bad feeling surrounding the Vera saga is over and I can look back on it as a lesson. I don't think you had the faintest idea of what I went through. Thank God that episode is closed."

"I hope it is," said Jiffa.

"It really is over, Jiffa. The day Vera walked into the house, I wished I had never seen the daylight of this earth. I will forever cherish you. My mother always warned me of the danger of treating you badly, but being human I took it for granted. But I tell you, I have paid a heavy price. You don't hate me for it, do you?"

"Why should I? We're all human beings and nobody is perfect. I have also made mistakes in life, so who am I to judge you?"

"Jiffa! You, make mistakes? No. As far as I'm concerned, you are perfect. In fact, I'm going to start calling you Mrs. Perfect." He kissed her.

There was a knock at the door.

"Come in," Vincent called.

Ajovi entered with Essenam, to say that Mama was calling for help. Vincent and Jiffa dashed into Mama's bedroom. She was lying on her bed, sweating profusely.

"What's wrong, Mama?" Jiffa sat on the bed, looking worried.

Vincent helped his mother to sit up.

"My heart was beating very fast and suddenly I felt sick."

"Has this happened to you before?" he asked.

"Yes, my heart beats very fast these days, but I have never sweated like this and normally I don't feel sick."

Jiffa held Mama's hand and rubbed it gently.

"Do you want me to take you to hospital?" asked Vincent.

"Don't ask her," Jiffa said, "Let's take her now."

"You decide what is good for me," said Mama.

Vincent shook his head, he had never heard his mother talk like that before. It was a bad sign. "Alright," he said. "Jiffa, you help Mama dress while I get the car keys."

Within minutes they were on their way to the hospital. When they arrived, Mama felt very tired. Vincent suggested a wheel chair, but she refused. Instead, Mama held Jiffa's and walked slowly and steadfastly into the hospital. After she had been examined and taken into a ward, the doctor told them that she had suffered a heart attack.

"How bad was it?" Vincent asked.

"Quite bad." Jiffa held Mama's hand and rubbed it gently while she talked to her.

"So what should we do now?" Vincent asked.

"We're going to keep her in for a few days and monitor her condition. One of the nurses will come in soon and put her on a drip. I will be here, so if you have any questions, please come and ask me." Then the doctor left.

Vincent turned to look at his mother, who was chatting peacefully with Jiffa. His mind was split between his mother and his work. He had a couple of crucial meetings on Monday and it would be difficult to cancel them. But he also had a commitment to stay and look after his mother. How could he leave her on her own without feeling guilty? He would discuss it with Jiffa, and see whether she will offer to stay behind. Mama fell asleep after the drip, so Vincent asked Jiffa to come outside for some fresh air.

They walked side-by-side around the hospital deciding on what to do about Mama. Vincent suggested that Mama should be moved to a hospital in the city so that he could keep an eye on her. Jiffa disagreed saying that she was already receiving treatment and moving her would just bring more complications. Then he asked whether she would stay and look after her.

"There is no question of me leaving Mama alone here. I shall stay in Kpetwei until she's better. In fact, I'll sleep in the hospital every night just in case she needs me. In the mornings, I'll dash to the house and see Essenam and Ajovi, then I can bring her some home made soup."

"Oh Jiffa, you can't do that," said Vincent. "You - "

"Of course I can. Mama has been my mother ever since I was a child. She has looked after me wonderfully. Today, if she needs someone to look after her, why should I wait to be asked?"

So Jiffa stayed at the hospital and Vincent went back to his mother's house that evening to be with Ajovi and Essenam. The following day, he drove to the hospital to see them and to say goodbye.

A couple of days after Mama had been admitted, she called Jiffa to her bedside and asked her whether she had been to thank the Chief on her behalf.

"No, Mama," Jiffa replied. "Vincent and I were going when we had to rush you here. To be honest, it had escaped my mind."

"Don't worry," Mama said, "We all forget things. But please try and see him tomorrow morning when you go to the house. I do not want him to think I am ungrateful. He has been very kind to me, and it would be terrible not to thank him properly."

"I will do it, Mama. But meanwhile don't worry about what he may think of you."

"Oh, Jiffa." Mama offered her hand and Jiffa rubbed it gently. "It gave me such pleasure to see you and Vincent looking happy. I hope he now has the brains to treat you properly."

"Yes, Mama." Jiffa could see she was having difficulty speaking.

"It has taken him so many years to realize that his parents chose the best woman for him," Mama whispered. Jiffa smiled. "I don't want you two *ever* to separate. If there should be a separation I don't think it will come from you. You may therefore wonder why I am talking to you, instead of Vincent. My answer is simple. You are by far cleverer than he is, so you must help him. He has displayed his weakness with women, as we have seen recently. I want you to promise me that you will never ever leave him, because if you do he will be destroyed forever."

"I promise Mama"

"I would be very happy if you went and thanked the chief now."

Jiffa alighted from the taxi in front of the palace and opened the gate. A young man asked her who she wanted.

"Is Chief Mawusi in?"

"Yes. But he is in a meeting at the moment. Do you want to wait?"

"Yes." Jiffa followed the man into the sitting room.

"Can I offer you something to drink?"

"Yes please - a glass of water will be fine." Jiffa sat down and looked round the sitting room. The old furniture had all been replaced by new pieces. The young man came in with the water and told her the meeting would be over shortly. Jiffa sat wondering what Mawusi's reaction would be when he saw her. Would he recognize her? Would he be cold towards her? And how should she react if he was cold? Should she just give him the message and leave? No, whether he was cold or cheerful, she was not going to walk out on him. He had helped her in the past and circumstances had not permitted her to choose her husband. That was not her fault. It was life.

After waiting for a while, she heard voices coming from the meeting and knew the advisers were leaving. She now felt uncomfortable knowing that in a few minutes Mawusi would appear. Soon after the voices had died down, Jiffa heard footsteps approaching the sitting room. Mawusi entered, tall and elegant in his adinkra cloth. He opened his mouth and eyes very wide when he saw Jiffa. She looked at him and smiled.

"Am I seeing a human being or a ghost?" he asked, walking up to her.

"You're seeing a human being alright," said Jiffa. She stood up and curtsied, but Mawusi hugged her so tight they could feel each other's heartbeat.

"Jiffa, Jiffa, Jiffa!" His voice rose louder and louder. "What has brought you back to me?" They sat on the sofa. "You have not changed a bit. In fact, your beauty seems to grow with every passing year."

"I thought you would not recognize me," she said in a childish voice.

"Me! Not recognize you!" Mawusi laughed. "Jiffa, I would recognize you in darkness, let alone in broad daylight." He embraced her. "Oh, my Jiffa, my own Jiffa.

"Where is your wife?" Jiffa was getting nervous. She did not want Mawusi's wife to walk in and see them hugging and embracing each other.

"In Segakope with the children. But she knows all about you. I have never stopped mentioning your name. I told her that there was a particular woman in my heart whom I will never forget."

"Wasn't that tactless?" Jiffa asked.

"Isn't it better to tell her the truth than to lie?" Mawusi looked very happy and Jiffa remembered what Vincent said about old love burning quickly once it is rekindled.

"Yes, but would you have been happy if she had said the same thing to you?"

"Oh, Jiffa, you of all people should know my character by now."

"I know your character alright. But people change, and it's over eighteen years now since I last saw you, so - "

"Yes, eighteen years have passed since you broke my heart into pieces. I never thought I would survive that pain."

"Please, don't talk about it, it's in the past."

"Oh Jiffa! It's like a dream seeing you today. I want to hear all about life with the schoolboy and everything, everything that has happened." Mawusi was so excited.

"Now, Chief Kushieto, what number are you in the chieftancy?"

"Third."

"So I have to address you as Chief Kushieto the Third?"

"That's right. And you have to do whatever I say," said Mawusi, laughing.

"Yes, chief, I'll do anything you say. But things like what?"

"The first thing will be to leave your husband. And marry me" They laughed and embraced each other again.

"I knew that was what you were going to say. Alright, chief, I will leave my husband, but meanwhile let me tell you why I have come." There was some seriousness at last. "Mama Agawu has asked me to come and thank you for everything you have done for her."

"It's my pleasure. She was wonderful to me when my father died, it's the least I could do for her. Where is she?"

"In hospital," said Jiffa.

"What's wrong with her?"

"According to the doctor she had a heart attack and she is on admission at the general hospital for more tests."

"Oh dear, what a worry. Are you staying on to look after her, or will you be going back?"

"I'm staying on. I have been here since last weekend. During the night, I sleep at the hospital in case she needs me."

"My God, you have been loyal to that woman. Well how can I help?" Mawusi asked.

"I have to collect some soup from Mama's house and take it to the hospital," said Jiffa.

"How do you get here?"

"By taxi"

"Then I'll drive you to the house and collect the soup, take you to the hospital and visit Mama."

"No, Mawusi, I can't have your driving me round. You are not my chauffeur."

"Come off it, Jiffa. Will today be the first time I have driven you around? Wait a moment, I'm going to get changed."

Jiffa was pleased to see Mawusi. She realized that there was no ill feeling towards her and that gladdened her heart. He was now like the brother she never had. Also she could trust him totally and talk to him about anything.

Mawusi and Jiffa drove to the hospital in joyous mood. They talked about Togbi and the furnishing work he had done for him. Then they talked about their lives at length and laughed over the funny bits. Mawusi told her he had hated Vincent when he heard that she was pregnant. Jiffa had thought her rape was secret, but since Mawusi knew about it, she told him what happened. Mawusi told Jiffa about his wife whom he loved dearly, but during the early days of their marriage he was only able to make love to her if he thought of Jiffa. It did not mean he loved his wife less, but that was how he coped with his feelings. They both wished Togbi was in the car with them. Mawusi promised to take Jiffa to Adidome before the end of the week.

When they arrived at the hospital Jiffa led the way to Mama's ward and, seeing that her bed had been screened off, she asked the doctor what was wrong.

"I'm afraid her condition has suddenly deteriorated and we are monitoring her heart beat. Jiffa was terrified to see tubes in Mama's nostrils and her eyes firmly shut. She took Mama's icy hands and realising that her condition was serious, she went out to phone Vincent, leaving Mawusi with her. She rushed back into the ward to see the doctor looking worried as the heart monitor gave out a long high tone. It was a confirmation too appalling to be accepted. Mawusi comforted Jiffa as her screams filled the ward.

Printed in the United Kingdom
by Lightning Source UK Ltd.
132369UK00002B/1-39/P